The House at the Edge of the Jungle

ALSO BY *MARY MORGAN*
Willful Neglect

The House at the Edge of the Jungle

MARY MORGAN

St. Martin's Press

New York

THOMAS DUNNE BOOKS.
An imprint of St. Martin's Press.

THE HOUSE AT THE EDGE OF THE JUNGLE. Copyright © 1999 by Mary Morgan. All rights reserved. Printed in the United States of America. No part of this book may be used or reproduced in any manner whatsoever without written permission except in the case of brief quotations embodied in critical articles or reviews. For information, address St. Martin's Press, 175 Fifth Avenue, New York, N.Y. 10010.

Design by Ellen R. Sasahara

Library of Congress Cataloging-in-Publication Data
Morgan, Mary.
The house at the edge of the jungle / Mary Morgan.
—1st U.S. ed.
p.   cm.
"Thomas Dunne books."
ISBN 0-312-19898-1
I. Title.
PS3563.O87125H6   1999
813'.54—dc21   98-44010
CIP

First Edition: February 1999

10 9 8 7 6 5 4 3 2 1

This book is dedicated to the cherished memory of my parents, Jean and Cyril Braund, who taught me to love words and to laugh at life.

Author's Note

The House at the Edge of the Jungle is fiction, the characters and situations entirely my own invention, but the invasion of Malaya in 1942 was all too real. A large number of civilians and soldiers suffered greatly in a period of history almost forgotten by the rest of the world. I want to acknowledge the heroism and bravery of those who survived the dark days and to honor the memory of the many who died.

I would like to thank Ruth Cavin, my editor at St. Martin's Press, who believed in this book, and my agents, Anna Cottle and Mary Alice Keir, who constantly sustain me with their enthusiasm.

Through the jungle very softly flits a shadow and a sigh—
He is fear, O little Hunter, he is fear.

— RUDYARD KIPLING

*The House
at the Edge
of the Jungle*

1

VICTOR CARTWRIGHT was fond enough of his sister, Isabel. His only sister. His only relative, come to that, apart from Isabel's husband and children, who somehow didn't count. Victor didn't use the word "love" for the sibling relationship, because love wasn't a word he used easily. His fondness for Isabel was purely the result of that accident of birth with which he'd inherited a brother's responsibility.

How else, except responsibility and a degree of fondness, to account for the suggestion that Isabel accompany him to Malaya? He knew he must have been out of his mind.

The trip had been planned for weeks. Merely business. Someone had to go to Singapore and Kuala Lumpur and pass a trained eye over the books at the Far East offices of Parker and Dellworthy. Not an audit; just a reminder that London was watching what they were doing out there. Victor hadn't mentioned it to Isabel. He didn't keep his sister informed about his every move, but the fact that this trip was to Malaya was different. That dim and distant country filled a special place in her mind, and the merest mention of it invariably brought on tiresome tears and recriminations, yet as he sat at his desk with the airline tickets and hotel reservations in front of him, he found himself quite suddenly dialing her number, the sort of uncontrollable impulse not at all in his nature.

"Izzy. Victor."

"Victor, darling! How lovely to hear your voice! I was having a cup of coffee, all alone in the kitchen, feeling sorry for myself, and now there you are, like a ray of sunshine in a gloomy day."

The exclamation marks and emotional overstatements came pouring out of the telephone. Victor could picture, only too easily, the pale oval face, the flying rambunctious hair, the great shining eyes.

It wasn't necessary to ask why she was feeling sorry for herself, because any moment now she'd tell him. Victor thought that if he were married to Adrian Bennet, he'd feel sorry for himself too.

"The house is so empty, Victor, now the boys have gone off to school. I really don't know what to do with myself all day."

"You could get a job," he suggested, not for the first time.

"I could, couldn't I? But who would employ me? And it'd mean going up to London every day, and the thought of that awful commute absolutely shrivels my innards."

"Adrian does it," Victor pointed out. "You could also move nearer to Town."

She laughed. Her laugh was infectious, deep-throated and burbling, and it made Victor smile in spite of himself. She said, "Can you see Adrian leaving his beautiful house? God, he'd sooner leave me."

Which was probably true. What Victor didn't see was why Isabel didn't leave Adrian. He, Victor, could never have put up with those constant remodeling projects, that obsessive collecting of dubious and expensive antiques. He believed the persnickety Adrian looked upon his wife more as a housekeeper for his precious objets d'art than anything else. She was a lousy housekeeper anyway. Marriage was such a mysterious state of affairs.

When Isabel sighed and said, "But the house is dreadfully empty all day, Victor. I do so miss the boys," it was then he told her about the trip to Malaya and made the fatal suggestion.

"Izzy, next week I have to go to Singapore. On company business. Then to Kuala Lumpur. I'll be gone about ten days."

He heard the indrawn breath, the catch in her throat. As long as she didn't start crying.

"How'd you like to come with me?" Why in God's name had he said it?

"Kuala Lumpur? Victor! Would I like to? Oh, God, Victor, you and me, going back there together? Oh, heavens, it's an answer to a dream."

He knew that, of course: her dream, her obsession, to return to that far-off country where they were born, to see again the house where they lived when they had parents. The parents only she could remember. She'd worried that bone all their lives.

"You'd have to pay your own airfare," he said firmly. "Though I suppose you could share a hotel room with me. The firm will pick up the tab for that, naturally." He was digging a deeper and deeper hole for himself.

"Don't worry, I'll find the money. Somehow. Who cares what Adrian says?"

Victor could imagine what Adrian would say. It gave him some satisfaction that his brother-in-law might have to forgo a piece of silver or another useless painting.

She laughed again, joyously. "Victor, it's unbelievable—one minute sitting here depressed and unhappy, the next an offer like this, out of a clear blue sky. Though the sky is by no means blue down here. Victor, you're my savior. My angel! My darling little brother. I love you, Victor."

Love. That overused word. Defiled and denigrated by the constant babblers of radio and television. A word that made him perspire.

"No need to overdo it, Izzy. Nothing stopped you going yourself, you know. You could have gone anytime if you'd really wanted to."

He thought he detected, then, the dreaded sound of a sniffle, a whine in her voice. "No, it had to be you and me together. We left together; it's only right we should go back together."

"Sentimental nonsense. I want no weeping and wailing on this trip, Izzy, you understand? Otherwise I will regret ever having suggested it." He already regretted it.

"Not a peep, Victor. Not one single damp eye. I promise."

He didn't believe her.

"Let me know when you've got your ticket," he said. "Friday week. The sixteenth. British Airways from Heathrow to Singapore. It's a hell of a long flight. Bring something to read."

He put the phone down, appalled by his own foolhardiness. There was just a faint hope she might not be able to get on the flight.

Victor left for lunch immediately, to the familiar watering hole, the Bull and Feathers, around the corner from the office. Lord knew he needed a drink. He fought his way to the bar and downed a pint with some degree of relief. The Bull and Feathers was packed as ever at lunchtime with the usual City crowd of secretaries in too much makeup and with fresh-faced minions in dark suits and striped ties, the volume of braying laughter and shouted conversation deafening, everyone jostling at the bar for food and drink. Usually he came earlier, before the real crush began. He thought it was a wonder anything was achieved in the City in the afternoons, with the amount of beer poured down the throats of the workers between one and two P.M. He looked forward to getting out of London in this dark month of November, in this dark year of 1973, out of the grimy streets and the chilly winds picking up strength for the winter ahead, out of these overcrowded, smoke-filled drinking places. He was afraid he may have ruined the escape by burdening himself with Izzy.

Though the truth was, he admitted, watching the giggling girls and the occasional male hand straying down someone's skirt, that the Far East was a long way to go all by himself. They'd sent him to America earlier in the year to learn a new bookkeeping system on Wall Street, and it'd been an uncomfortable time, the canyon-like streets of New York intimidating to an Englishman, the hotel room sterile, impersonal, the bars dark and unfriendly. He wasn't a good traveler, was not open to easy conversation with strangers, not interested in museums or people-watching. Ten days alone in the heat and foreignness of Malaya might be bad for his sanity. He had to watch his sanity.

And he owed Izzy. He thought about it sometimes, now and then, particularly after she'd irritated him beyond bearing. It's a burden to owe one's life to someone, let alone to your sister. Not that she ever reminded him of it; he gave her that. But it weighs on a man to have to look at a woman and know that but for her he wouldn't be around today. Much as one must have to look at a mother, Victor supposed, though he never had to deal with that, which was a relief to him.

Apart from Isabel, he'd been able to live his life free of such onerous considerations.

A girl pushed past him and jostled his elbow, slopping beer over the edge of his glass. "Sorry," she said carelessly, with a sideways indifferent glance across her shoulder. She was so near to him that her perfume overwhelmed the masculine smell of malty beer and ham sandwiches.

"Why, Victor, it's you!" She smiled and fluttered eyelashes thick with blue mascara. Why blue, in God's name? What creature in nature has blue eyelashes? For a moment, he couldn't imagine who on earth she could be, and then he dimly recognized her as one of the clerks down the hall in the office and was amazed that she not only knew his first name but was using it, as though she were some sort of intimate, some kind of equal. Victor found the usage of first names distasteful, yet another blurring of the parameters between those he was forced to be acquainted with and those he wanted to be acquainted with.

"I wouldn't have thought I'd find you in here at lunchtime, Victor." She had one of those excruciating Home County accents. "Not quite your scene, is it?"

He looked blankly at her. What did she mean, his kind of scene? "I've been coming in here most lunchtimes for the past five years, Miss . . . er . . ."

"Bette," she said, and drooped her blue eyelids. "With an *e*. Bette Lumley. I'm in the European Division. I'm an accountant too, you know. Sorry about your beer. I was in a hurry to get to the loo."

Victor stepped carefully out of her way, practically onto someone else's toes. She put one hand on his arm and slid past, her breasts brushing against him. The place was altogether too crowded, bodies forced against one another, soft flesh pressing against soft flesh, and suddenly it was airless and fetid in there, too much female scent, too much masculine breath. Women never used to come into pubs like this. Once, one could get a halfway quiet drink and sandwich at lunchtime and not be exposed to girls on the way to the loo, as they called it, wriggling their behinds and thrusting their tits against you. Once, firms like Parker and Dellworthy didn't have giggling female accountants or female lawyers one mistook for clerks. It must have been easier in the old days.

He left without finishing his beer. Somehow he almost looked forward to Malaya.

2

"Y<small>OU DID WHAT?</small>" Adrian lowered his glass and stared at her in disbelief, his mouth drooping open so that he looked for a moment like an idiot. "I can't believe I heard what I think I just heard."

She'd had trouble deciding whether to tell him before dinner, during dinner, or after dinner. Then she watched as he fixed his gin and tonic and settled into the chair by the kitchen table, comfortable and complacent, and she knew no time would be a good time.

Repeating the statement calmly, Isabel said, "I booked a ticket to go to Singapore with Victor. Friday week. The sixteenth."

Adrian buried his head in his hands. "Good God almighty, Isabel! Without even discussing it with me first?"

She was stirring the roux for the white sauce, whisking it around in the small copper pan with a wooden spoon. She didn't look at him. "I was afraid you'd try and talk me out of it."

"Too right I would. I'm still going to try and talk you out of it. I never heard such nonsense, leaping on a plane to the other side of the world without a moment's notice."

"You've got ten days' notice. And you can't talk me out of it. The ticket's nonrefundable."

"Damn it, Isabel. Look at me while you're talking to me. How much did it cost?"

She raised her head and looked at him. His thin brown hair stood on end, spiky, where he'd been pushing his fingers through it, and his mouth had drawn into a sulky and petulant pout. God forgive me, she thought, I'm not sure I can live with him anymore. She beat furiously at the thickening mixture in the pan. "Don't worry. I took the money out of my own account."

He threw his hands apart, almost knocking over his glass. Grabbing at it, he banged it down on the table. "You know we agreed to keep that money in reserve for emergencies."

"This *is* an emergency. I'll never have another chance like this. You know Victor would never go there unless he was sent on a business trip."

Adrian shook his head in a pitying manner, drained his glass, got up to refill it. "What sort of company do you think Victor will be, for heaven's sake? You think he's going to take you off sightseeing? Think he'll spare the time of day to look for relics of the past? You really imagine he's waiting eagerly to wallow in the mysteries of family history? Victor has absolutely no interest in all that stuff."

"Victor only pretends not to be interested in all that stuff, as you call it. Once I get him there, I know he'll want to find out things just as much as I do."

"Isabel, you have a foolish romantic view of your brother's nature. He's nothing but an old woman. Thirty-two years old and already dried up. Totally without juices."

She was always having to defend Victor to Adrian. And vice versa. They could at least pretend to like each other.

"Victor's wary of life, that's all. How would you be if you lost your mother soon after you were born? If you'd been shunted around a dangerous world as a tiny baby, no one to love you or comfort you? If you'd waited and waited for your father to come home from the war and he never came? If you'd spent all your childhood in a boarding school? He's lucky he's as normal as he is."

But Adrian had heard it all before. He snorted. "Normal? Victor? He's a prude, a lemon. Terrified of women. Look how he is with you. Keeps even his flesh and blood so far away you almost have to shout to get him to hear anything. When the feelings were handed down in your family, you got them all, Isabel. All the raw ends and all the imagination. It's you that agonizes about what happened to your parents, not Victor. Victor doesn't give a damn. I can't believe he even asked you to go with him." Stopping short, Adrian peered at her. "Did he ask you? Or did you invite yourself along?"

"Adrian, I swear he called me up this morning out of the blue. I could hardly believe it myself. Which just goes to show he wants it—doesn't he?—in spite of himself. Oh, I know Victor's a funny old stick. But he's my brother, and I love him. And he loves me, I know he does, however much he tried to pretend he doesn't."

"And I'm telling you you'll have a miserable time with him. Why, I'm more interested in your family saga than he is. You could at least have waited until I could go with you. I'd have thought you'd want me with you on a trip like this."

But that was exactly it. She didn't want Adrian with her. She wanted to be away from him. Since the boys went off to school, he'd stifled her with his unrelieved presence and insatiable sexual needs, as though getting rid of his children had released him from the constraints of fatherhood and transformed him into some kind of priapic stud. She'd been sleeping with him and eating meals alone with him in the empty beautiful house, listening to his views on the economy, the state of the nation, the political process, the Common Market, the immigrant situation, the stock market; his idea of conversation was to read an article aloud out of the newspaper over the breakfast table, an article that coincided with his views, of course. Isabel supposed she should count herself lucky he wanted to share his interests with her, except she'd discovered she had no interest in his interests. A great yawning gulf stretched before her.

She kept busy with preparations for dinner, fetching dishes, opening and shutting cupboard doors, clattering around the kitchen to make it seem warm and friendly. "Victor only pretends not to want to know. But he *has* to find out. I have to. We can't get on with today until we come to terms with what happened yesterday. We have to unbury the dead to truly believe they are dead."

Across the kitchen, Adrian watched her warily, his face pinched and exasperated. "That's you talking, Isabel. Not Victor. He knows that what's gone is gone. Over and done with. In the past."

She shook her head stubbornly. "They were his parents too. Flesh of his flesh. He needs explanations. We both need explanations."

Folding his hands on the table, Adrian bent his head over them and was silent for a long few moments. When he looked up again, the anger had left his face, crumpling it into the semblance of the young man she'd once known and loved. Getting up slowly from the chair, he walked across the room, put his arms around her. "I'm just afraid it will lead to more pain, my darling. You should let go of it. You should have let go of it a long time ago."

Isabel rested her head on his shoulder and tried to feel comforted. He wanted to do and say the right thing, she knew that, but she blamed him for the old nightmares that had come crowding back. If only he hadn't insisted on sending the boys away to boarding school. She'd argued against it endlessly, but Adrian truly believed it was the correct thing for them—to attend his old school, learn the same lessons, be brought up the way he'd been brought up. The way Isabel had been brought up too, which was why she was so opposed to it. But he'd planted it in the boys' heads for so long, they wanted it too, and now they would grow into strangers with masculine secrets and different loyalties, pressed and molded into a class of males beyond the reach of their mothers, a select band who would henceforth only dimly understand people like their mothers.

And once the boys—with their noisy laughter and their quarreling and their dirty clothes and their constant need for food—were gone from the house, a stony silence had descended on Isabel. Her sleep grew haunted not by her own children but by her dead parents. By her mother, whom she could hardly remember, not the shape of her or the sound of her. By her father, abandoned in that foreign place so far from England, deprived of the comfort of *his* children. Never to see them again. Never to see England again. Left to rot by an ungrateful, impotent country. Her father had been taught the same lessons the boys were going to learn, duty and loyalty and unquestioning conformity, and where had it left him? Where had it left her and Victor?

Her dreams were filled by the white house on the lawn carved out of the jungle, with the heat and the rains, with the questions buried so long by the waiting and the sense of abandonment, the lingering grief. She'd almost succeeded in growing into a whole person with marriage to Adrian, whom she once loved, and with children she adored. But not quite. Because there was a void, an emptiness at the core of her life, questions she was certain could be answered only by her returning to that white house in the jungle.

Isabel and Adrian sat opposite each other at the table in the dining room. She lit the candles in the silver candlesticks as she always did at dinnertime, and their light flickered around the room, off the old beams and the mahogany sideboard, off Adrian's things, glinting and gleaming around Adrian's beautiful house. He poured two glasses of wine, unfolded his napkin, picked up his knife and fork, cut one corner of the veal chop, laid down the knife and fork. "You will come back, won't you?"

She was watching the candles, thinking of the heat of Malaya, the sound of cicadas in the trees, the soft clicking of a fan in the ceiling. She was remembering her amah, with soft brown hands and long rustling sarong.

"What did you say?"

His face across the table looked almost unfamiliar, as though she had not lived with him for fifteen years, as though he were some stranger she had just met and had not yet learned to know well.

"You will come back, won't you, Isabel?"

"What a strange thing to say! Whatever would make you say something like that?"

3

ISABEL WAS ON time at Heathrow, surprising him. He thought of her as late for everything, dropping things as she ran, edgy and disorganized, but as she crossed the concourse toward him, she appeared calm and almost serene. It was difficult for him to focus on someone as close as a sister, but when she came at him like this, from a distance, Victor suddenly felt he was watching a stranger. The wild flying fair hair and the huge melting eyes gave her an air of deceptive fragility; in reality she was tall and sturdy, with big, strong bones. Today the thick curling hair was tied behind her long neck, so that she no longer seemed disguised as a Botticelli angel, and she was wearing a pale-green linen skirt and jacket that gave her a businesslike air, unusually cool and neat; even among the rushing crowds, Victor noticed heads turning to watch her pass.

Stopping before him, she smiled, the shining gray-green eyes alight. "Victor! I'm so excited, I can hardly walk straight."

"Save your energy. The flight is very long."

She grabbed his arm and pulled him toward the stairs and the bar on the next floor. "Let's have a drink to celebrate our journey."

He went with her unwillingly. "I don't know that drinking is such a good idea at this time of day."

"Come on, Victor. Let's get in the holiday mood."

"I'm not on holiday," he pointed out. "This is work for me."

In the bar, crammed with travelers in various stages of exhaustion, it took a while to find a couple of seats together. The table was still wet with someone else's beer, and a dark-skinned woman in baggy pants, a grubby white scarf draped around her head, came to mop it in a desultory and resentful fashion, crashing the glasses onto an overloaded cart. Among the throng, the dark skins far outnumbered the white.

Victor remarked, "Looks as though we're in the Far East already. What can they all hope to gain by coming here?"

Isabel dropped her bags at her feet and ignored the disorder. "Food and shelter, perhaps? . . . What about champagne?"

"Champagne? At eleven o'clock in the morning? The firm would never tolerate champagne."

"The firm? I don't expect the firm to buy my drinks, thank you very much. This is on me. And eleven o'clock in the morning is absolutely the best time for champagne."

She handed him a couple of ten-pound notes, and he reluctantly fought his way to the bar, stepping over suitcases and backpacks and brown paper packages, maneuvering between crying children and bad-tempered parents. He paid an exorbitant price and struggled back with a bottle of second-rate champagne. No matter what, it was good to be getting out of England. England was never at its best in November, but he was fed up with the whole country anyway—with the strikes and the complaining, the general level of sloppiness and inertia. He was sick of the political arguments, the constant chopping and changing of the system, one minute denationalizing everything, the next renationalizing it. He loathed the new money, the floods of Indians and Pakistanis, the thought of the Common Market.

He dumped the bottle and glasses on the table. "You have to wonder where everyone is going, don't you? Why can't people just stay at home quietly? Whittle did a great disservice to the world by inventing the jet engine."

Seizing the bottle, Isabel stripped off the gold foil and fumbled at the wires. She had large, clumsy hands and always dropped things, but this time she popped the cork quite expertly, pouring the frothing bubbly into the silly little glasses without spilling a drop.

She raised her glass. "Cheers, Victor. Here's to our great adventure." She gasped as the bubbles hit the inside of her mouth.

"Izzy, there's nothing remotely adventurous about Singapore anymore, unless you're talking financial markets, which somehow I doubt you are. And there never was anything like that about Malaya. Malaya is a small, jungle-infested, swamp-ridden, malarial nowhere." He sipped the champagne. It wasn't a drink he cared for. "Did you remember the chloroquine?"

Fishing in her carry-on bag, she rattled a handful of plastic containers at him. "I've got enough tablets to save the entire population of Asia. Antimalaria, antibiotics, antidiarrhea, vitamins, tranquilizers, and I've had my yellow fever, typhoid, and cholera shots."

"Tranquilizers? What on earth do you need tranquilizers for?"

She smiled at him, slightly, over the edge of the glass. Her eyes were astonishing, the color of the North Sea in winter, fringed with very black lashes. When she turned them on him like that, he almost had to look away from her. Izzy had a photo of their mother, and she'd seemed to have had the same kind of eyes. You could almost feel they saw things no one else could see. Demons and devils, probably. Isabel saw that sort of thing when no one else did.

"Sometimes," Isabel said, "I have trouble sleeping."

She *was* neurotic. "It's very bad to take stuff like that, Izzy. But if we have to share a room, I sincerely hope you won't tramp around all night, disturbing me."

Nothing he said seemed to squelch her determined good humor. "Sharing a room will be fun, Victor. Just like when we were children, remember?"

"I don't remember," he said, firmly, not wishing to get started on reminiscences.

Immediately she looked rueful, disappointed. "You wouldn't, I suppose. You were just a baby. But don't you even remember Aunt Lucy's house, before we went off to boarding school, when it was so cold you and I had to get into bed together to keep warm? I remember lots of things from when I was five and six years old."

"No." But of course he did remember. His memories from that age were quite as good as Isabel's; he just didn't choose to make a meal of them. Aunt Lucy, who wasn't a real aunt but a second cousin or something to their father, had taken them in when they first arrived back in England during the war, into her miserable little house in the wilds of Somerset, cold as death. They'd lived with her until their father was officially declared dead and there was money to send them off to boarding school. It came just in time, because Aunt Lucy, the only relative the authorities could find for them and a poor old duck anyway, died shortly afterwards. God knew where they'd have gone if there hadn't been some inheritance. The bedroom where he and Izzy slept was close under the roof, with a sloping ceiling and dark splotches of damp on the walls and a tiny little window that faced north, so the sun never came in. Izzy and he would cuddle together under the eiderdown, fully clothed because it was too cold to undress, watching their breath vaporize in the tomblike bedroom. Boarding school seemed almost warm and cozy after that.

"Where's Adrian, by the way?" Victor suddenly realized he should have been there to see his wife off. If Victor had a wife, he supposed he'd want to see her off.

"He has a meeting at noon, so he dropped me at the entrance. He said to say he's sorry he couldn't stay to wish us bon voyage."

Victor wasn't sorry. Adrian was a fussbudget, always checking details, worrying about papers and other minutiae. He'd have been asking if they had their tickets and passports and rushing them into the departure lounge. Victor supposed that's why Isabel married him, to have someone take care of the details of life she wasn't capable of taking care of herself.

"You do have your passport, Izzy?"

"I have my passport and I have my ticket and I've already checked in. And we've got seats together."

"I hope you're not going to talk the whole way to Singapore. I generally sleep as much as I can on an airplane."

"Well," she said, "I was hoping we might pass the time of day with a little conversation now and then, Victor. Even you can't possibly sleep for the whole journey."

"Maybe I'll try one of your tranquilizers."

"You just said that sort of stuff was bad for one."

That was another thing about Izzy that irritated him, the way she never seemed to forget when one contradicted oneself. Victor leaned back in the chair and took a gulp of the sweet champagne. Actually, it was making him feel quite cheerful. "It could be an interesting experiment. To see if that sort of thing has any effect on me."

"I won't guarantee it," she said, and laughed.

Out of the corner of his eye, Victor caught sight of an Indian at the next table, grinning as Isabel's laughter bubbled up, saw the way he was looking at her fair hair and pale skin. Victor glared at him, and the man turned his too-black, too-smooth head away, still smiling, his teeth very white in his dark face. Indians were a filthy, lascivious lot, Victor thought, with their *Kama Sutras* and erotic temples. Came of eating all that hot, spicy food. You could smell the curry and garlic on their breath if you got too close.

"Oh, Lord," Isabel said. "There's the announcement for our flight. We'd better get a move on." Scrabbling for her bag, she knocked back the rest of the champagne and jumped to her feet eagerly. Victor hadn't heard the announcement and had almost forgotten what he was doing at London Airport at eleven o'clock in the morning. When the Indian at the next table stood up too, he recalled with sinking heart that the flight went through Karachi and Bombay and so would doubtless be full of Indians and Pakistanis. It also stopped at Bahrain, which meant there'd probably be Arabs on it as well, and if there were any people that made Victor more uneasy than Indians and Pakistanis, it had to be Arabs. Arabs were buying up all of England these days.

Isabel hiccuped slightly and took hold of his arm.

"Tell me you're excited, Victor."

"When you have to travel as much as I do," he said, "there's not much to be excited about."

Then he thought perhaps that made him sound more of a wet blanket than he meant it to, and so he smiled down at her. "It will be exciting for you, I expect." He should stay on the right side of her. He would need someone familiar to keep him company among all those foreigners.

4

ADRIAN WAS RIGHT about Victor as a traveling companion. Laconic and uncommunicative, he did nothing to help make the endless journey any shorter. Isabel was determined not to mind. She sat beside him, watching him as he slept, which was a great deal of the time, and was grateful just to be with him. She found Victor's physical presence oddly comforting; merely by existing, he validated her own existence, his large, gawky body proving that those mythical people, his parents and hers, had actually lived and breathed outside her own mind.

Since their long-ago, disrupted childhood, they'd spent little time together, each shunted off to different boarding schools, Victor when he was only seven years old. Poor Victor, such a baby to be sent off to the regimented, deprived life of a boys' school. At least her own boys were spared until they were eleven and twelve—still only babies, too, but not fearful little scraps, as Victor was then. And at least the boys were together, not separated the way she and Victor were. It had been a terrible wrench when she didn't have her brother to take care of any longer.

In the seat next to her, his head rested at an uncomfortable angle, his mouth slightly open, his shortsighted eyes closed behind the glasses, the red hair growing too long over the back of his collar. The day they'd both gone off to school, his face was wretchedly pale, the freckles vivid across his forehead, the carroty hair cut so short his ears protruded, vulnerable and ugly. The regulation gray uniform had been bought one size too large so he could grow into it, and he was pathetic and faintly ridiculous in the baggy flannel shorts, his white neck sticking out of the loose gray shirt, the knee-length socks already rucking around his thin ankles. She'd bent down and pulled them up for him, knotted the striped tie. He couldn't tie ties then. He could hardly manage his shoelaces.

"I'll write to you every single day, Victor," she'd whispered against his fragile, pink-rimmed ear. "It won't be so bad. You'll learn to play cricket, just like Daddy, and you'll have lots and lots of friends, boys like you. Not just a sister."

But he never learned to play cricket like his father, or rugby, or any of those other games British schools considered essential for health, *mens sana in corpore sano*. He was too uncoordinated for games; it was probably just another agony to be made to join in the compulsory team sports. He'd never had many friends, either, as far as she could tell.

That first year, before Aunt Lucy died, at least they'd been together during the school holidays, Christmas and Easter and half-term. After that it was more difficult, for there was no one to go home to, no home to go to. Kindly parents, sometimes from her school, sometimes from his, occasionally took them in together, but they felt awkward, burdensome, intrusive. The children in whose homes they stayed never failed, in the way of children, to make them aware they were there on sufferance, as an act of charity. There was something shameful in being orphans, as though their parents had betrayed them by dying. Victor had turned into a phlegmatic, silent child, suffering indignities with silent stoicism, and Isabel couldn't wait to be able to provide a home for him herself. It was the first thing she thought of when Adrian asked her to marry him, though by then Victor was on his way to university and self-sufficient. At least that's what he said.

The aircraft bored across the roof of the world, through the heaping dramatic clouds, the Mediterranean unseen somewhere below. It put them down in Bahrain, and they stumbled out into the fierce desert heat. After a couple of hours, the plane flew on to Karachi and then to Bombay and down the length of India to Colombo. The crews and the passengers changed, day gave way to brief night and back to day again. The hours blurred together in a miasma of sleeping and waking, eating and drinking, swollen feet and aching head, not exactly discomfort but not comfort, either. The droning of the engines, the lack of fresh air to breathe and space in which to move about, dulled Isabel's mind and senses until it seemed she'd spent all her life enclosed in the metal tube of an aircraft.

Once, it took weeks to make this journey. Once, great ships carried the British to the far corners of their empire, steaming sedately through the Mediterranean and the Suez Canal and across the Indian Ocean for many languid weeks, with the empire builders partying and dancing their way to strange distant destinations. Isabel liked to think her parents had danced under the light of the moon on their way to Malaya, leaned on the rail and watched the ship's wake leaving England far behind, that they were happy then. At least they were happy enough to conceive her on the journey, one more in a generation of English children who'd sprung into being in the wombs of English women as they traversed the high seas.

Isabel, trapped in the confines of the airplane, felt that an ocean liner would have been a much more civilized way to travel. Though the only time she'd traveled that way, it had been far from civilized. She was six years old when the Japanese invaded Malaya and the British fled in unseemly haste. Those who could flee. She and Victor were crammed onto an old cargo vessel, which was supposed to take them to Australia but somehow became part of a convoy returning to Britain. That journey was very vague and confused in her mind, the months and months adrift on the dangerous oceans, dangerous enough for them to be torpedoed and rescued once more, out of the ocean. Rescued for what? She often wondered what their lives might have been if they'd reached Australia instead and spent the remainder of the war there. Perhaps the remainder of their lives. There'd be a different husband and different children, with sunburned skins and funny accents. Maybe even Victor would have turned out differently. But Isabel was sure she'd not have been much different, because even in Australia she would have waited for her father to come and get them, and when he didn't, she would still have wanted to know what happened and how.

Reaching into the bag beneath her feet, Isabel pulled out the small precious relics of her parents' lives, the few old photographs that once belonged to Aunt Lucy. Wrapped in tissue paper for preservation, they were brittle now, sepia colored, fading with age, half a dozen snapshots all that remained of two people's ambitions and emotions and desires. Yet she felt lucky to have even a tiny record like this. Before there were photographs, earlier generations had no images to gaze upon, nothing but slipping memories to mark the passage of life.

These photographs were so familiar she hardly needed to look at them anymore. Her mother posed in a chair somewhere, hands resting lightly in her lap, glowing eyes turned directly into the camera. Her father standing alone, arms folded, rather arrogant, so much like Victor, leaning against the veranda of the house in Kuala Lumpur. Isabel was sure her mother had taken that photograph; there was something about the expression in her father's eyes, a possessiveness that a man has when looking at a wife. There was one of herself as a toddler, her mother in a flowered dress, the sun harsh on their faces. A gathering on the lawn of the house, formally arranged, her parents among servants and guests, and her amah, Ayala, holding Isabel against the long skirt of her sarong. And her favorite photograph, her parents on their wedding day, her father smiling down protectively at the woman beside him. On that long-ago summer's day, the lacy brim of a hat shadowed her mother's face so the camera caught only a curving mouth uplifted in a tiny secret smile. Though Isabel had looked at that photograph many times, only now, suddenly, did it occur to her that she was already years and years older than that elusive figure was then, that death had already claimed her mother before she reached the present age of her firstborn child.

Victor stirred in his seat, and Isabel turned her face away so he wouldn't see the inevitable tears. She knew she cried much too easily. She tried to hide the photos in her lap, but he was already peering at them over her shoulder. "You brought those?" he said, as though amazed she would think to do so.

"Who knows? When we get to Kuala Lumpur, perhaps we'll find

someone who'll recognize someone. That one on the lawn, especially. Some of these people could still be alive."

He took the snapshots from her, staring at them. He hadn't lived with them as she had. "Hardly likely. It's more than thirty years ago."

"But when you come to think of it, people who were twenty, even thirty years old in those days would only be fifty or sixty now. If they'd lived, Mummy and Daddy would be in their sixties. That's not so very old." She knew he thought "Mummy and Daddy" was a childish way to speak about them now she was an adult, but that was how she thought of them. Mummy and Daddy, fixed in a child's mind, never growing old, never changing, just like their photos, just like her memories of them.

Victor studied the group photograph intently, bringing it close to his myopic eyes.

"Funny, that, come to think of it. It's all so long ago, so far in the past, you can't imagine anyone still being around who'd remember those times."

"I remember those times," she said.

"You only think you do, Izzy."

"I remember," she insisted, as she always did. "Why, it's even possible Ayala could still be alive." That unbidden thought, a sudden surprising idea, made Isabel's heart leap, driving away the tears and the aching boredom of the journey. "She was probably only a teenager when she lived with us. I thought of her as so grown up, so wise, but that's because I was only a child then."

"Which is Ayala, again?"

"There. I'm leaning against her. She was so darling, so sweet. I adored her. And she loved you, Victor. You were her precious new baby." Ayala, calm and beautiful Ayala, the one true constant in Isabel's life in those days, the presence she mourned perhaps above all others.

"She'd be old now," Victor said. "An old Malayan woman. Probably can't even speak English. She wouldn't be able to remember us."

"Of course she would. How could she forget?"

"Perhaps we didn't fill as big a part in her life as she did in yours."

Isabel thought about it. "That could be true," she agreed reluctantly. She didn't want to believe it.

Victor turned over the last photograph. "And this is Marike, of course."

It was the one photograph Isabel never quite liked to look at. Her father stood in the same place as before, against the white rails of the veranda with the white house in the background, but this time he had his arm around a dark-haired girl, very pretty, her thick springing hair curly and shoulder length. There was love in their eyes, unmistakable joy on both faces, and they laughed confidently into the camera.

"Yes, that's Marike."

"How pretty she was. They look pleased with themselves, don't they?" Victor handed the photos back to her, carelessly, without bothering to rewrap them in the tissue paper. "Didn't take him long to find someone else, did it?"

Isabel folded the crumpled paper around the photos and put them in her bag. Carefully. "You can't blame him. He was lucky to find someone who'd want to take on two small children. And Marike was as dear and kind to us as he could ever have hoped for. I can't remember which of the Dutch colonies she came from, but if she hadn't married him, she'd probably never have been caught up in the Malayan invasion, so sudden, so little time to escape. It just makes everything so much sadder, don't you think?"

Yawning, Victor stretched his arms above his head. "But there was something indecent about it, if you ask me, so soon after his wife died. You'd think he could have mourned a bit longer. You'd think he could have looked unhappy a bit longer."

She didn't want to hear him say that. But sometimes she thought it too, sneakily, treacherously. Too soon, too quick.

"It was wartime. People couldn't afford to waste time in the war."

"You always want to think of people as perfect, don't you, Izzy? Can't bear to believe that someone might not be wonderful and flawless. Maybe there was more to our father than you believe. You've built him up in your mind as an angel of rectitude and duty, a hero, a martyr, but he was flesh and blood, Izzy, just like the rest of us, with warts and all. And if you don't want to believe that, you shouldn't go asking questions, because you mightn't like the answers."

But there were questions to which she needed to find the answers.

Maybe the answers lay hidden somewhere down below the clouds there, in the heat and the dampness and the jungle, maybe in the house in Kuala Lumpur. There had to be some reason she dreamed of the house so often. She might be afraid of the answers, but she was even more afraid of not finding them.

When she looked at Victor, he was asleep again.

5

WHEN THEY FINALLY emerged from the airport building, Victor immediately felt even more exhausted. There was a pitchy blackness to the sky, quite unlike northern latitudes; the heat and humidity wrapped around them like a wet blanket, stifling and draining.

With a tone of astonished outrage, Isabel asked, "You know what the name of this airport is?"

"Singapore, I hope."

"Changi! It's called Changi! Where that dreadful prison was, where all the soldiers died during the war. You'd think they'd want to forget that name, wouldn't you?"

He pulled out a handkerchief and wiped his brow, then he undid his tie and slung his jacket over his shoulder. "You've got to forget the war, Izzy. It's ancient history now."

A taxi drew up beside them, and a small Chinese driver leapt out and seized Victor's bag.

"The Raffles Hotel," Victor shouted. He always shouted at foreigners, as though by raising his voice he would make them understand him better. Pushing Isabel ahead of him, he fell into the back seat.

He'd forgotten, if he ever knew, that they drove on the left in Singapore, like civilized people. The taxi proceeded at a sedate pace, soothing to Victor's nerves, except that Isabel, perched on the edge of the seat, alert and bright-eyed, started a conversation with the driver almost immediately.

"Tell me," she said, "what's Singapore like now it's independent?"

Victor groaned to himself, and the driver glanced cautiously at Isabel through the rearview mirror, as if suspicious of her question. "We've been independent since 1965, madam. You will find it very different if you knew it before. You been here before, madam?" He spoke surprisingly good English.

"A long time ago," she said. "I don't remember it."

That was a relief. At least it didn't sound as though she was about to embark on colonial recollections with someone who was probably glad to have seen the back of the British.

"Singapore is going to be an important country, madam," the driver stated with pride. He seemed gratified to have an audience. Taxi drivers always wanted to tell you more than you wanted to hear. Victor closed his eyes. "We are building oil refineries and big banks and offices. Yes, madam, Singapore is a very different place from when the English were here. Our prime minister, Mr. Lee Kuan Yew, is a great man, very forward thinking, very ambitious for our country. He is strict with the people, and so there is no more prostitution, no drunkenness and gambling, not like the bad old days. Yes, madam, Mr. Lee is a very great man."

A bloody dictator, that's what he was, Victor thought. Not that dictators didn't do a good job here and there. He'd heard that Lee Kuan was running a tight ship in Singapore, the days of vice and corruption apparently dead and gone. Britain could do with a dictator to shape it up.

Maintaining an incessant chatter now that he knew no one was going to stop him, the driver pointed out sections of the city as they drove through, this section Chinese, this one Malayan, this Indian. Isabel nodded as he talked, peering out the windows into the inky blackness and pretending she could see something.

The Raffles Hotel, into which Parker and Dellworthy had booked Victor, looked exactly as he'd imagined: slightly down at heel, rattan furniture and circling fans, no air-conditioning, old colonial types sitting around as though they'd been left over from the twenties. It didn't occur to Victor until he stood in front of the registration desk that perhaps it was not quite appropriate to turn up there with someone he claimed was his sister. Taking Isabel's arm, he pulled her to one side.

"All in all, Izzy, it might be better if we had separate rooms. God knows what the firm might think if it got back to them that I'd shared a room with a woman."

She actually laughed. She looked incredibly fresh after so many hours on that infernal airplane, her hair neatly combed and tied back, her lipstick glossy, even her clothes not too crumpled. Victor scratched at the stubble on his chin. Women had it easier than men— just add a fresh dab of lipstick, and they looked almost like new.

"Oh, Victor, you are a stuffpot! We're thousands of miles away from London. Surely we can please ourselves."

She leaned her elbows on the high counter and asked the clerk waiting behind it, another neat little Chinese man, who wore a uniform and a stiff polite smile, "Is there a suite we could have?"

"A suite?" Victor was shocked. "Parker and Dellworthy won't go for a suite."

The clerk flipped the pages of his book. "We do have a two-bedroomed suite with adjoining bathroom, madam. You are staying three nights?"

"Three nights. That's right, isn't it, Victor?"

Turning back to the clerk, she smiled winningly, and he seemed flustered for a moment, his black eyes sliding away from hers. "Is the suite available for three nights?" she asked.

"Certainly, madam." Now his smile was almost genuine. "If you would please sign the register."

Too exhausted to argue, Victor signed his name and trudged behind the bellman, up the stairs and along a wide corridor. Isabel whispered, "Don't worry, Victor. I'll pay the difference. I thought it would be fun to live in style while we're here."

"You didn't even ask what the rate was," he grumbled. But if she wanted to throw Adrian's money around, he supposed it was her business. He just hoped there wouldn't be a fuss when the firm found out.

The large rooms were nice, Victor had to admit, with chintz slipcovers on the chairs and thin white curtains fluttering in the movement of the fans; a huge old-fashioned bathroom had a deep freestanding tub and brass taps and a cool tiled floor. Isabel tipped the bellman and Victor stretched out on the bed, thankful to get his feet on the same level as his head after so many hours of sitting. He had no idea what the local time was.

Isabel inspected the rooms, opening and shutting doors, peering into closets. She pulled the curtains aside and leaned against the window. "People are having dinner out on the lawn. It looks nice. I think we should shower and go down to the bar for a drink, walk around a bit. I'm desperate for some fresh air and exercise, aren't you?"

Dear God, he had a maniac on his hands. "No. I have to rest."

"Oh, Victor, you slept and slept on the plane. Don't you want to see a bit of the town?"

"I'm here on business," he pointed out again, "not pleasure. You go and see the town, though I doubt you'll get much fresh air. It's hard to breathe out there. Tell me all about it tomorrow."

Removing his glasses, he closed his eyes.

He could hear her moving about, the water running in the bathroom, more doors opening and closing, and he was irritated that she wouldn't lie down and take it easy. It must be hell having to live with someone with too much energy. Isabel's energy was the nervous kind, not the accomplishing kind; she spun wheels and fiddled around for the sake of doing something, not with any object in view. She was just totally unable to sit quietly and silently. It disturbed Victor to have another person so close at hand; she was an intrusion on his territory. He should have insisted on separate rooms. He'd lived alone for too long to share living quarters with anyone else. The day he left school, he swore never to live again in close proximity with another human being. Not that he considered schoolboys human beings. Those years and years of communal bathrooms and sleeping spaces, the noisy hordes of unwashed and idiotic youths who considered a desire for privacy an affront to their masculinity, or their esprit de corps, or some other outdated notion, as if those who didn't want to join in all the time couldn't be normal, had put him off cohabitation forever. Most of the boys at his school had gone on to the army, where they could continue their institutionalized, unprivate lives, where they could spend the rest of their days marching and countermarching in formation, dressing alike, behaving alike, thinking alike. In Victor's opinion, the British boarding school system turned people into useless worker ants. If there was one thing the British didn't need anymore, it was surely an army.

But even as he rested his aching eyes and longed for some real sleep in a real bed, to restore his sagging flesh, he found something oddly comforting in the sounds from the other room, in the thought of his sister changing her clothes and spraying herself with perfume, tarting herself up for an assault on the colonial types in the bar down below. He hadn't, after all, been washed up alone on a foreign shore. There was someone around who'd care if he lived or died.

The door of the bathroom opened, sending a stream of light into his quiet haven.

"I'm changed and unpacked and ready for a bit of action. Are you sure you wouldn't like to come with me, Victor? Don't you fancy a nice gin and tonic? A Tom Collins?"

"Singapore Slings," he said, eyes still closed. "That's what they drink in Singapore, I believe."

"A Singapore Sling, then. Do come down with me, Victor. I can't bear to think of you lying here alone, missing life."

"Didn't look like much life in that bar." He thought about it, about getting off the bed and standing upright, placing his worn-out behind on yet another seat, considered his unshaven face and stiff neck and swollen feet, the wrinkles in his trousers, the tightness in his scalp, the general feel of staleness, furred teeth, diminished lung capacity.

"Oh, all right, please yourself," Isabel said. "See you later."

He opened his eyes. She'd changed into a flowered dress, soft and flowing, totally correct for the Raffles Hotel. He stared at her for a moment. "Now I come to think of it, a gin and tonic sounds pretty good. I wonder if the ice will be safe." He swung his swollen feet to the floor. "You'll have to wait while I shave."

It turned out to be only eight-thirty in the evening. The bar in the hotel turned out to be not so bad. Expatriates sat around in the cane chairs in linen suits and sunburned faces, the waiters were Indians and Malays in short white monkey jackets, there was even a string orchestra, for God's sake, sawing away in a palm-fringed corner. But he had to admit there was an air of civility to the place, no braying laughter and raised voices and crushing bodies, not like the Bull and Feathers. No over-made-up secretaries in the bar of the Raffles Hotel, thank God. No fighting your way to the bar here. Here a man came and took your order, in a subdued and polite manner, and brought it to the table, one of those glass-topped kind over a rattan base. The chairs were comfortable and spacious. The fans clicked gently overhead, created a pleasant stir in the warm air.

"Not so bad," Victor said, and decided not to worry about the ice.

Izzy appeared unbowed by the dreary flight and the time changes. She nursed her drink, and the flowered dress floated around her in the chair, and her hair was pinned up at the back of her long white neck. She gazed about the room, and quite a few of the sunburned faces stared back at her with interest. "Think of it," she said. "Mummy and Daddy might have sat in this very place, in these very chairs, having drinks just like these."

"I rather like your hair like that," Victor said. "Quite suits you."

Her eyes swiveled back to him, wide and surprised. With their fringe of thick black lashes, the washed gray-green irises surrounding deep, dark pupils, they were eyes that always made him believe she was about to say something startling, even though she never did.

"Why, Victor! That's almost a compliment."

"It wasn't meant as a compliment. It was merely a statement of fact."

Isabel pulled her mouth down and then smiled. "Well, thanks anyway. I'm so glad you decided to come downstairs. It wouldn't have been the same sitting here all alone." She took a deep breath and let it out slowly, her breast heaving under the filmy flowered material. "I like this place. It's exactly how I thought it would be. It smells of the old days, doesn't it, when Britain ruled the Empire and all was well with the world. When you've finished your drink, let's go outside and look at the lawn. And then we should step out a bit, don't you think? Stretch our legs."

There it was again, that inability to sit quietly and enjoy the moment.

"Just do me a favor," he said. "Please don't refer to our parents as Mummy and Daddy. It's not seemly at your age, Izzy."

She gazed at him gravely. "Perhaps you're right," she said. "I'll try, Victor."

Eventually he let her drag him out of the bar. He plodded across the cricket ground by the great white colonial city hall or whatever it was, his legs stiff and swollen, past a church that looked as though it belonged in Somerset, down to the river, where the city reverted to its Oriental origins: crumbling Chinese godowns and food stalls and flaring burners and the smell of cooking rice and curry and hawkers with cheap clothes and heaps of jewelry and crowds of polyglot natives pushing and shoving.

"Oh, God," said Isabel. "I love it, Victor. The warmth and the smells and all these people. It's like coming home. And when we get to Kuala Lumpur, it will really be home."

Exaggeration again.

6

*W*HEN SHE AWOKE in the night, Isabel couldn't at first imagine where she was. She listened for the sound of Adrian's breathing in the bed beside her and heard instead a mechanical, clicking sound, strange and yet dimly familiar; opening her eyes into the blackness, she saw disembodied red numbers floating in the dark near the bed and stared at them uncomprehendingly. Then the numbers became a digital clock telling her it was two A.M., and she remembered. Singapore. The Raffles Hotel. Fumbling for the light by the bed, she slowly realized that the clicking sound was a fan turning above her head, and was surprised by her second thought: she missed Adrian in the bed beside her.

In the lonely empty bed in the hotel, she thought about her bed in the house in Kuala Lumpur. The bedroom there hadn't been so different from this one. It was smaller and lower, less grand, of course, but there was a shining wood floor like this, and curved rattan furniture, slatted louvers at the windows, and flimsy curtains stirring ever so slightly in the breeze of the fan. Except in Kuala Lumpur the heat was heavier and more breathless, and there had been a white mosquito net draped over her narrow bed like a tent. Getting into bed was a tiny adventure, to dive in fast before the mosquitoes got in with you, to close the net quick. But before she leapt into bed, she'd kneel beside it and say her prayers while Ayala waited, and then she would jump in and Ayala would tuck the ends of the net under the mattress and blow kisses through the cloudy filmy material. Each night, Isabel placed her hand against the netting, and Ayala held it until she drifted into sleep. She asked Ayala why it was the mosquitoes didn't bite her, and Ayala shrugged and said, "Little mem, who knows? Maybe they like better your yellow hair."

Her father explained that mosquitoes bit everyone, but the natives didn't make so much fuss about being bitten because they didn't understand the dangers. Everyone got malaria, he explained to Isabel, though perhaps the English seemed to suffer more from the disease. But everyone should be careful of malaria, he said, because a lot of people died from it.

It was thirty years since she'd heard her father's voice. Now, closing her aching eyes, Isabel could still hear the light amused tones, see the small gestures, the way he pushed his glasses back on his nose with two fingers, the way he thrust his hands deep into his pockets and rocked backward and forward on his toes when he was thinking. Thirty years since the Japanese invaded Malaya and tore her life apart. She should have recovered from it by now, and she wondered how all those other people out there in the world whose lives had been distorted by war and death and irretrievable loss recovered from it. Or did they? Didn't such traumatic events always leave scars? Didn't the wounds just heal over superficially, become hidden beneath layers of living and grow obvious only when one was naked or tired or life turned difficult? The world understood and forgave the victims of the Nazis for suffering long afterwards, but there were other victims who still carried wounds. From other corners of the conflict. The world seemed to have forgotten about them. They'd been expected to return to normal quickly and quietly. The forgotten war, that's what the British war in the Far East was called. Forgotten by some. Not by those who lived through it.

After a while, Isabel drifted once more into sleep, a child again, her hand drooping out of the bed. In her sleep, she smiled, imagining she felt the touch of her amah's hand, warm and brown and reassuring. Keeping her safe.

In the morning, Victor was so jet-lagged, Isabel was sorry for him. She had to shake him to rouse him, and when he groaned awake and put on his glasses, his eyes were bleary and red-rimmed, the gingery stubble sprung again on his chin. "Oh, God, I'll be late," he muttered, when she told him what the time was. He fell out of the bed and stumbled his way to the bathroom.

"I was awake half the night," he complained, through the door. "Why do we have to do this to our bodies?"

"You were awake? So was I. We could have kept each other company."

He came out of the bathroom, still swaying on his feet. "Isabel, with all due respect, that's not the sort of company I want at two o'clock in the morning."

She grinned up at him from the sofa, drinking tea she'd ordered from room service. "Why, Victor, what sort of company were you thinking of?"

He plucked haphazardly at the clothes still packed in his suitcase. "Izzy, you have a dirty mind. I was thinking of a nice undemanding television program or a friendly game of bridge."

"Oh, Victor! I imagined you were going to surprise me with some wild and exotic fancies. You disappoint me."

"Yes, I know," he said flatly.

As usual, she chose to ignore his ill temper. It took three cups of the hot, sweet liquid from the large pot of room-service tea to restore some color to his cheeks, a hint of intelligence to his face. "At least they know how to make tea here," he acknowledged. "Not like America. You can't get a decent cup of tea there for love or money."

When he started dressing, with much cursing and many muffled exclamations, Isabel got off the sofa and peered out the window to watch the army of hotel staff on the lawn below, sweeping, tidying, straightening chairs, laying fresh white cloths on the tables. They moved slowly and deliberately, not rushing, each performing a small task in a ballet-like routine, something soothing and reassuring about their languid, unhurried movements. She turned back to the room and saw the disorder that Victor was creating as he rooted around in the suitcase, flinging clothes onto the bed and the floor.

"What you need, Victor, is a wife. Why don't you find some nice girl to marry?"

He groaned aloud. "Because a wife would almost certainly insist on talking in the morning, just like you."

At last he'd battled through the morning preparations, but he emerged still disheveled and frazzled, his thick hair straggling over his collar, his shirt and suit wrinkled.

Isabel said, "My God! You look like a crumpled heap. I'll unpack the rest of your clothes for you while you're gone and get them pressed."

"I'm quite happy with the way I look, thank you. Why do women always try and remake people?"

"Because it doesn't do to be too self-satisfied with your own product, Victor. What time do you think you might be back?"

He shuffled through his briefcase to check his papers. "That's another thing a wife would say. 'What time will you be home, dear?' I don't know what time I'll be home. I don't even know how much there will be to do. You'll just have to amuse yourself for the rest of the day, Izzy."

"Don't worry about me. I can manage perfectly well. I do it every day, you know. But if you're back in the hotel by five o'clock, we can have dinner then so you can go to bed early."

Picking up his briefcase, Victor placed it under his arm, armed and ready for London, not the tropics, in his creased gray suit, striped shirt, and striped tie. Even his tie was a mess. She restrained herself from smoothing and reknotting it for him.

He paused with his hand on the doorknob, delaying his entrance into the outside world. His shoulders sagged. "Don't you feel even a bit tired?" He asked the question hopefully. "It's not natural to be this cheerful in the morning."

"Must be adrenaline or something. I feel marvelous."

"At least you can go back to bed." He slammed the door shut.

Isabel poured herself another cup of tea. She knew she, too, would be grumpy if she had to sit and look at ledgers and accounts all day, when the Orient was waiting to be explored just beyond the door. Perhaps it was because she had no head for figures. Figures were dull and unexciting, not worthy of the close attention her brother paid to them. As brother and sister, they'd inherited not only different personalities but also the right brain/left brain functions that went with those personalities. She knew that Victor probably didn't want to explore the Orient; he probably wanted to sit all day in an office, where he felt safe.

If Isabel had a head for anything, it was music. She'd never completed the music degree she was attempting when she met Adrian. Because she was aware that her talent was minor, her ambition had been low-key, so to speak, but she still sang and played the piano when the mood took her. Her small talent had promised such an uncertain way to make a living, she'd been relieved never to have had to test the market. However, it worried her now that as a result of her incomplete studies, she was not capable of earning her own living; she'd put herself on an insecure footing in life and in marriage. Not that Adrian didn't earn more than enough for all of them. Or would if he didn't spend so much on the house. It also worried her that she didn't care as much about the house as he did.

It was a beautiful house. Adrian had made it beautiful, lavishing all his free time and energy and finances on restoring it to a never known former glory. Once the coachhouse of the estate at the village edge, it was crumbling and decaying when they bought it, over her objections. "So much work, Adrian. We'll never be able to do anything but take care of it." He hadn't listened, of course. Adrian appeared to listen to her, but he never heard what she was saying. Now the old coach house was a showplace, with great oak beams and odd-shaped rooms, bedrooms converted out of haylofts, a kitchen with stone flags and hooks in the ceiling where tackle once hung; there were even roses around the reconstituted stable door. Isabel admired the results and hated the process, the eternal hammering and disorder, the plumbing that never quite worked properly, the uneasy sense that the occupants of the house were less important to Adrian than the house itself. It was Adrian who reveled in the details, who browsed through antique shops to find the exact and perfect fittings, the correctly dated pieces that would make the "right statement." Isabel wasn't interested in statements. She'd just wanted a home. She'd wanted to take vacations in France and Italy. She wanted to go to the opera. She supposed she was lacking in some way.

That house on the edge of an English village, the house that wasn't quite a home, seemed incredibly distant now. Which it was, of course, literally thousands and thousands of miles away. But it also seemed a lifetime away, as though just one night in the heat and humidity of the tropics had wiped clean all her existence since she was last in this place. Even the boys seemed a distant regretful memory, gone from her, departed into their masculine separate world, never to be her little boys again, her darlings, her babies. Maybe she'd used up all her love on their childhood, and there was none left over for Adrian or for the rest of her life. At thirty-seven, Isabel found that an alarming, desolating thought.

She filled the bathtub in the splendid bathroom, tipped in the complimentary bath salts, and lay for a long time in the silky tepid water, soaping her long white legs, massaging her belly, idling when she should have been dressing and getting out there in the heat and the crowds. Maybe she was saving herself for Kuala Lumpur, storing up energy to spend on her journey of rediscovery. Singapore was merely a way station, a pause in the real journey.

What did she expect from Victor? That he would suddenly become close and warm with her? The sort of brother she thought she deserved? Would he ever find a wife? Or was he so flawed by his childhood or by his innate nature that he would never learn to love anyone enough to want to marry, to have children? The very idea of Victor having children of his own made Isabel gasp with sudden laughter. Would they look like tiny versions of the grown-up Victor, ponderous and unhumorous, or would they look like him as he was when he was small and skinny and vulnerable? The way she still thought of him. She was constantly surprised and shocked by the change in his appearance, as though he should somehow have remained the baby brother she'd loved and cared for. Males made such a terrifying transformation at puberty, a totally alarming change from clear-skinned, clean-limbed angelic creatures into overgrown spotty monsters sprouting hair everywhere. Sadly, it would happen to her own boys, and then she'd never know them again.

Eventually Isabel got out of the bath. She dressed slowly, still wondering about Victor and his future. She knew that marriage and children didn't automatically bring happiness. But they fulfilled a certain predestination, a perpetuation of life without which existence made no sense. Not that her own existence made much sense. Isabel knew in her heart that she'd rushed into marriage, into having children, so that she could reinvent a family to replace the loss of her own. Trying to create a little order out of disorder, as though the passing on of her genes could somehow make up for the people who disappeared into the thick green blanket of jungle so many years before.

She would go out and look at Singapore, but she was waiting for Kuala Lumpur.

7

*V*ICTOR REALIZED he was a mere token at the Singapore branch of Parker and Dellworthy. In a couple of days, he couldn't possibly uncover any perfidy. Not that there was a question of perfidy, because most of the chaps running the show had gone to school in England; the head of the office was an Englishman, Oliver Bailey. Bailey was your old-fashioned colonial administrator, dedicated, loyal, honest; though he'd been here so long, some people said he thought like an Oriental. But it didn't hurt the Singapore lot to know London was keeping an eye on them. Every six months, someone came out to check the books; it just happened to be Victor's turn. He plowed his dutiful way through stacks of ledgers and bookkeeping, checking the accounting, not the operations side, and found everything in order, all the correct steps followed, no signs of double bookkeeping or false entries, nothing to raise the hackles.

He knew accountancy was considered a dull trade by some, but to Victor the neatly balanced rows of figures, the profit and loss columns, the breakdown of expenses, were akin to reading music. A musician looks at a sheet of music and hears the sound the notes make, and that's what figures did for Victor—played a tune in his head, sometimes discordant but usually Mozartian. Lots and lots of notes, all making sublime sense in the long run.

But the jet lag had rendered him wretched. It baffled him how the human race survived the unnatural business of screaming around the earth, thousands of miles above it. He couldn't imagine how that chap

Kissinger hoped to solve anything with his "shuttle" diplomacy; surely he must be on automatic pilot at the negotiating table, praying for his next cup of coffee, counting the minutes until naptime. No wonder the stupidity in Vietnam was dragging on for so long. And how could the Americans trust someone whose first language wasn't English to negotiate for them? As if a non-native speaker could possibly understand their point of view. That sort of understanding wasn't acquired, it was inborn. It was a simplistic notion that heritage and birth and centuries of culture didn't count for anything. Americans didn't understand Vietnam or the Vietnamese, and now they were allowing a foreigner to try and straighten out the mess for them.

In Victor's opinion, the Americans should have asked the British to help. The British had been around these parts for so long, they understood how Orientals thought. The British got the Communists out of Malaya without all the fuss America was making in Vietnam, just swept through the jungle and cleaned them out, no agonizing, no beating of breasts, no negotiating. And it hadn't taken hundreds of thousands of troops, either, just one good soldier who understood what he was up against. Good old Templer. At least the British could hold their heads up in Malaya now, not remain abject for the way the Japanese beat the shit out of them in those same jungles in 1942.

Victor was proud of the way Parker and Dellworthy jumped right back into the Far East after the war, took up the reins of commerce exactly where they left off. No head hanging for them. Parker and Dellworthy had been trading around the East forever: rubber, tin, copra, tea, silk, coal, shipping—you name it. Now they were into oil, and they were still a mighty operation, even if the Empire had gone by the board, even if these tin-pot countries were claiming these lands as their own. Their lands were nothing before the British organized them; there was no India or Burma or Malaya until the British put down the warring factions, built roads and bridges and railways, gave them some semblance of law and order. Colonialism might be a dirty word in this day and age, but the British didn't have too much to be apologetic about.

Victor considered Singapore. Leaping into the twentieth century with the speed of light. They'd shucked off their colonial overlords and taken on a dictator. Now it was all cleanliness and new buildings and anticorruption and jailing people with long hair, locking up anyone who dared to disagree with Lee Kuan Yew. Victor thought they might come to rue the day the British left. At least the British left them to think what they liked as long as it didn't interfere with business. Now the people were mouthing slogans and pretending they lived in a democracy.

On Victor's second day, Bailey, the big boss, treated him to lunch at his sedate, deferential, and men-only club. The way of life couldn't have changed much for people like Bailey, even if the high, cool dining room, once for Brits only, now contained several Chinese in expensive dark suits. For Victor's taste, the food wasn't up to much, too many spices and odd things floating around the plate, but the beer was good.

Bailey seemed a nice enough chap, with a Marlborough tie and a respectable accent, but he was quiet and reserved, and for a while the conversation lagged. However, when Victor mentioned, to make sure no one got the wrong idea, that his sister was with him because she wanted to trace some family history, find out about the people who never made it out of Malaya, Bailey suddenly lost his sleepy, disinterested manner.

His blue eyes gazed intently at Victor, studying his face. "Your last name's Cartwright, isn't it? Victor Cartwright?" Emphasizing the surname as if hearing it for the first time, he put down his glass of beer and peered more closely at Victor. "You're not by any chance related to Rodney Cartwright, are you? The Rodney Cartwright who was at the Centre for Tropical Studies in KL before the war?"

Victor blinked in surprise. "As matter of fact, my father's name was Rodney. And yes, he was at the Centre."

Bailey's face lit up in what seemed genuine delight. "Good Lord! I had no idea. My dear chap, he was a famous man."

Victor was taken aback by the enthusiasm. "I can't say I knew he was famous."

"You didn't? Good God, man, Rodney Cartwright was a hero in this part of the world. You know how important the rubber trade is in Malaya? How terribly important it was to the war effort? It was devastating to the Allies when the Japanese captured Malaya's productive capability. Those who know say that if it wasn't for your father's work, the war could quite well have been lost. He had some technique for new trees or grafting or something like that, which resurrected the rubber industry in other parts of the world. They say he deserved a medal for his work. And for making sure his results got out before the Japanese discovered them. There's some story . . . I can't remember all the details now, but apparently he collected all his research together just before the Japs got to KL, and he smuggled it out. Something like that. Anyway, it's said that if it hadn't been for him, we'd have lost a vital commodity." He stared at Victor in polite astonishment. "Fancy you, of all people, not knowing all that."

Victor, though gratified to learn he had a famous father, felt obliged to explain why he didn't know about him. "I was less than a year old when we left, and I've never been back." Of course, Izzy had always insisted their father was an important man, but he'd thought it another of her romantic fantasies. And as to what techniques Bailey was talking about, Victor had no idea.

Bailey shook his smooth gray head. "Rod Cartwright's son not knowing about his father's work! I can hardly credit it. When you go to KL, you must visit the Centre. They'll fill you in. In fact, I'll give them a call when we get back to the office. They'll make a hell of a fuss of you—you'll get the royal treatment."

"Oh, no." Victor was immediately alarmed at the thought of fuss and royal treatment. Izzy would be blubbering all over the place. "That's really not necessary. My sister just wants to have a look at the house where we lived, that sort of thing, you know. Personal stuff, no pomp and circumstance."

"You'd go all the way to Kuala Lumpur and not see where your father did his research? That hardly seems natural, if I may say so." Bailey's eyes, the limpid pale blue typical of colonial Englishmen, the color washed out from too many years in the sun, fixed on Victor. Disapprovingly. "Wouldn't your sister like it?"

Victor shrugged. "She probably would. Women like that sort of thing, don't they? It's all more real to her because she remembers those times. That part of my life means very little to me. It was over before I knew who I was or where I was. Life for me started in a boarding school in England."

"My dear chap," Bailey cleared his throat, as though expressing sympathy. "I forget exactly what happened to your father. Did he end up in a prison camp?"

Suddenly Victor felt a twinge of regret about his ignorance. "We don't know, as a matter of fact. My sister and I were evacuated with other children just hours before the Japanese reached Kuala Lumpur. After the war, when Malaya was finally liberated, we expected—that is, my sister expected—to hear something, but the War Office couldn't find any trace of my father anywhere. Eventually he was declared dead, and we inherited his estate. It all took years and years, of course."

Bailey looked distressed. He signaled for another beer, as if to assuage some sort of guilt. "It's not an unusual story, unfortunately. But many of those we'd believed lost were found after the war, in places like South Africa and Australia. You know, they'd got out on ships and been torpedoed and things like that. They turned up years after everyone believed they were dead. You and your sister were some of the unlucky ones."

"Yes," Victor agreed. "I suppose you can say that."

"And your mother?" Bailey asked. "What about your mother?"

It wasn't a story Victor thought needed retelling, and as though Bailey could read his mind, he said, "I'm interested, you see, because I was in Malaya at the same time. As a matter of fact, I met your father once. I remember the occasion because he was really quite well known."

"You met him?" Victor stared at the unlined English face with astonishment. A survivor of that time still alive, still alive and kicking? "But you don't look that old." He stumbled for the right words. "I mean, it was all so long ago."

Bailey smiled briefly. "Long ago to you, perhaps, but twenty or thirty years are only the middle part of life. Hopefully, there's a lot left to go after that. I came out here straight from Cambridge. People did that in the old days, you know, aiming for a career in the colonial service. But my timing wasn't quite right, to say the least. I was caught almost immediately in the invasion. No one expected it, you know. We thought this part of the world was far away from danger. My poor mother was grateful I escaped serving in the army in France, but by the time I was less than your age, I'd already spent three years in a Japanese prison camp." He toyed with his knife and fork. "Sometimes those years seem only like yesterday. One tries not to dwell on it, of course, but occasionally I'm surprised to find myself still alive. A lot of people didn't make it."

The Japanese prison camps had been notorious for their death rates. Victor, for one, knew he'd never have survived. He looked at Bailey with renewed respect. "But you stayed on afterwards? I think I'd have wanted to go back home, get as far away as possible."

"Oh, I went home. But I'd changed too much. I was no longer the callow youth who'd left in 1941. And England wasn't home anymore. You won't remember what it was like just after the war. Gray and dismal and cold. I was always cold. Couldn't stand it."

Victor waited for him to go on, but Bailey seemed lost for a moment in another life.

"So you came back?" Victor prompted.

"Yes," Bailey said simply. "When my health recovered. Been here ever since. And that's why I'm interested in people like your parents. One can't help feeling a bond with those who went through the same experiences. You didn't tell me what happened to your mother."

Victor struggled to imagine a young Bailey enduring a Japanese prison camp: the starvation and disease, the ill treatment, the heat, the despair. It was only natural Bailey would feel a bond with those survivors. And with those who didn't survive. "As a matter of fact, my mother was dead before the Japanese came. She died soon after I was born. My father remarried shortly afterwards. And that complicated things even more, because there was the question of his new wife. If she had survived, Izzy and I might not have inherited."

Bailey must have heard the same sort of story a hundred times before. It was surely not unusual in the far reaches of the British Empire, in the aftermath of a distant war.

"The War Office didn't find your stepmother, either?"

"Absolutely no trace. Both she and my father disappeared completely."

Victor had never used the word "father" so often. It felt strange on his lips, unnatural.

Sipping thoughtfully on his beer, Bailey said, "That's surprisingly uncommon. The War Office did a good job, all in all. It's amazing how many people they were able to account for, through witnesses and survivors, villagers, guards, that sort of thing. Naturally, you and your sister want to try and find out what happened to them."

To Izzy it was a consuming, nagging question. Victor explained. "My sister would like to know. For myself, I accept that circumstances overtook them. They probably died in the jungle, far from anyone. Or in Japanese hands. Does it matter how it happened?"

Bailey raised his eyebrows, brushed crumbs from his jacket. "It's the sort of thing most people would want to find out."

"I see no point in hashing over it myself. It's over and done with. Nothing we find out can bring them back or alter it, can it?"

"The moving finger writes?"

Victor was puzzled for a moment. "Yes, I suppose. That sort of thing."

"I used to read the *Rubáiyát* when I was your age," Bailey said. "You know how it goes on?"

Poetry wasn't Victor's thing. He shook his head.

" 'The moving finger writes, and, having writ, / Moves on: nor all thy piety nor wit / shall lure it back to cancel half a line. / Nor all thy tears wash out a word of it' "

It made him uncomfortable to have the boss of the office quoting poetry at him. "I guess that's my philosophy," he agreed.

Bailey looked at him for a moment, then waved his hand to the waiter. "Maybe you're right, but I'd like to think my children would shed a few tears for me after I'm gone."

"The tears are my sister's department."

An elderly dark-skinned Malay in a short jacket came to the table, bowed as he presented the check. "I hope you enjoyed your lunch, Mr. Bailey," he said, politely.

"Thank you, Pran. Excellent, as usual."

As the man left, Bailey said, "*There's* someone who's been here forever. He was here in the club before the war. Amazing to think that, isn't it?"

"Amazing," Victor agreed. He began to feel as though he was wading in ancient history, caught in a mire of memories and regrets.

Signing the scrap of paper, Bailey stared at Victor again with the washed blue eyes. "And you, young Cartwright? Have you never shed any tears?"

Victor didn't want to offend him, but how he felt was how he felt. "What's the point? Tears are a fearful waste of energy."

They went down the steps of the club into the thick afternoon sunshine, and Bailey put a hand on Victor's shoulder. "We humans do use up a lot of energy on unproductive emotions, don't we? However, I've always associated tears with the human condition. Do any other of God's creatures have the capacity to cry?"

Victor assumed the question was rhetorical. In any case, he had no answer. He wished Bailey would drop the subject. Good job Isabel hadn't been with them. Together, Bailey and Victor walked back to the office, slowly, because no one walks fast near the equator, and as they passed the Raffles Hotel, Victor couldn't help wondering how Izzy was spending her day.

"Your accommodations comfortable there?" Bailey asked.

"Oh, yes, thanks. Very good." He didn't elaborate on the suite deal.

"Everyone who's anyone in British Singapore has stayed at Raffles," Bailey remarked. "It's seen a lot of people come and go. No doubt your parents would have stayed there once."

"Funny," Victor said. "That's just what Isabel suggested."

He glanced up at the faded elegance of the white facade and all at once realized he could be walking on the very same ground where his dead and distant father might once have walked. A small, uneasy sense of connection stirred in him.

Bailey said, "I *will* give the Centre in KL a call. You might find it an interesting experience."

8

THE CONICAL HILLS were draped in a dense green blanket of forest: trees, trees, and more trees. Isabel sat with Victor in the back of the car, and the weight of her thoughts reduced her to silence. The car and driver were an offering from the Centre, so they could go and see the house in the hills today. They'd been made so welcome at the Centre, more than she'd ever expected; at the Centre, people had spoken the name of Rodney Cartwright with reverence. In England, his name was forgotten.

The driver, a thin young Indian with a thick black mustache, was named Singh. He drove furiously and talked constantly, impervious to the lack of response from his passengers. "Soon to be there, lady and gentleman, very soon now," he repeated frequently, but when he slowed the car minimally and threw it into a narrow opening hidden between the ranks of trees, Isabel knew that now, they would indeed be there soon. The long years of anticipation crushed the breath out of her.

As they left the highway, the jungle descended upon them. Beneath the arching canopy, the road to the house was a thin layer of crumbling tarmacadam barely covering the soil. This lane was once unpaved, rutted, the red earth clogging and sliding under the wheels of her father's car; in the rainy season, the ruts turned into small racing rivers, so his car was completely mud-spattered by the time it reached the house. Every day, when he arrived home, the vehicle was ritually washed by one of the gardeners, a man with missing front teeth whose name she couldn't recall and whom she'd forgotten until this very moment. Today, a car still bumped and rattled over the uneven surface, just as in the old days, and Isabel clutched at the seat in front to steady herself, her fingers slippery with sweat.

Sunlight flickered through the thick layer of leaves, flashing hypnotically, unfolding the road like an old film at the wrong speed. Bamboo and palm pressed close against the sides of the car so they traveled in a green tunnel, then they lurched around a bend, and the sun filled the end of the tunnel in a burst of painful fire. Isabel flinched away from it, her eyes hurting.

"Almost there, lady and gentleman," Singh called out, as triumphant as if he had navigated them safely across an unknown and dangerous land. They were no more than five miles from the center of Kuala Lumpur.

Beyond the arc of light lay the house.

"Stop," she called to Singh. "Please stop the car. Victor, let's walk the rest of the way."

When the vehicle slowed to a skidding halt, Victor looked startled, as though he'd been asleep. He blinked through his glasses. "How far is it?"

"Only fifty yards or so."

"Christ, Izzy, it's too bloody hot. You walk if you want. I'm staying with the car."

Singh was already out of the driver's seat, running around to open her door. He extended a slender hand to help her down and smiled dazzlingly, his eyes very dark brown and bold, as though she were his special property. "I didn't think English ladies like to walk. Your feet in those nice sandals will get dirty."

"English ladies like to walk," she said, setting her feet firmly on the familiar path. "Wait for me at the house."

Shrugging his shoulders under his thin shirt, an exaggerated gesture that conveyed the strangeness of foreigners, Singh got back in the car and bumped slowly forward into the blinding glare and out of her sight.

The sound of the engine died away, and the silence of the jungle descended upon her. Not quite silence; the jungle was never silent; it was filled with little creaks and groans and whispers, flutterings and slitherings. Isabel stared into the tangle of leathery succulences that once held such terror for her. She was still afraid of it: the hanging strands of liana like snakes waiting to strike; the high, sun-spotted branches hiding shadowy leopards; the thick carpet of undergrowth a cover for monstrous insects. She wasn't a child anymore, but her heart still thumped too loudly inside her chest, banging away with a jungle beat all its own.

Under the trees, it was humid and airless. The fabric of her dress clung to her body. When she moved into the sunlight it would be even hotter and stickier, the sun a malignant force. She put on the hat she'd bought in the market in Singapore, drew the steamy air deep into her lungs, waited for her thundering heartbeats to subside, and then could wait no longer. She stepped through the barrier of light.

Even with the hat and dark glasses, the sunlight assaulted her eyes and washed all color from the scene, as though she were looking at an overexposed photograph, pale, shadowless, and unfamiliar. She'd expected the recognition to be instant, believing her heart would break immediately, and was almost disappointed that nothing cracked inside her. For a moment, she couldn't even see the house and felt a stab of panic, imagining it gone after all, then the grass beneath her feet became green, as green as she remembered, stretching in a long, gentle slope carved out of the jungle, down to the house where she was born.

The house itself swam into view, shimmering, floating, insubstantial, unbelievably familiar, square and white in the expanse of lawn, shaded by tall, feathery trees, veranda on all four sides, neat beds of rosebushes flaring into improbable brilliance. The house was unchanged, even after all these years. In her heart, she'd feared that war and time and different circumstances would have altered it beyond recognition, but it was exactly the same, as though thirty years were nothing, as though it had been waiting for her to come and reclaim it. Carefully—as if a sudden movement might cause it to vanish like a mirage—she moved across the grass toward it, then walked faster and faster, almost running in the cloying heat. As she came closer, the house grew solid and real, almost ordinary, until it resembled any other old colonial house in a strange foreign land. She slowed her headlong rush.

On the lawn beside the house, a large hand-painted sign said "Malayan Craft Centre. Batiks and Hand Crafts." "You will find it very different, I am sure," the director of the Centre had said. It didn't look at all different, but the people waiting on the veranda were not the ghosts she half expected to be waiting there for her. She saw Victor and Singh standing near the sign, under the shade of the trees, Victor wearing a panama hat that covered his red hair and shaded his eyes. He was rocking backward and forward on his heels, gazing up at the house, and for the first time, Isabel saw in him a resemblance to their father.

When she reached Victor's side, she took hold of his arm to walk up the steps with him. Out of the sun, the shaded veranda, dark-green paint on the wooden floors, was almost cool; the doors to the inside of the house were wide open and inviting, drawing her eyes.

"It hasn't changed," she said, "not at all. It looks exactly the same."

Four women in sarongs, small and fine-boned, with shining black hair and brown smiling faces, stood waiting beside the open doors. Singh announced, self-importantly, "The mem and the tuan have come all the way from England to see this house because they used to live here once upon a time. Before the war. Before the Japanese came."

Once upon a time, Isabel thought. As in a fairy tale.

The women bowed and pressed small hands to their chins, glints of gold in their smiling mouths, their eyes not quite meeting those of the visitors. Beside them, Victor loomed huge and untidy, face flushed scarlet from the heat, clothes rumpled, unsuitable black shoes splaying across the veranda floor. He took off the panama hat and fanned his face with it. "Christ, it's hot," he said.

One of the women rustled forward, in her hands a tray with a tall glass pitcher and thick tumblers. "Please. For the mem and the tuan." She giggled nervously and glanced sideways at Singh, said something to him.

"It is lemonade," he said. "They made it themselves. It will be quite safe."

"How kind." Isabel took one of the glasses and handed it to Victor. He gulped the lemonade down and grinned at the women. "Thanks," he said loudly. "Very nice." The women turned their heads away and looked at the ground.

"These ladies are working here," Singh explained. "They are most happy to show you everything. This house which once was yours is where artists bring their work and where these ladies weave the cloth in the old methods. You see, they wear traditional dress from the cloth made right here. Perhaps you remember this kind of dress?"

Yes, she remembered. Each of these women looked like Ayala, the same graceful movements, the tiny hands, the smooth brown face, the long elegant sarong. Ayala's feet were bare, and her silent feet had trodden the boards of this very same veranda, her hand holding Isabel's. Before these women would have been born.

"The tuan and mem's father was a very important gentleman at the Centre," Singh said importantly. "Everyone has heard his name."

It was true. Everyone at the Centre for Tropical Studies knew of Rodney Cartwright. They'd been astonished to find the great man had living descendants, and had shown his desk, the laboratory where he did his experiments, even a fly-spotted framed photo of the prewar staff, grave young Englishmen in colonial uniform, long khaki shorts and knee-length socks. Rodney Cartwright's memory was praised and extolled, a triumphant affirmation that her father's worth was not a mere figment of her imagination. Even Victor was impressed.

The women on the veranda rustled and smiled and gestured, inviting them into the house. Isabel would have preferred to make her own tour, but they were already leading the way and Victor was following, bending his head to duck through the door. She hesitated, took a breath, and stepped over the threshold.

She pulled off her dark glasses, but it still took a moment for her eyes to adjust to the different light. "This was the sitting room," she said to Victor. "I think."

The rattan furniture with the bright cotton covers was gone; there were no gleaming tables with oil lamps and trinkets, no pictures of England on the walls, no tigerskin rug with gaping fanged mouth and watching glass eyes. Now the space was filled with hand looms and heaps of material; shelves stacked with bolts of cloth lined the walls, and there were long wooden tables with lengths of cloth pegged out on them. A child stood beside one of the tables, bowls of dye on the floor beside her, her little hands stained blue, her huge black eyes fixed on Victor and Isabel. One of the women touched Isabel on the arm and said something to her.

"It is her daughter," Singh explained. "She is learning to make batik."

The mother spread her fingers and Isabel counted. "Eight?" She herself was six years old when she left here.

The woman spoke again, and Isabel had to wait while Singh translated. Once, she could understand the language herself, but it was lost to her now, as so much was lost from that time.

"She wants to know if the mem has children too."

"Yes, I do. Tell her I have two boys. One is eleven and one is twelve."

"Ah, sons." Singh nodded approval. "That is good. Your husband will be pleased."

Victor laughed, a sudden noisy bark of amusement. The woman shied away from him, but Singh grinned, knowingly, as if it was something only men understood. He took charge then and led the way, escorting the towering figure of Victor in front. The women hung back with Isabel, and she felt huge too, monstrous and pale beside the fragile Malays. She'd never felt as enormous as this by Ayala's side, but of course she was only a child then. The little girl reached up and touched Isabel's white arm, a small fluttering caress like a butterfly, and Isabel smiled down at her, regretful she couldn't ask her how it was to be a child today in this house.

The women seemed eager to demonstrate the techniques for making the batik, pulling open lengths of cloth for the visitors to admire, showing blocks of wood and different colors of dye. Progress around the room became slow and deliberate. This wasn't what Isabel had come for, and eventually she drifted away to the windows to gaze out at the garden, closing her eyes to remember the room with the furniture and the people in it. She was beginning to feel light-headed and disoriented, the soft murmurings of the women and the long translations from Singh buzzing in her head. The house was cool but she was hot, small waves of dizziness washing over her. She wondered if she was getting sick or whether it was the jet lag catching up at last. Last night, in the hotel in Kuala Lumpur, she'd slept badly, the noise of the air conditioner disturbing her, the room so cold she had to get up and find a blanket for the bed. It didn't feel right to need a blanket in this part of the world.

The small procession moved into another room, which may have been her father's study, and Isabel felt cheated, unable to see the house in the way she wanted, to catch the memories she knew waited somewhere. This room had shelves laden with paintings and carvings, the paintings brightly colored, garish, the carvings overelaborate, but the writhing Hindu figures and mythic jungle creatures struck a chord in Isabel, as if, perhaps, pieces like this had once decorated the house. She wondered if she and Victor were expected to buy something and grew indecisive and bothered about what to choose from among all these things she didn't want.

At last the tour of the house seemed finished, and they all emerged out onto the veranda. Isabel hadn't found what she was seeking; she didn't know what it was but knew there had to be something, a small memory that would illuminate an emptiness at the core of her life, a clue to some strange blankness.

On the wide, shady veranda, on a low table, the tall pitcher of lemonade was waiting for them, covered by a net weighted with colored glass beads. Isabel stared at the blue and green beads hanging from the edges of the white netting and in an instant recalled her mother sitting in a long chair at this very spot, face pale, eyes dark, fanning herself with a round rattan fan, a tall white pitcher beside her, covered by that same kind of net with the same colored beads. She could hear her father's voice calling and her mother crying. . . . Crying? No, she was screaming. Her mother had been screaming, high-pitched, penetrating screams, which terrified the child hiding her head in her amah's skirts. . . .

The sudden memory made Isabel's knees fold beneath her, and she sat quickly in a chair. One of the women poured her a glass of lemonade. As Isabel took it, she saw her own hand shaking in a betraying manner, and when she sipped at the tepid liquid, the glass banged painfully against her teeth. The heat rose in shivering waves off the grass beyond the veranda.

Victor said, "You okay, Izzy?"

She lifted up the hair clinging in thick clumps around her neck, wiped her shaking fingers across her forehead and around the collar of her dress, where the sweat ran in rivulets. The woman who'd poured the lemonade put a soft hand on Isabel's forehead and began to fan her face, murmuring in a soothing voice. Isabel closed her eyes gratefully. She heard the sound of the Malayan voice, felt the cool breeze of the fan on her cheek, and quite suddenly she was a child again, safe in the care of a gentle Malay woman, a lamb returned to the fold. A lamb, a darling, Ayala's beautiful little English mem, with eyes like the ocean, sea green and cool, with the strange hair that tangled in the damp heat so the knots must be brushed from it, tenderly, lovingly. Ayala's little English mem, precious and adored.

It was inevitable, she knew. She started to cry, the tears surging under her closed lids and running down her hot face, as she sat on the veranda of her once-upon-a-time home, weeping for those who had lived in this house, for all the years she'd waited to come back, for everything she'd missed and could never regain. She cried and cried, as she'd never allowed herself to do so before, and even as the hot tears cooled her aching heart, she knew the tears could not regain one moment of those years or bring back more than a sorrowful shadowy flicker of those distant beloved people.

But there is a finite amount of tears. When at last she opened her drained eyes, she saw that two of the Malay women remained, one still fanning her, one with her hands folded at her waist, watching Isabel as she would a child, without condemnation. Singh had retreated to the shade of the trees, and when Isabel turned her head, she caught sight of Victor at the far edge of the lawn, hat tipped over his eyes, jacket slung across his shoulder, walking the perimeter of the property like a landowner.

She sat for a long time, looking at the grass and the green jungle on the pointed hills, as she knew her mother must have done all those years ago. There were birds singing in the garden, and she was surprised to remember their names: bulbuls and sunbirds, a black-and-white magpie robin. Above her head, a tiny flicking movement caught her attention, and a gecko darted up a post, paused with swelling throat and jeweled eyes, clicking its odd call in the still air. Extraordinary how familiar that sound was, as though it hadn't been so long since she had heard it.

She said, "I would like to go upstairs, to see the rest of the house."

The woman with the fan shook her head.

Stubbornly, Isabel said, "I'm going upstairs," and stood up from the chair. Her legs ached as though she'd run a great distance.

Clucking and murmuring together, the women called to Singh, who came up the steps, peering warily at Isabel, listening to the women. Their voices were like those of baby chickens, small incomprehensible chirpings.

"It is not safe upstairs, mem," he said. "The ladies say it is not used. No one goes there anymore."

"I'll be careful. I've come a long way to see this house."

Singh nodded his head, uneasily. "That is true. If you want to see it, then you must see it. But I think you will be disappointed. There is nothing there."

The three of them followed her to the foot of the wide wooden staircase and watched as she climbed the stairs, heavily and slowly, her sweaty hand clutching the banister. "Be very careful, mem." Singh's face tilted upward, anxious like the women's faces, his thin brown neck straining out of his white collar. "The ladies say the floor is rotten in places."

"I'll be careful," she repeated.

At the top of the stairs, the landing divided into two corridors, one on each side of the length of the house. Up here the air was thick and stifling and still, the heat trapped under the roof, no fans working. Isabel turned to the left, without hesitation, to where her own room had been, here, behind this first door. At the further end of this corridor was the room where Ayala was supposed to sleep. Usually she slept at the foot of Isabel's bed, so that when the little girl woke in the mornings, she could stretch out her hand and find Ayala's immediately, reassuringly. Ayala. The one constant in her life.

Isabel pushed at the door of her room, but the door was stuck; she put her weight against it. It flew open suddenly, and she fell forward. Beyond the door, the room was bare, the floor planks uneven and curling in spots, the ceiling lower than downstairs, a broken fan hanging crookedly, the one small window covered with brown paper, so the light was very dim. A strong smell of mildew, as though the air hadn't stirred for a long time, filled the room like a presence. Her bed had been over there, against the wall near the window, so she could see the morning dew on the grass when she pushed aside the white mosquito netting. The heat when she took a nap in the afternoons was like today, heavy, silent, and sinister.

Isabel stared at the room for a long while, then she backed out of it and returned along the landing, past the top of the stairs to the other side of the house. She felt huge again, like Alice, grown too tall for the low ceilings. The ceilings had seemed high to her once, the corridor very long. A long and dangerous journey to the room where her parents had slept.

Standing in the empty doorway, looking over the empty space, Isabel knew it was still a long and dangerous journey. Once, there'd been a big double bed, a dressing table with a glass top and chintz drapery, silver-backed brushes and a jewel box with pearls, a round leather box for her father's collar studs, photographs in silver frames, her mother brushing her hair with long, mesmerizing strokes. Her mother? Or was it Marike, who replaced her mother? Whose voices was it she could hear, sobbing and pleading, the low angry buzzings? Did it matter? They were all gone, lost forever in the thick green blanket of jungle.

Someone was calling her name. "Isabel? Isabel? Where the hell are you?"

At last they were coming for her, at last, those ghosts she was seeking. And she was suddenly afraid, as she'd been afraid then, so she ducked inside the room and hid behind the door that no longer existed and imagined no one would find her. But of course she was found, as she'd always been found, and of course it wasn't her father. It was only Victor, thumping into the room on heavy, impatient feet.

"Oh, for God's sake, Izzy! Why are you hiding up here? We'll never get away from this damn place at this rate."

And before she could move, his large, clumsy feet in the unsuitable black shoes went crashing through one of the rotten floorboards she had been warned about, and he fell with a curse into a gaping hole that had been waiting for both of them for a long, long time.

9

H<small>E WAS FELLED</small> like a sacrifice on Isabel's altar of memory. For a moment, Victor could only curse, then he grew painfully aware that his leg not only was secured like a rabbit's in a trap but was also hurting abominally.

Isabel came leaping at him from her strange lurking place beside the doorway and bent down to drag his leg from the shattered floorboards. Yelling at her, Victor fought her hands away. "Leave it alone, for God's sake! I think the bloody thing is broken."

They both stared into the hole in the floor. His leg was trapped almost knee-deep in the gaping space, and the dusty boards had splintered and torn through the material of his trousers, into the flesh of his calf. Blood was pouring out of a jagged tear from ankle to knee, and the blood was running into his shoe, warm and wet and terrifying. Almost worse than that, his foot was twisted at an agonizing unnatural angle.

"Oh, God, Victor, I'm sorry!" she cried. As well she might. "We've got to get it out of there, quick, before your foot swells too much. Sit down and I'll pull the boards away from it."

But the splintered boards were gripping his leg in such a way that he couldn't even sit down. Cold sweat soaked through his shirt. "Get the driver up here," he moaned. "He might know what to do. God knows what's lurking in these floorboards. I'll be dead of tetanus before we know it."

Isabel shot out of the room. Gritting his teeth, Victor leaned down and struggled to pull apart the broken wood that was clamping his leg in a viselike grip and managed to drag his foot out of the hole. The sight of his own blood and torn flesh made him feel faint and queasy enough, but when he saw the way his foot flopped at the end of his leg and felt the agony of the movement, he was afraid he might really pass out. Dropping to his hands and knees, he lowered his head on his forearms and wondered how in the hell he had got in such a fix. All Isabel's fault. Or perhaps his own. If he hadn't been fool enough to bring her with him, this would never have happened.

After what seemed an eternity, Singh came sidling into the room behind Isabel, his mouth a wide pink O, his hands flapping. At the sight of Victor crouched on the floor, he shrieked in a high thin voice, "Oh, mem! I said not to go up here. This is a bad place. What will they say at the Centre?"

Victor snarled at him. "Never mind the bloody Centre! Help me out of here, for God's sake." The man was as useless as a tit on a bull.

Kneeling beside Isabel on the floor, Isabel looked into his face. "I'm going to take your shoe off."

"No! Leave it alone. Haven't you done enough damage?"

"I think I must," she said, and she took hold of his leg, unlaced his shoe, eased it off his foot, peeled away the blood-soaked sock. Victor moaned and swore and swiveled around to survey the damage. His ankle was swelling alarmingly, and he groaned again. "I know it's broken." It served her damn well right. But at least she'd had the presence of mind to bring a length of cloth with her, and though her hands shook, she managed to wrap it around without hurting his leg too much. He no longer had to look at all that blood, but he was still aware of the warm, sweet smell of it.

"We'll have to get you to a hospital. Singh, go and ask the women if there's something we can use as a splint—anything. And something more for wrapping. Then we'll have to help him down the stairs and you can drive us to a hospital. The nearest one."

"Yes, mem. Yes, I will do that. The hospital in Kuala Lumpur is a very good hospital, tuan. They will look after you there."

"First, a splint," Izzy said, calmly enough, though her face was whiter than he thought his own must be. When the helpless Indian ran out of the room, Victor was relieved to see him go; his air of hysteria was contagious.

Cupping two large white pills in her palm, Isabel showed them to Victor. "Codeine," she said. "I had them in my bag. It'll be all right, Victor. We'll get you to a doctor, and everything will be taken care of." She handed him the pills with a glass of the lemonade they'd had downstairs.

He forced himself to swallow the codeine and the tepid drink, probably thick with typhoid or cholera. "Some bloody wog doctors. God knows what a cock-up they'll make of it. You'll have to get me back to London, fast, before it goes septic."

She spoke in a crooning voice, as though to a child. "Let's see what they say at the hospital, shall we? I'm sure they can stitch it up and put a cast on. And lie down, Victor. It would be better if you keep your head low. You're very pale."

"Of course I'm bloody well pale. You'd be pale, too, if half the blood in your body had disappeared down a sodding hole."

But he did lie back and allow his head to rest on the floor, because the stuffy room was swirling around him and the pain was overwhelming. The next thing he knew, his leg was bound between two crude pieces of wood, the unbleached material used for batik bandaged around, blood already seeping through. The driver was hovering over him, and Isabel was urging Victor to stand. He couldn't stop groaning, but somehow or other he forced himself upright, with Isabel's help, and soon they were maneuvering awkwardly and painfully along the corridor and down the staircase he'd run up so easily half an hour before. His arms on the shoulders of Singh and Isabel, Victor was fearful they'd fold beneath his weight, let him fall and break something else. Under his right arm, the bones of the Indian felt fragile and insubstantial, and the man's breath was sucking between his teeth with the effort. Under Victor's left arm, Isabel felt sturdier and more reliable. At the foot of the stairs, the Malayan women clustered, faces upturned, politely impervious as ever, and he wanted to tell them to bugger off if all they could do was stand around to watch the fall of yet another imperialist. The situation was farcical and demeaning.

The three of them struggled crablike along the veranda and down the steps, and at last Victor could ease himself gingerly into the back seat of the car. Isabel climbed in beside him, though there was hardly room for her, and put a cushion on her lap, lifted his leg onto it, and held it firmly. Victor found it hard to breathe, and the sweat running inside his shirt was cold and uncomfortable.

"Tell him not to drive like an idiot," he gasped. He leaned his head against the upholstery and stared accusingly at his sister. "So, Izzy, we say farewell to our birthplace. Such a jolly little visit."

She turned her head to look back at the house, her eyes huge and dark, her face startling in its pallor. She whispered, "It was trying to tell us something, Victor, I know it was."

"Not to traipse around on rotten floorboards, that was the message."

Singh threw the car into gear and jolted it along the rutted lane beneath the trees. Instant roaring stabs shot through Victor's ankle. He yelled at Singh, "Slower, damn it."

The journey was going to be endless.

"What the hell," Victor demanded, "were you doing up there anyway?"

Isabel stared at him across the width of the back seat, her pupils enormous, blacking out the gray-green irises. Her voice dropped to a lower whisper. "You know what the women told Singh? They said the house is . . . haunted . . . up there. That's why no one goes upstairs anymore. They hear sounds when there is no one there."

"Oh, what rubbish! That's just the sort of thing you'd like to hear. What are those Malayan women? Buddhist? Don't tell me Buddhists believe in ghosts."

He raised his voice to shout to Singh. "Buddhist don't believe in ghosts, do they, Singh?"

"Tuan?" Singh shot a nervous glance over his shoulder, his face blackened with misery. He'd get in trouble with his superiors back at the Centre, and Victor wasn't sorry about it. He should've stopped Isabel in her foolish perambulations.

"I said Buddhists don't believe in ghosts, do they?"

"I am Hindu, tuan. Hindus don't believe that spirits roam the earth.

Hindus believe that when people die, they take on another earthly form."

He hadn't damn well asked him what Hindus believed, but the effort of carrying on a shouted conversation was too much for Victor. The lurching of the car made more sweat pour from him before they reached the end of the bumpy lane, when Singh paused to turn onto the main highway. The ride should be smoother from now on, if the damn fool just took care. A huge lorry hurtled past, and Singh accelerated jerkily into the road behind it.

"It is true what the mem says. The ladies are afraid of that part of the house. They feel bad things may happen to people up there."

"Well, they're bloody well right about that, aren't they?"

Isabel said, still in the stage whisper, "I felt it, Victor. As though they've not been released from there. Do you think they may have died up there? Daddy and Marike?"

Victor closed his eyes. The pain was receding a little, probably the codeine taking effect. Resting his head against the shuddering upholstery, he tried not to think about her fantasies. But when he'd walked across the grass to the edge of the lawn where the jungle began, he had the odd feeling that he'd looked at the house from that particular place and distance before, a sudden sensation of déjà vu such as other people said they experienced and which he'd never believed in. Of course, he could have seen it before. He was less than a year old when they left, an age before recall begins, but someone could well have carried him around the lawn. It was as if he'd seen it from the exact same six-plus feet as now, maybe from the height of someone's shoulder. The way people carry their kids on their shoulders. As a father might. Victor opened his eyes and glared at Isabel. Her head hung down and her hair was loose, flowing in a canopy over his leg, and she clutched his leg close to her like a baby. Christ, she was infecting him now, putting thoughts and memories in his mind where there mercifully had been none before. If there was anything to remember, he wanted no part of it.

"More likely," he said, and he wanted to be cruel, "our mother would have died up there, don't you think? Where did she die? Do you know?"

Raising stricken eyes, Isabel said mournfully, "I don't remember."

"Funny. You remember so many *unnecessary* things."

Her voice came at him, distant and sorrowful. "Yes, it *is* funny that I don't remember anything about it. That's what's so awful, isn't it, not to remember your own mother when she was dying? One day she just wasn't there anymore. If she'd been sick in bed, wouldn't I have been taken to see her?"

"You're probably blanking it out." He meant it sarcastically, but Isabel didn't react, just stared at the road, her forehead creased with a painful concentration. The jungle hurtled past them on their way back to civilization.

She looked at Victor. "But I do remember the day we left, you and me."

"Oh, spare me," he muttered.

Then quite suddenly he thought he wanted to hear about it. For all these years he'd shut out her memories because they had nothing to do with him, but now, after seeing that house, there were faint uneasy stirrings of curiosity. They should never have gone there. He should have trusted his instincts, not allowed himself to be taken along for the ride. It seemed innocent enough—awkward, even, to get out of it—when the people at the Centre offered the car for the day. When Bailey had set up the visit for them.

Now, his resolve sinking, Victor thought that maybe the house had trapped him, too, in its web of memories.

10

IT HAD RAINED very hard that day. It rained often in the monsoon time, but on that particular day the rain was heavier and more thunderous on the tin roof than she could remember. Leaden clouds coalesced earth and sky into one gray solid mass, and the sound of the rain was so loud, everyone had to shout to be heard. The noise of the rain, the raised voices, the crackling of the radio, that's what she remembered most. A hurtful, anxious cacophony.

And she remembered the clothes. Strewn everywhere. Heaped on beds and on the floor, overflowing from drawers and suitcases and boxes, more clothes than she ever knew were in the house; her own and Marike's and Victor's, odd heaps of baby jackets and dresses, muslin diapers, leather shoes, silk frocks, a pair of riding breeches she'd long grown out of, things she hadn't seen for ages, some she was sure she'd never seen before. In one of the piles she found a long blue chiffon dress with sequins around the neck, and she draped it against herself, retreating from the turmoil into dress-up games, only to have the dress snatched away and thrown back onto the floor.

Her father was shouting. He so rarely raised his voice that the mere pitch of it alarmed her. "For God's sake," he yelled at Marike. "Forget the clothes—they aren't important. There isn't time."

Marike was kneeling in the middle of the living room floor, thrusting roughly folded garments into suitcases, the lids of the cases gaping open to swallow Isabel's life.

"Roddy, if they go on a boat, the children must have something warm to wear. And if they get to England, I must find the right things for them."

Marike wore a white dress that day. With her thick black hair and her dark eyes, she looked like Snow White, and Isabel loved her. She also loved Ayala, who was rushing distractedly from room to room with yet more clothes. Isabel ran after her, up the stairs, down again, into the living room, back up the stairs. "Wait for me, Ayala, wait. Where are we going? I don't want to go anywhere. I want to stay here with you."

Normally Ayala carried Victor on her hip all the time, but that day she'd put him down on the floor and left him, as he was never left, as though forgotten, to cry alone in a corner. The unaccustomed sound of the screaming baby added to the fury of all the other sounds.

Reaching up from the floor beside the cases, Marike caught hold of Isabel, stopping her in her headlong flight, clutching her close so Isabel could smell the perfume in the crumpled white linen. "Darling, Ayala is going with you, to look after you and Victor. Everything's going to be all right. Don't be frightened."

But she *was* frightened, frightened by Marike's pallor, by the hair that flew in a wild black cloud around her head, by her unusual tears; she was frightened by her father's tight jaw, the hard line of his lips, the way he wiped his forehead and his glasses, over and over again. By the strange way Ayala would not stop still and speak to her, no one smiling or listening, all the other servants vanished, the disorder in the house. By some deep and unknown betrayal taking place.

"They won't take natives on the boat, Marike." Her father was still shouting, pacing the floor, his feet dragging clothes after him, unnoticed. "You will have to go. Who'll take care of the baby if you don't go?"

Marike released Isabel and stayed on her knees as if she was about to pray, folding her arms across her breasts, hugging herself as if in pain. "The children will be safe with Ayala. She's always taken care of them."

He was never angry, especially with Marike, but he was angry now. "You don't seem to understand Marike. There's no room for natives. And suppose they don't get a boat, suppose there is no boat? What then? They'll be all alone."

"Please, please, Roddy. Don't ask me again. They're not my children. I love them, Roddy, but I love you more."

He stopped the compulsive pacing, looked down at her with weary eyes. "If you love me, you'll go with the children. For my sake as well as theirs."

Isabel's safe little world was splitting further and further apart. She started to scream, threw herself at her stepmother. "Marike, please don't leave me." She wound her arms in a fierce grip around Marike's neck to keep her close, burying her head in the folds of her skirts, banging her forehead against her breast. She could feel Marike's body shuddering under the blows. "I love you, Marike. And Daddy too. I love Ayala and Victor. I want to stay in my house. I'll be good, I promise. Just don't send me away."

Loosening the clutching hands from around her neck, Marike stared into Isabel's face, folded her back in her arms again, smoothed her hair. "Hush, darling, hush. You're a good girl, we all know that. But you can't stay here."

Isabel had always adored the way Marike said "Darlink" in her funny accent. Now, suddenly, it enraged her and she raised her head, yelling what she knew were forbidden words. "I want my real mummy."

"Darlink, your mummy went to heaven to be with the angels. We talked about it, didn't we? You understand, don't you?"

Her father groaned. "For God's sake! There's no time for that now. We'll all be with the bloody angels if we don't get out of here. At least the angels might be a sight better than the bloody Japs. And shut that racket, Isabel, for Christ's sake."

But Isabel couldn't stop the racket. Hurling herself out of Marike's arms and into her father's, she pressed her face into the vee of his open shirt. "Don't send me away, Daddy. I'll be good."

His hands gripped her so hard it hurt, and there was comfort in the hurt. "Hush, Isabel, there's my girl. We must all be brave. We're all soldiers now. You know how soldiers have to behave."

Lifting her head, she peered up into his face. "I can't be a soldier. I'm only a girl."

For a moment, she'd made him smile again, a fleeting warming of his eyes behind the glasses, a softening of his mouth. Gently, he said, "Everyone has to be a soldier in a war, my darling child."

The rain drummed on the roof and Victor howled in the corner and Ayala scurried in to drop more clothes in the center of the room. From the radio on the table at the end of the settee came urgent cracklings.

Suddenly Marike leapt to her feet, scooped Victor from the floor and bounced him in her arms, then collapsed on the chintz settee as though her legs wouldn't hold her up, even for a few minutes. Clutching the baby against her breast, she rocked him backward and forward, patting his back, and he gasped and hiccuped, nuzzled into her, and finally stopped crying. Marike blinked at their father over Victor's soft carrot-colored head. "I think we must all go together or we must all stay together," she said. "That is decided, Roddy."

"I'll be able to follow. In a few days. It'll be easier alone. I beg you. Take the children, take them back to England. I want you to be safe. This madness will be over soon, and then we'll all be together again."

Marike's mouth set in a firm unhappy line. "We won't be safe in England, either. Look what's happening in Europe. We'll never be together again, Roddy, if you make us go away without you."

There was a stubborness in her voice but also a terrible defeat, and Isabel turned from the comforting close smell of her father's skin to stare at Marike's bleached tearful face, the hollowness in her cheeks, the droop of her mouth. Her father let go of Isabel so abruptly she slid to the floor among the clothes, and he crossed the room with heavy feet to sit beside Marike on the sofa and put his arms around her instead. Victor began to cry again, and Ayala went over and lifted him off Marike's lap. Marike didn't seem to notice, just draped her arms around her husband's neck and hid her face in his shoulder, and for a moment the room was almost quiet, the baby not crying, her father not shouting, even the radio silent. There was only the sound of the rain drumming on the roof.

Ayala jiggled Victor in her arms, shushing him—"Diam, diam,

baby, baby"—and when she carried him out of the living room and up the stairs, Isabel went running after her. In Isabel's bedroom, Ayala put Victor down on his back on the bed to change his soaking diaper, and he smiled up at her with his few baby teeth, waved his fat baby hands.

"Hungry, poor baby," Ayala said. "Poor baby. He need makan."

Isabel understood perfectly her amah's mixture of Malay and English. Food was what the baby needed. "But tell me, why must we leave?" she wanted to know.

Ayala's face wasn't white like Marike's. It was warm and brown and round; her eyes were still soft and black, not red with tears. "Soldiers come," Ayala said, whispering. "Japanese soldiers. English tuans very afraid, they say Japanese very bad. Soon I must go home to my kampong. Japanese won't hurt my peoples, only English peoples. That is why you leave."

"But Marike isn't English," Isabel said. "She's Dutch."

"She is orang puteh."

"They'll hurt her because she is white?" Isabel was astonished. She'd never heard such a thing. Everyone loved white people; they were loved by God, especially the English. And the English, she knew, weren't afraid of anyone or anything. The truth was that everyone was afraid of them, of their king and the great English army, of people like her father, who was a kind of king himself.

"You can't go back to the kampong, Ayala. This is your home now." Isabel kept hold of her hand. "Where will you sleep? Who will teach you English? Who will feed Victor?"

Ayala only shrugged her smooth brown shoulders and shook her gleaming head. "Little mem, saya tidak mengerti."

"But you must know, Ayala. Someone must know."

But all Ayala said was, "We go find some makan for baby," and she took hold of Isabel's hand and they went downstairs together to the kitchen, where everything was in strange and shocking disarray, the breakfast dishes still littering the table and piled in the sink without being washed, as though the servants had dropped everything straight after breakfast. Isabel hadn't seen the houseboy all day and knew Marike would be very angry with him; his disappearance and the mess in the kitchen was almost more alarming than the noise and disorder in the living room. Victor's bottles were stored in the refrigerator, and Isabel fetched one for Ayala, who thanked her—"Terima kaseh"— politely, as though this were an ordinary day. Ayala poured water from the kettle into a bowl and stood the bottle in it, then she carried Victor out to the veranda, where the sound of the rain was very loud. She sat in the wide swinging chair, cradling the baby in her arms as he sucked at his bottle, and Isabel sat close by her side, the chair rocking gently in the gray damp light. Ayala began to croon a familiar song in Malay, and life seemed almost returned to normal. Reassured, Isabel shut her aching eyes, leaned her head against Ayala's bare shoulder, comforted by the feel of the soft, familiar skin. Everything would soon be all right. Ayala would never leave them.

The rain continued to fall.

A different sound jerked Isabel's eyes open, and she saw a lorry, dark green and canvas covered, emerging out of the thick sheet of rain, lurching along the muddy lane, steam rising from the radiator. Ayala stopped her song and gave a small cry—she jumped to her feet, holding Victor in one arm, and Isabel against her skirts with the other. Almost too afraid to look, Isabel whispered, "Is it the Japanese?" and then, before the lorry came to a complete halt, she saw a British soldier leap from the cab at the front. He ran up the steps of the veranda, his heavy steel-braced boots thumping on the floorboards, shaking the whole house. His khaki shirt was black with rain, his short hair plastered to his head.

"Come on!" The soldier was shouting, his voice harsh and urgent. "We've got to get out of here. In the truck, quick."

He grabbed Victor out of Ayala's arms, took firm hold of Isabel's hand, and pushed Ayala aside roughly. "No Malays," he said.

But Isabel wasn't afraid of British soldiers. She held on to Ayala with one hand and tugged at his hairy, unresponsive arm with the other. "She's coming with us. We're all going together or we're not going."

Grinning down at her with crooked teeth, unamused, the soldier said, "Where's your mum and dad?"

"My real mother's dead."

Now her father and Marike appeared at the sitting room door. Their eyes were oddly blank, without expression, and puffy, as if they had woken from sleep too early, the way they looked sometimes on a Sunday morning after being out late. Each of them held one small suitcase.

"These your children, sir? If you want them out of here, we got to leave right away. The Japs are no more than thirty miles up the road. We might make it to Singapore, if we're lucky."

When her father spoke, his voice was flat and toneless. "Then you'd better get going, hadn't you, Corporal?"

"Your wife can come, sir, but no men, I'm afraid. Orders. You'll have to take your chances, sir."

The same dead tone was in Marike's voice. "I'm not going. We're taking our chances together." She put one of the cases down on the veranda. "These are some clothes for the children. They will need something warm."

Hesitating, the soldier cleared his throat. "You're not going to let the kiddies go alone . . . ? I wouldn't advise it, madam."

"No, maybe not." Her eyes looked past Isabel and Victor. "But I'm not their real mother, you see. Someone will take care of them. Ayala, please get the rest of the baby's bottles."

Ayala let go of Isabel's hand and scuttled back along the veranda to the kitchen, returning with the wire contraption that held all the glass baby bottles in the boiler. Now Isabel could see tears glittering in Ayala's eyes, small silver streaks on the brown cheeks. Isabel began to cry again, silently now, the tears running into her mouth. She tugged futilely at her captor's thick wrist, and he suddenly picked her up in one swift, disorienting movement, so that she was dangling, head down, under his arm. He smelled of sweat and cigarette smoke.

"I don't have time to argue, sir, but I'd advise the lady to come with us."

"No," Marike said, and shook her head. "I'm sorry, I cannot leave."

Isabel swung in the corporal's arm.

"Very well, if you're sure, madam. We'll do our best to see the kiddies are safe."

Her father clutched the edge of the doorway, his face white and rigid, then he took off his glasses and wiped them on his shirt, abstractedly. Without his glasses, Isabel knew, he couldn't see her. "Thank you," he said. "Thank you very much."

The grip around Isabel's waist tightened so she could hardly breathe, and she stretched her hands to Ayala, to Marike, to her father, tried to call for them to help her, but she had no voice and she saw them turn away as though they couldn't bear the sight of her. Unable to cry or plead any longer, she allowed herself to be carried away, without struggling, down the steps of the veranda and to be heaved over the backboard of the lorry. From the darkness inside, a dozen hands reached out to pull her in with them, and then Victor was bundled in after her. In the airless black interior, a woman whom she couldn't see said, "Is this your baby brother? Such a lovely boy. Isn't your mum coming with us?"

Isabel only shook her head. She would have answered, if she could speak, "My mother's dead."

"Oh, dear me. Looks as if you'll have to take care of him, then, doesn't it? There's only you to look after him now. But you're a big brave girl, I can see that. Here, lovey, I expect he'd like to be with you," and the woman put Victor into Isabel's lap. She took tight hold of him, and he burped; he smelled of warm milk and wet diapers.

The suitcases came hurtling in after them, and Isabel could hear Ayala's voice, already thin and distant, calling, "Selamet jalan, little mem."

The woman in the dark snorted with ironic laughter. "Safe journey? Where the hell does she think we're going?"

Immediately the wheels of the lorry ground into movement, spinning in the mud, and the canvas was pulled down over the opening again, plunging them further into gloom, so that she couldn't even watch the house and the people on the veranda disappearing into the teeming rain.

"Selamet jalan," Isabel whispered, and pressed her face into Victor's warm baby flesh. "They'll be coming after us soon, Victor, I know they will. I'll look after you till then."

11

VICTOR LISTENED in silence, not once interrupting with some sarcastic remark, some throwaway line. Isabel thought he might even have gone to sleep in the awkward position, but when she came to the end, he opened his eyes. "She abandoned us, didn't she? Why did she do that?"

Isabel was trying to behave calmly for Victor's sake. Or was it for her own sake? She'd kept talking to keep at bay her fear of what might happen to his poor mangled leg, the obviously broken ankle. She was certain a raging and uncontrollable infection would set in, afraid that any moment now she would once again break into hysterical tears and upset him even more.

"You think she should have come with us?"

"For God's sake, Izzy! To let two small children go off alone under any conditions, let alone those . . . What was she thinking of? What kind of a woman was she?"

Strangely, Isabel had never thought of blaming Marike for staying with her father, never thought there was anything else she should have done. She thought of Marike as brave and resolute, choosing to stay behind when escape was offered. She and Victor *had* survived, hadn't they? Marike had been right, someone else had taken care of them. An assorted band of women, first in the bone-thumping journey through the rain and the darkness to Malacca, grinding away for hours and hours on a road crowded with bicycles and bullock carts, everyone sure they would be cut off along the way by the Japanese;

then on the ship that smelled of diesel fuel and seasickness, eight women and two children in a cabin meant for two.

It seemed to Isabel now, in the throes of another, less momentous, emergency in Malaya, that behind the chaos of those long-ago dark days must have lurked some hidden miracle of organization. How else could a small ship have reached England from the other side of the world? How could it have plowed through the dangerous seas to link up with a dozen other ships on a similar journey if a mysterious force hadn't been guarding them, bringing them safely, eventually, to their faraway destination?

Trying to focus on the half-remembered black-and-white figure of Marike, she realized the car was going slowly now, jerking as the brakes and then the accelerator were applied in quick succession. Victor groaned with the uneven progress. She saw they were caught in the midst of city traffic, rickshas and bicycles and handcarts, thousands of pedestrians, and impatient honking small cars that refused to give way. Singh leaned his head out of the window and screamed at the other drivers, waving his hand furiously, wrenching the wheel to the left and the right. "Soon to be at the hospital, memsahib. Very soon now."

She couldn't wait to get to the hospital and yet dreaded it, fearful it would be filthy and disorganized, that the doctors would be incompetent or worse and do something dreadful to Victor's poor leg. That Victor would be difficult and rude. Did they have antibiotics here? Were there doctors who'd know what to do? How would she know if they were doing the right thing? Should she try and get him somewhere safe? Where? Singapore? Australia?

Her mouth was dry, her hands were clammy. She wanted to stay cool and alert, but her mind was racing feverishly, her head swimming from the motion of the car, her stomach churning. It was unbearably hot in the back, but when she rolled down the window, the noise and fumes and dust made her feel worse. Please don't let me get sick, she prayed silently, don't let me be smitten with some dreadful tropical disease. Suppose she was getting malaria? She had no idea what the first symptoms of malaria might be.

Then the car lurched off the noisy, crowded city streets and pulled up between white pillars, under a wide shaded overhang, not unlike the entrance to the hotel they'd stayed in the night before. Peering up at the building, Isabel saw that it was reassuringly modern and sturdy and that above the glass doors where they'd stopped, a large sign said, in English, "Casualty."

Leaping out of the driver's seat, Singh opened the back door and stuck his head inside. "Please to wait there, mem, tuan. I will find a nurse. A wheelchair. Please do not move." There was a sheen of sweat on his anxious young face.

"Don't be long," she pleaded.

"I will be very quick." He ran off, leaving the door open. Hot diesel fumes swam into the car.

"How the hell does he imagine I'm going to move?" Victor muttered between clenched teeth. "Where on earth does he think I'm going to go?"

"He's doing his best, Victor. None of this is his fault."

Victor's face was an unpleasant pasty color, the blotches of freckles livid on his forehead and across his cheeks, like some nasty skin disorder; the hair at his temples had turned from ginger to black with sweat, and his glasses were slipping down his nose. Isabel knew what he was thinking, that it was all her fault, and he was right. If she hadn't gone up those stairs, if she hadn't come on this trip with him in the first place . . . "How does your leg feel now?" she asked, unnecessarily. The look of contempt he shot at her through the steamy lenses was unmistakable.

"Listen. I want you to call Bailey in Singapore before you let them do anything stupid. He seemed a sensible chap. He'll know what to do. I don't trust the kind of doctors they'll have here." Victor leaned sideways, picked his crumpled jacket off the floor of the car, and fished a business card out of a pocket. "Ring him. Oliver Bailey. If he's not at the office, get his home number. Speak to him before you let them do anything irreversible."

"It's your leg, Victor. You can stop them too. They're not going to cut it off or anything."

"Oh, very funny, Izzy. I do appreciate your sense of humor under such difficult circumstances." He gripped his thigh between two hands and groaned. "God knows what they'll do in a place like this, but with any luck they'll shoot me full of dope and I won't be able to think straight. Christ, I hope they do. It hurts like hell."

She was still apologizing when Singh reappeared with a man in a short white coat, pushing a wheelchair—an orderly or perhaps a male nurse; she didn't know which. He was another small, fine-boned man, no larger than Singh, and there was a great deal of discussion, in English and some other language, as to the best way to extract Victor from the back seat of the car. Taking the weight of his leg, Isabel tried to support it, to keep it from moving too much, but it was quite obvious the inept maneuvering was causing him pain. "Sod it!" Victor cried, as they inched him out. "Careful, for God's sake. Haven't any of you silly buggers ever seen a broken leg before, damn it!"

But he was finally in the chair, and the orderly inserted a metal extension under the seat and wheeled him into the hospital, the bundle of leg and towels and bloodstained cloth sticking out straight in front.

Isabel hadn't been inside a hospital for years. Not since Edward, her younger son, fell out of a tree and had to have stitches in his head. She'd been terrified then, certain he'd fractured his skull, absurdly grateful to the doctors and nurses who'd cleaned him up and attended to the bleeding mess, briskly and competently. This casualty department looked much like the one in England: tiled walls, bright lights, and curtained cubicles, hurrying nurses in white dresses. Except it seemed newer and cleaner than the English hospital. The voices were different, but somehow the sounds were the same—clattering steel and distant ringing telephones—and it all smelled of disinfectant and anesthetics. She was vaguely reassured.

The orderly wheeled Victor into a cubicle and went away. In the cubicle, a shiny high-tech examination couch, with levers and angled attachments, took up most of the space, so there was barely room for the wheelchair and Isabel. Singh stood by the curtains and wrung his hands. "I am going to telephone the Centre. To explain this very dreadful problem. They will not be pleased. Perhaps I should have telephoned from the house."

Victor stared at him, his face pale and expressionless. Isabel said, "Thank you for all your help, Singh."

"I think I will have to make a report," he said unhappily, as though making a report was the worst fate that could befall him. "I was only the driver."

A young woman in a white dress and soft-soled shoes came silently into the cubicle, closed the curtains behind her, and without a word began to unwrap the towels and bandages from Victor's leg.

"Are you a nurse?" Victor asked. "Or a doctor?"

Smiling up at him, the girl said something incomprehensible and continued unwrapping. Instantly, Isabel began to worry about the language barrier. How were they going to discuss the treatment if no one spoke any English? The nurse, if that's what she was, exposed the wound, clicked her tongue against her teeth, and said to Victor, in English, "Very bad, tuan."

"Thanks," Victor said. "It helps to know that."

He peered down at his extended leg with almost impersonal interest, and Isabel, who didn't really want to look, felt compelled to inspect it as well. A deep gash ran up the side of his calf, a ragged tear some ten inches long, the flesh on either side bruised and blackened, blood and serum still oozing from the wound. Isabel thought she caught a white glisten of bone and felt sick. She'd never have been any good as a nurse.

Taking a pair of forceps out of a container, the young woman prodded gently at the swollen skin around the wound, and Victor said, "I hope you know what you're doing."

She smiled at him again and patted the examination couch with a small hand.

"After the effort it was to get into this wheelchair, you really want me to get up there?" Victor asked testily.

She put one foot on a lever, which lowered the couch by several inches, and patted it again, like a schoolteacher instructing a small boy. Victor asked again, "Are you the doctor?"

With a flourish, the curtains were pulled aside. "Sir, I am the doctor."

A tall and gracefully thin man, an Indian, wearing gold-rimmed glasses and a long starched white coat, entered the already crowded space. "I am Mr. Ray. Mister, as in England. Please get up on the couch, sir. I know it may be a bit difficult, but it really isn't possible to examine a patient in a chair, you know."

His English was unaccented, public school, upper class, and at the sound of it, Isabel's first reaction was relief. Her second, almost instantaneous, reaction was mortification that she felt that way. Just because he spoke English well didn't mean he was any good as a doctor. She saw a similar set of reactions chase across Victor's face—amazement, hopefulness, a relaxing of the tension around his mouth—but when Victor opened his mouth, Isabel was certain he was about to say something tactless and rushed to speak first. "My brother thinks he's broken his ankle. We're just visiting from England."

"Ah, well," the doctor said, rubbing his hands together briskly. "Let's take a look, shall we?"

He waved her aside as he came further into the confined space, and she had to squeeze past him to get to the other side of the room. The nametag on his pristine white coat came within a few inches of her face, and she saw it said "Mr. Rei," not Ray, and that following the name was an impressive array of English degrees. He certainly had the superior demeanor of an English surgeon.

Mr. Rei grabbed hold of Victor's arm, obviously expecting him to do as he was told, and after a moment's hesitation, Victor obediently raised himself out of the wheelchair. He swiveled awkwardly onto the couch without further protest, his teeth dug into his lower lip, the sweat running down his face. Isabel could tell he was determined not to make a sound. When he lay down, his head and feet protruded from each end, and the nurse had to slide an extension into the end of the couch. She took a pair of scissors and slit his pants away from the wound, and the doctor bent down, peering at it intently. "Ah, yes, rather nasty. How did you do it?"

"He fell through some rotten floorboards," Isabel explained, as though Victor couldn't speak for himself.

"I fell through some rotten floorboards," Victor repeated.

The doctor looked amused. "Perhaps you'd like to wait outside while I look at this, Miss . . ."

"Mrs. Bennet," she said. "Perhaps I will. I'll make that phone call, Victor."

Straining his neck, Victor stared up at her. "Why don't you wait and see what the doctor says first, Izzy."

Outside the cubicle, she leaned against the wall, her legs weak with relief that she didn't have to stay in there to watch the prodding and poking, not sure if it was Victor's suffering she couldn't bear or whether it was the sight of blood. But surely no one enjoyed the sight of blood. She felt inept and incompetent, too tall and awkward and in the way, stranded in the middle of what was no more than a corridor of cubicles. A bevy of small, dark-haired people shuffled around and past her, like small boats avoiding an ocean liner, their eyes flicking in her direction and then away again, as if embarrassed by her presence. She looked about for Singh, saw no sign of him, and didn't know what to do without his guidance. Should she stay right here, where he could find her again? Should she go looking for a telephone? How did one make telephone calls in Malaya? She didn't have any coins on her—Victor was carrying the money, and it was in his pocket in the examination room. So she flattened herself against the wall and tried to be inconspicuous, waiting for someone to rescue her. Which made her feel even more useless.

She could hear the rumble of voices from inside the cubicle but couldn't quite make out the words. Thank God the doctor spoke English. Thank God. She should have been amused that Victor changed his tune so quickly when he heard Mr. Rei speak, but she was merely relieved. She and Victor were just ignorant English travelers who didn't speak the language of any country but their own. Whatever had made her think she was capable of tracing past history, even before Victor's accident? Of achieving anything at all? Why, she was even incapable of making a telephone call.

After what seemed an eternity, the nurse emerged through the curtains and beckoned with a slender brown hand, a beguiling gesture, as though Isabel were being invited into Aladdin's cave. Hastily but reluctantly, she pushed herself away from the supporting wall. In the cubicle, Victor was stretched out and covered with a sheet, his eyes closed; the doctor was washing his hands at a sink in the corner, his shirtsleeves rolled up to his elbows, his tie tucked into the front of the white shirt. He glanced at her over his shoulder and smiled, and a gold tooth gleamed. The nurse handed him a towel, and he dried his hands slowly and deliberately.

"I've given him some morphine," he said. "He was in a great deal of pain. He'll sleep for a while. I suspect his tibia might be fractured as well as the fibula, but we'll need an X ray to confirm that, of course. The wound needs cleaning and stitching. We'll have to do that in the operating room, then we'll either pin and plate the bone or manipulate it and put it in a cast. Either way, it means he'll have to spend some time in the hospital."

Isabel gazed down at her brother. His face was slackened and peaceful, and he was snoring, very quietly and gently. "Poor Victor," she said, and dared not touch him for fear of waking him.

"Oh, he'll be fine," the doctor said breezily. "But it always complicates matters when there's an open wound. I've given him a booster shot of antibiotics, and once the wound is debrided and stitched, everything should heal all right."

"Did you explain all that to him? About operating and everything?"

"Of course. I also told him I did my training in England. At Charing Cross Hospital, as a matter of fact. I think that made him feel better about things."

He smiled again, somewhat condescendingly. "I think you'll find we're not too far behind Western medicine here. Most of the staff have spent time in either England or Australia."

"Oh, I'm sure"—she stumbled over her words—"I'm sure you're all very capable."

"It can be worrying," he said, and allowed the nurse to help him into his white coat, "to be in need of medical care in a foreign country. Especially in some parts of Asia. But you'll find the standards in Malaya quite comparable to the National Health Service."

"Oh, I'm sure," she said again, and wasn't certain how good that was. "How long might he have to stay in the hospital? We were going to be in Kuala Lumpur just for a few days. I'll have to let his office know."

"You're alone here with your brother, Mrs. . . . . er . . . ?"

"Bennet. Yes. Yes, I am. We're staying at . . ." For a moment, her mind went blank. This was Kuala Lumpur, not Singapore. Where *were* they staying? "The Hilton. I'll have to make sure I can stay on, won't I?" The thought of remaining alone at the hotel without Victor was terribly uninviting. "How long will it be?"

"About ten days," he said, and her heart sank. "Maybe longer. Come with me, and we'll make a few phone calls. The nurse will remain here with your brother. He'll be going to X ray soon, in any case."

Sweeping her out of the cubicle and along the corridor, Mr. Rei was a commanding and imperious figure, nurses and orderlies and passersby stepping out of his way obsequiously. Isabel had to hurry to keep up with him. When another doctor in a white coat stopped to ask him something, he waved a thin hand impatiently. "Later," he said in English. "I am busy with this lady."

He held a door open for her and led her into another hallway—this one cool and quiet, black and white tiles on the floors, the ceilings high—down the corridor into a large office space. At a desk by the door, a young Chinese woman with blue-black hair and smooth alabaster skin stood up as he came in.

"She will bring some tea," Mr. Rei said, with another authoritative wave, and he ushered Isabel into the room beyond: spacious, book-lined walls, framed diplomas, armchairs, an Oriental rug in front of a large mahogany desk. The inner sanctum of an old-fashioned hospital consultant, a throwback to the days when the doctor was some sort of deity.

"Please make yourself comfortable, Mrs. Bennet."

She sank into one of the armchairs, gratefully, suspecting that not all relatives received such courtesies.

"Now, whom can we call for you?" he asked, and Isabel searched in her bag for the card Victor had given her.

"My brother wanted me to ring this man. He's the head of the company in Singapore. Victor was supposed to be at the office here in Kuala Lumpur tomorrow. I should let them know what's happened."

Taking the card from her, Mr. Rei smiled again, the gold glinting in his mouth. "Ah, Oliver Bailey. Of course."

"You know him?" She was astonished.

"This isn't such a big country. Oliver Bailey is quite an important person. I'll be happy to call him, if you wish."

It was as though he were descended from heaven to help her out of this mess.

"My secretary will get on to it, as soon as she returns with the tea. A nice cup of tea will not come amiss, I think."

He was so very correct, so precise. He must have gone to an English public school, with that accent. There was only the very faintest trace of an Indian intonation in his voice.

"Isn't there anyone else we can call for you? Here in KL? Elsewhere in Malaya? You would like to ring someone in England, maybe? Your husband? Your brother's wife, perhaps?"

It hadn't occurred to her to call England. To speak to Adrian? What would Adrian do except remind her she shouldn't have gone on this trip in the first place? "My brother isn't married," she said.

She saw the first flicker of curiosity on Mr. Rei's sharp-angled face. He put his elbows on the desk, his chin on his hands, the sleeves of his white coat slipping away from delicate brown wrists, and regarded her with polite, professional interest. His dark eyes were bright and intelligent behind the gold-rimmed glasses, his nose was narrow and high-bridged, his thick black hair touched with gray at the temples. She thought him handsome, distinguished, and elegant.

"It's a pity you have to stay here all alone at a sterile Westernized hotel, Mrs. Bennet. My wife and I would be happy to offer you the hospitality of our home. Would you perhaps consider coming to have dinner with us one evening?"

"How kind of you," Isabel said, faintly. "Perhaps later, when we know what's happening to Victor? Mr. Rei, when will he go to the operating room?"

"Oh, probably not until tomorrow. There's no rush, you understand. There's no need to be operating in the middle of the night."

He certainly seemed unhurried. Cool and calm and in command. The girl with the alabaster face came very quietly into the room, carrying a tray with a pot of tea, tiny, delicate china cups and saucers, and wedges of lemon. In deferential silence, she placed the tray beside Isabel, poured two cups of tea with quick, precise movements, presented the first cup to Mr. Rei, then one to Isabel. The tea was fragrant and hot and extraordinarily refreshing, and until Isabel sipped at it, she hadn't realized how exhausted she was. She wished she didn't have to move from this chair, wondered how long she'd have to wait at the hospital. The thought of a cool shower, an air-conditioned hotel room, and a long nap was very appealing, and then she felt guilty for thinking that when Victor still had hours of pain and discomfort ahead of him. Poor Victor.

The telephone rang at Mr. Rei's elbow, and he spoke into it in English. She heard him explaining about Victor and asking for Mr. Bailey, listening and nodding. He put down the phone. "Unfortunately, Bailey is not in the office in Singapore. It's now nearly six o'clock, after all. But they'll look for him and get him to call me. Someone will be in touch with you at the hotel. I'll send a car to take you back there."

"But my brother? I can't just go off and leave him."

"We'll take care of him, Mrs. Bennet. There's really no point in your hanging around the hospital." Though he smiled benignly at her, she could tell he didn't want her hanging around. "Don't worry, I'll make sure he's comfortable. I believe in plenty of pain medication. You can always come back later if you wish."

Weakly, letting him take charge of her, she said, "I came in a car. From the Centre. I don't know what happened to the driver."

"The Centre?"

It seemed so long ago already, the day too filled with events and places and people: the Centre for Tropical Studies, the house, the women on the veranda, the ghosts in the bedrooms. Putting the teacup down on the small side table, Isabel rested her head against the back of the chair and tried to focus on the doctor. His white coat and dark face, the gold-rimmed glasses, blurred and flickered in a haze behind the shiny mahogany desk. She was supposed to be asking intelligent questions, and the best she could do was trust in his English accent.

He said, "You're tired. Go back to the hotel and rest. I'll call you later and let you know what time we'll be taking your brother to the operating room."

"You're very kind." When she stood up, her knees felt wobbly.

Mr. Rei escorted her to the entrance of the hospital, put her in another car, with another driver. She couldn't even be bothered to ask what might have happened to Singh. At the hotel, she fell across the bed in the cool white room, and as she closed her aching eyes, her last, unreasonable thought was that in spite of everything, she felt strangely secure. As though it had all been meant to be.

Somehow it was like being home, and she didn't know which home she meant, England and Malaya all mixed up together, the English accents, the letters on Mr. Rei's nametag. But she was sure she would be taken care of. Like a child again.

She was asleep in seconds.

12

WHEN THE RINGING of the telephone woke her, Isabel had absolutely no idea where she might be. For a moment, she floated, disembodied, above a strange bed in a strange room, looking down on a young woman with a disorderly mass of light hair, fully dressed in clothes she didn't recognize, white arms and white legs stretched out in some kind of abandonment. A woman who, if she had had no clothes on, might have sprung from an erotic painting. She heard the familiar tone of a phone but had no reference to place or time, and then she thought: Why, that's you, Isabel Cartwright! Whatever are you doing there? Then she hurtled back inside her own skin and snatched the phone off the hook.

"Yes?"

"Is this Mrs. Bennet?"

Yes, she thought, yes, that's who I am. Not Isabel Cartwright. Isabel Bennet. "Yes."

"This is Oliver Bailey, Mrs. Bennet. From Parker and Dellworthy in Singapore."

"Yes?"

"I just spoke with Hari Rei. He told me about your brother's accident."

Harry Ray? Who was Harry Ray?

"Oh, yes?" Oh, yes, my God, Victor! She woke up fully then, sat up straight on the bed, hung her legs over the edge and felt the blood rushing to her feet. "I'm sorry, Mr. Bailey, I was sleeping. . . . I think the jet lag must have caught up with me."

"I do apologize if I woke you. But of course I was most concerned to see what I could do to help. I'm flying up to KL tomorrow. Mr. Rei tells me he'll have to operate. How very unfortunate."

Staring down at her toes, Isabel wriggled them. Sometime, somewhere, she'd painted them. She couldn't quite remember when or where. "This Mr. Rei . . . You know him? He's a good surgeon?"

"Very competent, I understand. Chief of orthopedics at the hospital. Trained in England. Your brother is in good hands."

"You're sure? Victor was anxious that I find that out from you."

"It's an excellent facility. As good a place as anywhere." He had a nice voice, this Mr. Bailey. Soothing and reassuring, fatherly. "But I'm coming up to check on you both anyway. After all, this is a foreign country for you, isn't it?"

Isabel started to say no, not really, and you don't have to come, then remembered how lost she'd been, how she couldn't even go to a phone and ring him in Singapore. "That's awfully kind of you. But I hate to put you to any bother."

"Really, it's no bother. I come up to Kuala Lumpur all the time. I want to make sure you're both all right." There was a pause on the other end of the line, and then the voice that sounded so familiar said, "I feel a sort of proprietary interest in the two of you, after all. No doubt your brother told you I once met your father?"

Isabel heard the words and couldn't believe she'd heard them. She snatched the receiver away from her ear and stared into it, as though the words might make more sense from a further distance, words that made her heart thump alarmingly, a wild banging inside her breast, as if someone had risen from the dead and was speaking to her.

"I'm sorry," she said, replacing the receiver. "Would you say that again?"

"I didn't connect the name until your brother told me why he had his sister here with him. I was surprised that he didn't seem to know too much about your father. I told him I'd met him once. Not a very significant meeting—I don't want you to think that, Mrs. Bennet—but . . ."

Isabel tried to listen to what this man was saying and could hear nothing but the blood pounding in her ears, a raging against Victor's thoughtlessness. Suddenly she was furious with her brother. Livid. Leaping to her feet, she crammed the phone against her head. "As a matter of fact, Mr. Bailey, no, he didn't mention it. But I'll be delighted to meet you, and perhaps you can tell me more. Thank you so much for ringing. I'll see you tomorrow sometime. Either at the hospital or at this hotel."

She had to slam the phone down quickly before she screamed. Then she screamed. "Goddamn it, Victor. Goddamn you, you rotten, mean-spirited swine. How could you not tell me? How could you?"

Isabel couldn't remember when she'd been so furious. Not, for once, upset or tearful or blaming herself. Just plain furious. She stamped around the room, flung off her clothes until she was naked, banged into the bathroom, and turned on the shower to a high speed, soaking her hair and her face in the stinging water jets. She swore, using idiotic words she normally never used, but there just weren't enough swear words in her repertoire. "I'm not sorry you broke your fucking sodding ankle, Victor. Serve you right, you bloody stupid moron."

She was still angry when she turned off the shower. Snatching up a towel, she was irritated that it was soft and fluffy. She needed something harsh and unforgiving, like the old worn towels they used to have at boarding school, washed until they were thin and abrasive. She wanted to scrub her flesh until it tingled, a masochistic urge to flagellate herself in lieu of Victor. Bundling one of the too-gentle towels around her head, she thumped back across the bedroom, unlocked the minibar, and poured herself a brandy. "And don't worry, Victor. This will be on your bill."

She never got angry like this. Never. Certainly not at Victor. She'd been forgiving him ever since that day when they left the house in Kuala Lumpur. Her poor little deprived baby brother. She'd promised then to look after him forever and ever, be kind to him, and she'd kept her promise. Until now. Now he could rot in hell, as far as she was concerned. She wouldn't even go and see him at the hospital. She would never forgive him for not telling her this important information. Never.

As she stood in the middle of the room, knocking back the last of the brandy, the phone rang again. "Damn it!" She couldn't even be angry in peace, not even here in Malaya. Except this didn't feel like Malaya, this cool, generic hotel room, a room like a million others around the globe. This one might be furnished with fancy cane furniture and local prints so it could pretend to be in the Far East, but it might just as well be London or New York or Cape Town. Not that she'd ever been to New York or Cape Town.

The phone continued ringing.

It was Mr. Rei. Another smooth educated British voice. "I just wanted to let you know that we decided to fix your brother's leg tonight and not wait until tomorrow. There was some free time in the operating theater, so we went ahead. My list is rather long in the morning. All went well. We've cleaned it up, pulled the bones back together, and sewed up that wound."

Sitting naked on the edge of the bed, Isabel started to shiver. She dragged the counterpane around her body, feeling as though she were shielding her bare body from Mr. Rei's amused black eyes rather than from the air-conditioning. Her rage melted as suddenly as it had begun. "He's going to be all right?"

"Oh, yes. You can come and see him tomorrow."

"Thank you." She tried not to cry. "Thank you very much. I'm very grateful to you."

"The least I can do for visiting dignitaries," he said.

Visiting dignitaries? Who ever did he imagine she and Victor were?

"If you have any questions," he said, "I'll be around the hospital all day tomorrow."

Dropping the phone back on its hook, Isabel turned the clock on the bedside stand to check the time. Surprisingly—she'd had no idea what time it was—the clock said ten-thirty, and so she climbed between the sheets. Perhaps she should go and find something to eat, but she wasn't hungry. Lying flat on her back in the wide bed, she stared up at the ceiling, her mind almost blank. Hotel rooms had that effect on her, so impersonal, so devoid of the stuff of real life, of books and clutter and the debris of living, everything cleaned away every day. Someone in an office somewhere bought the furniture, not because the person loved it or it was all they could afford, but because it fitted corporate thinking. If she had to wait around for Victor for ten days, she might have to find somewhere different to wait, otherwise she'd lose ten whole days out of her life, lying on the bed like this with her brain on hold.

The hotel furniture made her think of Adrian's compulsive collecting, which suddenly seemed warm and desirable. Adrian! She hadn't given him more than a passing thought since she'd left home. She tried to stir her mind to think of the boys in their boarding school and was alarmed to find she could hardly remember what they looked like, as though they were characters from some other life, some other story. Not her story. Hers was in the house in Kuala Lumpur, in Malaya, a country she didn't recognize, with a language she didn't understand. What she'd understood, dimly, in the upstairs of the house, was that her childhood was a mysterious country; *that* was the land she needed to revisit, that was the language she had to learn again, the code she had to break so that it was no longer foreign but translatable.

She slid out of bed to get another brandy from the minibar. It was a terrible thing for a mother not to be able to recall the faces of her own children. She wondered if it was an inherited defect.

VICTOR LOOKED perfectly dreadful. He lay on his back in a high white cot with his leg strung high in a monstrous white cast, caught up in a medieval contraption of bars and chains and pulleys. He was wearing a ridiculous white hospital gown, and even his hair seemed devoid of color, pale and disheveled, sticking to the pillow in a wild halo. There was a faint gingery stubble on his cheeks and chin. His green eyes, bleached out behind steamed-up glasses, regarded her balefully.

"How did you get here?" he asked.

"In a taxi."

"But you didn't have any money."

"I changed some traveler's checks at the hotel."

"You don't get a good rate in a hotel, you know."

She had meant to be angry with him, to retain her righteous rage from the night before, but of course it had evaporated even before she laid eyes on him. "God, Victor! What a mess. How are they treating you?"

He caught hold of the chain above his head and rattled himself to a higher position on the pillow. "Well, to tell the truth, Izzy, not so bad. It's just like being in an English hospital—Indian doctors and foreign nurses, lousy food. Can't tell any difference, really."

"You've never been a patient in an English hospital, have you?"

"No, but one hears things."

"Mr. Rei seems to know what he's doing."

"He was at Oxford, he says. Did his training at Charing Cross. Can't be all bad."

She examined the huge cast, smooth and white, with an opening in the side, all signs of broken skin and suturing well hidden under a thick wad of cotton wool and gauze. She sat down in the hard blue vinyl chair beside the bed. "Your Mr. Bailey rang up last night. He says this is a good hospital."

"Bailey?" Victor raised his eyebrows. "Decent of him to call, I must say."

"He says he's coming to Kuala Lumpur today to check on you."

"Really? They're probably worried what this is costing."

"Victor, he said he told you he'd met our father once."

"Really?" he said again. "Yes, that's right. He did mention it, now I come to think of it. At that luncheon we had in his club. Funny sort of a place, like going back a hundred years."

"Why didn't you tell me?"

"What? About the club? I wouldn't have thought you'd be interested."

She would keep her temper. She would. "About meeting our father."

"Our father who art in heaven? Izzy, pour me a drop of that water, will you? I'm parched. They tell me it's safe, but I'm not sure I believe them. I'll probably get some ghastly intestinal infection on top of everything else."

Standing up, Isabel filled a ceramic feeding cup with water from the covered glass pitcher on the table by his bed. The pitcher reminded her of the one at the house. She thought about dumping its contents over Victor.

"You know, Victor, you are quite the most infuriating person I have ever met. Haven't you got *any* feelings? If you don't want to know what happened to your father, it's okay, I suppose. Unnatural but okay. But you are very well aware, Victor, that I came here to find out. Any clue, any hint. You deliberately withheld that information from me, didn't you?"

She thrust the feeding cup at him. He took it between his hands and sucked on the spout, like a baby, water dribbling down his neck. She resisted the temptation to wipe it away for him.

"I forgot. That's God's own truth, Izzy."

Plonking herself down in the chair again, she tried not to weep from frustration. "That's worse. That means you're just thoughtless and heartless. I prefer to think you're cunning and devious."

He held the silly cup against his chest. "Think you could find me something to read? They must have English books here."

"Victor, you felt something there, didn't you? At the house? I'm sure you did. Why do you insist on pretending you sprang into life in some kind of immaculate conception? You had parents too, just like the rest of mankind. You've inherited genetic material from someone, just like the rest of us." Except she'd like to understand how his particular genetic mix had turned out to be so different from hers.

"Parthenogenesis," he said. "I think that's the word you're looking for."

"While you're in the hospital, Victor, I'm going to use the time to try and trace them. I'll start at the Centre. There are bound to be documents of some kind. There are bound to be more people around here like Oliver Bailey."

Victor closed his eyes. There were dark shadows beneath them, deep lines around his mouth. She felt an upsurge of familiar protective pity.

He sighed. "You know I've never wanted to know, Izzy. Perhaps there's something that neither of us really wants to know."

At last he was talking about it. At last. A tiny crack in the armor. But his words made her flesh prickle. As though he had knowledge she lacked of something she might not want to know.

"What do you mean by that? Why do you say that?"

"Ignorance is bliss, they say. What you don't know can't hurt you."

She snapped at him. "I don't believe in that philosophy. Neither do you, Victor. You're only pretending to believe it."

He opened his eyes. "What makes you think you know what I believe in, Izzy? It's the only exercise your mind gets, jumping to conclusions."

Of course she knew what he believed in. He was her brother, wasn't he? Brothers and sisters shared deep impenetrable bonds; no one could be closer, no husband or wife, not even one's own child; no one could reproduce the shared genetic material of a brother and sister. It was what she'd always believed and what she would continue to believe. It was what had sustained her through all the years of being Victor's sister.

He rattled the chain above his head again. "They had a nice little aphorism in New York when I was there. Life is a bitch, and then you die. It happens to everyone, Izzy. Everyone's mummy and daddy are going to die, sooner or later. Ours happened to die a little sooner, that's all. You'll die one day. It happens. You've got to get used to it. Accept it."

She stared into his pale-green eyes and received nothing back in return. It was true: men *were* different from women. They had different concepts of life. They didn't weep or wail or remember; a man who wept wasn't considered a real man. That's how they could go off to war, because they could contemplate a world of slaughter and destruction and not be paralyzed with regret. What did it matter, if that's what life really was? A bitch and then you die? My God! What sort of standards were those?

She stood up to leave. There seemed no point in staying any longer. Someone else could look after Victor; his leg would heal in the hospital. His heart would never heal properly. There was hard scar tissue all over it.

As she was gathering her things together, her hat and sunglasses, her bag with her passport and her small stock of Malayan dollars, a tall, gray-haired man came through the door. He wore a cool linen suit, a striped shirt, and a striped tie, his hair very smooth, his eyes very blue. He gave Victor a quick glance and held his hand out to Isabel. "You must be Cartwright's sister. I'm Oliver Bailey."

She took his hand. It was firm and strong, and as she held it, a tiny shock like electricity ran up her arm, a connection stretching over the years, through war and peace, a thread linking her to this man, to her father, to her own beginnings. She held on to his hand for a long moment.

13

OLIVER BAILEY took her to lunch. Not, as with Victor, to a private club, but to a large, airy restaurant. In place of windows and walls, bamboo screens were propped open to a thick stand of luxuriant plants and flowers, and at the entrance to the green shady space, a girl with flowers at the back of her hair greeted them and bowed them to a table next to the rustling forest. Orchids tumbled from mossy trees, huge butterflies and tiny birds flitted among the branches; the roof was thatch, and fans circled gently in the sticky air. They were near the center of Kuala Lumpur, but the cacophony of motor vehicles and the rising swell of concrete buildings were hidden by the bamboo and palm trees and gigantic ferns rioting around the exterior, protecting and cooling the interior.

Isabel was enchanted. "How beautiful! It's exactly how I pictured Kuala Lumpur, hot, quiet, and peaceful. It must all have been like this once. Of course, I don't remember it, but if I did, isn't this what I'd be remembering?"

Bailey seemed pleased that she was pleased. "Alas, yes. It's what we colonial types would like to hang on to and preserve. The heat will always remain, but the peace and quiet is rapidly disappearing. This city will soon be as vulgar as the rest of the world. I've even heard rumors there are plans for the world's tallest building in this very spot. An inappropriate ambition, I would say. As if progress consists of removing what's indigenous and charming and replacing it with something that approximates New York. As if New York should be the standard for anything."

It was a blessing to be in a dim, cool place, out of the snarling traffic, out of a sterile air-conditioned hotel, away from the fluorescent-lit hospital and Victor's irascibility. Her body was beginning to recover from the air travel, but for the past twenty-four hours, when she wasn't sleeping she'd been hurtling around in cars, crisscrossing the city against the alarming traffic. Easing the damp hair away from the nape of her neck, Isabel slipped her feet out of her sandals beneath the table.

"Kuala Lumpur's not quite how I thought it would be. So many modern buildings. So much traffic. I imagined I was coming to a quiet backwater."

Oliver Bailey made a small gesture, a raising of his hand that somehow evinced sympathy. "You haven't had much chance to see it properly yet, have you? But it *is* a busy place. Malaya's a stable, thriving country, and everyone wants a piece of it." There was a hint of both modest pride and regret in his voice, as though he were personally responsible for an otherwise deplorable fact. "KL's already changed out of all proportion, but I bet if you come back in just a few years, you won't recognize it. Maybe you should go to East Malaysia. It remains a lot more primitive and underdeveloped."

His face was smooth and suntanned, hardly lined at all. He had a gentle, unaggressive smile and a courteous, slow manner, as though there was all the time in the world to chat with her. His speech was somewhat formal, a little old-fashioned, more like a kindly academic's than that of a high-powered and important businessman. Isabel supposed he must be high-powered to be head of Victor's company, but she felt uncommonly comfortable with him. Only one thing made him important in her eyes, and she waited for her chance to talk about it.

"But I can't complain about the changes too much," he said, and raised his hand to signal a waiter. "I consider it fortunate that people like me weren't forced to leave. That the company can carry on in much the same old way. When you see what's happened to the rest of the region, it's something of a miracle Malaya's survived as a democracy. Look at Vietnam and Cambodia; God knows what goes on in Burma. Malaya is one of the rare success stories. It's handled the transition from colonialism to democracy without collapsing into dictatorship or anarchy. It all hung in the balance in the 1950s, you know, when the Communists could easily have won power."

Isabel wasn't interested in discussing Communists or power struggles, however. She knew a bit about the troubles in the 1950s, of course, the guerrilla warfare in the jungle, the Chinese bands that roved the countryside, attacking rubber plantations and Europeans. She'd always kept track of Malaya's progress.

"What I want to remember is the country as it was. Before Communists, before wars. I get these odd flashes, when something seems so familiar I know it's all still there, locked away inside me. A sort of imprinting. I was born here; therefore it will always be a part of me."

Bailey seemed amused. "I understand your brother was born here too. He doesn't seem imprinted."

She leapt instantly to Victor's defense. "Oh, but he was merely a baby when we left. Less than a year old. He had no chance to be imprinted with anything." She gazed down at the white tablecloth. "Or anyone."

A waiter came up to the table, smiling, salaaming, handing out large, elaborate menus with a flourish. Isabel began to read the long list of unfamiliar dishes—satay, nasi lemak, rendang, roti canai—and was dismayed to discover she couldn't recognize any of them, another small example of how foreign she really was, not imprinted at all but a stranger in a land that had slipped away from her.

Oliver Bailey seemed to sense her difficulty. "May I suggest something for you, Mrs. Bennet? Do you like prawns? Curried prawns are a specialty of the house."

"Isabel, please. Somehow my married name doesn't fit here." She dropped the huge menu gratefully. "I'd love to let you choose."

She was starving, actually, had eaten nothing since yesterday lunchtime. Now she'd caught up with her sleep and was refreshed and hungry. Ready for the world again.

"And a cold beer, perhaps? Beer is awfully good in the heat."

After giving the order to the waiter, Oliver Bailey rested his elbows on the table and leaned forward to peer into her face. "I hope you don't mind my saying this, Isabel, but you have quite the most unusual and beautiful eyes." He cleared his throat, as though he might have embarrassed her. Or himself. "I told your brother how I met your father once. I didn't mention to him that I also met your mother. I recall it quite clearly now, because your eyes are just like hers. Quite unmistakably so."

Shocked, Isabel felt the heat run into her cheeks, the easy tears into her eyes.

"Oh, dear," he exclaimed. "I didn't mean to upset you."

The oddest sensations coursed through her, little surging waves up and down the back of her arms, along her spine, a mixture of disbelief and surprise overlaid with—what was it? Was it delight, this sudden pounding of her heart? Or was it a type of panic, some sort of dread? She had trouble controlling her lips, stammering and stumbling over the words as she tried to explain. "It probably sounds ridiculous, but you're the very first person I've met who actually talked to my mother. She's such a mystery to me, a shadowy figure, someone I have trouble remembering. Victor, of course, doesn't remember her at all. The one relative we had in England, on my father's side, had never even met her and said no one knew anything about her. They ran off together, I believe. At least that's what Aunt Lucy said. Perhaps it was a scandal. Aunt Lucy was very respectable." Isabel laughed suddenly, thinking of poor Aunt Lucy, and Oliver Bailey looked startled. "My father could've told us, but of course he never had the chance. It's almost as though my mother never existed. That's strange, isn't it? To know absolutely nothing about one's own mother. It makes me feel guilty. And I know that's silly. It's hardly my fault I don't know, is it?"

Bailey removed his arms from the table and leaned away from her, sliding back into his chair as though to give her space, as though not to crowd her. His intent blue gaze slid slightly off to the side, into the tumbling greenery. "Of course it isn't. But it's said that survivors suffer from guilt feelings, however unreasonable they may be." The blue eyes wandered back to her. "I find that to be true in my own case. Many of my fellow prisoners died in the prison camps. Those of us left behind always felt there was more we could have done, should have done, to save them. The truth was, there was nothing we could've done. We were just lucky to be alive ourselves."

There were many stories worse than hers, Isabel knew that. Hers wasn't that bad; she'd been spared the deprivations and suffering he was remembering. She'd been rescued and kept safe in England. Her war was an easy one compared to his, her loss a tiny one compared to others' losses.

The beer arrived in tall frosted glasses. Lifting his glass, Oliver Bailey touched it to hers. "Cheers, my dear. To us, the survivors."

Isabel drank some of the beer without tasting it. "I'd never have survived what you survived."

His smile remained gentle. Unaccusing. "That's what I'd have believed before it happened to me. It's astonishing what you live through when there's no alternative."

She wanted to express empathy but didn't quite know how to say it. "They were very cruel, weren't they, the Japanese?" She could hardly speak the word—Japanese—even today. For years after the war, she'd had nightmares about the hordes of sinister small figures creeping through the jungle toward her, a silent tide of khaki, a dreadful yellow fungus spreading over the land. Over her life. When people like Oliver Bailey were released from the Japanese prison camps, everyone learned how terrible their confinement had been, how they'd been beaten and starved and maltreated, how many of them died in those prison camps. The stories had kept her nightmares alive for years longer.

He sighed. "They weren't alone in their cruelty. War is a cruel, unforgiving business. Since then I've come to know the Japanese as ordinary people, not as captors or as enemies. I believe much of our problems were that we simply didn't understand each other."

Isabel wasn't as ready as he was to forgive. "Beheadings? Starvation? Beatings? You call that a lack of understanding? That type of treatment had only one explanation."

"It doesn't account for it all, of course. Not all." Shrugging his shoulders as though to shake off blame, Bailey said, "Soldiers do things they wouldn't do in normal life, things that haunt them when they get back to the real world. I don't let myself be crippled by the memories. I can't."

Suddenly she saw him as a different person: not merely a little mannered, as she first thought, consciously and deliberately English. Behind that polite exterior, he had to be tough-minded and strong. A real survivor. All the same, he could account for every day of his life, terrible though it may have been, while she still didn't know how to account for the people who disappeared from her life. Was it worse to know or not to know? Was Victor right, that what you didn't know didn't hurt you? There was only one way to find out, wasn't there? "Please," she said, "tell me about meeting my mother."

Bailey put his glass of beer down carefully, moved it round and round in small circles on the tablecloth, contemplated it for a few more moments, and then smiled, somewhat sadly, as though at a distant but fond memory. "It was rather a long time ago, and I was just down from Cambridge. It would've been July 1941, soon after I arrived out here. At some party at the club. That's where everything happened for the English in KL. It was a much smaller city then. I can't recall what the occasion was, but there were always parties in those days, three or four a week. They weren't particularly exciting affairs—the British circulated in restricted circles, and there were always too many young men and too few young women—but I thought it all rather glamorous and a little risqué, you know. I was not yet twenty-one, and it was the Empire in full swing. Life went on just as it had gone on for nearly a hundred years, people gathering for cocktails and gossip and to introduce the newcomers to the local bigwigs. There was little else to do, in any case, once darkness fell. Anyway, at this party, someone introduced me to this beautiful young woman with the most extraordinary eyes, and we danced and talked for a long while, and I remember how disappointed I was to find out later that she was someone's wife. Not just anyone's wife, either, but the famous Rodney Cartwright's wife."

Drawing in her breath, Isabel waited for him to tell her more. She watched the memories catching up to him, as he smiled at her across the table, not seeing her. He was seeing another life, another woman.

His smile grew rueful again, and he shook his head. "Disappointed is perhaps an understatement. I'd fallen in love, you see. Instantaneously. Falling in love was an occupational hazard at that age, in those circumstances. But as it happened, I never saw her again, and with everything that transpired after that, I must admit I'd almost forgotten her. Until today. Looking at your eyes. Now I can recall that evening quite clearly. As though it was yesterday."

The little story thrilled Isabel. She imagined how he must have looked then, twenty years old, fresh from England, probably in uniform, dark-haired maybe, his blue eyes not yet faded from the sun. She imagined how her mother might have looked. Was she really beautiful? Did she flirt with him? Was she trying to ensnare a susceptible young man, years younger than she was?

Across the table, Oliver Bailey's present-day face swam through her sentimental tears. She wiped her eyes with the back of her hand. "I haven't been thinking about it all my life, you know. Only lately, for some reason. I've been happy, married, children. But somehow, maybe, I've always hoped to meet someone who could tell me something about my mother and father."

His bleached eyes came back from the past and focused on her. Straightening his shoulders, he picked up his glass again, took a long draft. "Unfortunately, I can't tell you anything more illuminating. Very soon after that, I was sent up-country. And then the Japanese came and I spent three years in the prison camp."

Scrabbling in her bag, Isabel unfolded the tissue paper from the precious photographs, handed them across the table. "Do you recognize anyone? Those people on the lawn, are any of them familiar to you?"

Bailey brought out a pair of half glasses from an inside pocket, placed them carefully on his nose, peered at the photos one by one. "Yes, that's your mother. Indeed, it is. But it doesn't do her justice. She was very, very pretty. And fragile. She gave me the impression that she could break into pieces at any moment. She made me feel that if I didn't rescue her that very evening, something terrible was going to happen to her. It was, of course, just what a chivalrous young Englishman wanted to think."

He spread the pitiful remnants of her childhood on the tablecloth, reverently, as though he understood what they meant to her, and bent closer to them. Clutching her hands in her lap to prevent them from shaking, Isabel willed him to recognize someone, but after a long, careful perusal, he shook his head. "I spent so little time here in KL. And it's odd, but most of these young faces look totally alike to me now. So stylized, hair done the same way, clothes the same fashion. How strangely sheeplike we humans are when it comes to fashion. Even men follow blindly, even though we pretend not to. Look at these men on the lawn. Nearly all of them have those silly toothbrush mustaches, and they're all wearing the same kind of shorts, the same kind of shirts. I find them quite indistinguishable from one another."

Gathering the fading snapshots together, he handed them back. "Perhaps I've lived out here too long. Nowadays I find white faces much harder to identify than Chinese or Malayan."

Isabel thought he was making fun of her. Reluctantly, she took the photos from his hand and before she wrapped them again in the tissue paper, she looked at them one more time. But why? They were engraved on her brain. "If I saw my amah again, I know I'd recognize her."

"And would she recognize you?"

Isabel sighed. "I suppose I'll have changed more than she will have. But I have this foolish idea she'd know me instinctively. Like a mother's instinct."

A fine statement coming from someone who couldn't, last night, raise the image of her own sons. Today she could remember them perfectly well, as though she had a photograph of them in front of her with these others, their blue eyes and light hair, their soft round cheeks and clear soft skin, the defiant square shape of Edward's shoulders, Jamie's thin, awkward knees. Today it was Adrian's image that was fading in the hot bright light, washed out like overexposed film.

"And this relative of yours, your aunt, she couldn't tell you anything?"

"She used to talk about my father. Told us over and over again how clever he was, how he'd been at Oxford, how he'd been sent to the Far

East to do important research. But she didn't talk about my mother. She never met her, and I always had the feeling she didn't approve of her. And after all, I was only a little girl, not old enough to be told grown-up stories. In any case, Aunt Lucy wasn't a gossip. A pity, don't you think? Gossips tell us about people, and what's more important than people?"

Steaming platters of rice and fragrant curried prawns arrived at the table, tiny assorted dishes filled with chutneys and coconut and bananas, more beer. Isabel regarded the heaping dishes with dismay, her appetite gone.

"How must it have been for someone like my mother to come to a country like this, so different from England? How did women like her get on? What was life like for them?"

Oliver Bailey reached for her plate and began to spoon the food onto it. "What was it like? Comfortable, of course, if comfort is servants and idleness. I happen to believe that's the way to boredom, sometimes madness. There were women who came out to these countries to work, teachers and nurses, for instance, but most women came with husbands and without jobs and were doomed to sit around, counting the days before they could get out of the debilitating heat and return to what they were used to. I don't mean it as a criticism." He shot her a quick apologetic glance from under his eyelashes. "It isn't easy to have nothing to do all day long. Believe me, I learned that in the prison camp."

He set the plate in front of her. Like a child.

"It's difficult now to realize how far away places like Malaya once were," he said. "There was no jumping on a jet to be here in a few hours. It took weeks and weeks, and once you were here, it was difficult to return."

He gestured at the food. "Eat up. You'll be hungry later on if you don't."

Obediently, Isabel picked up her fork, stabbed at a prawn. "The English have changed too, haven't they? They used to be so hysterical about the heat everywhere—India, the Far East, Africa. Now they seek it out, hop on a plane to Spain in the middle of summer."

He grinned. "Perhaps we'd never have founded an empire if we'd had a warm south coast. Now I come to think of it, most conquerors came from cold climates. The Germans. The Vikings. The British."

"Not the Romans," Isabel pointed out. She put a small amount of rice and prawns in her mouth.

He smiled at her approvingly—whether for her observation or her eating, she wasn't sure. "Now tell me, what are you going to do with yourself while your brother is in the hospital?"

"I'm going to try and find out what happened to my father. And my stepmother."

He raised his eyebrows. "That's a tall order."

"It's what I came for."

"And your mother? Do you know what happened to her?"

Isabel stared down at the pink curved prawns, the heaped saffroned rice, the ocher-colored curry sauce. She put down her fork. "I don't know what happened to her. Do you know, Mr. Bailey?"

He laced his fingers together, well shaped, neatly manicured. "Oliver. No, I don't, Isabel. But you have to realize that Europeans succumbed to all sorts of tropical diseases in those day. To other diseases too. Those were the days before penicillin. We take antibiotics so much for granted now, but not so very long ago people got sick and died from the kinds of things we just pop a few pills for today."

It was perfectly logical, of course. Her mother had just had a baby. Women died all the time from the aftereffects of childbirth in those days, in that other world, that other age. Infection, blood loss. Victor was born in 1941. June 1941. Oliver Bailey must have met her just a few weeks later. Fragile, he'd said. Brittle. Isabel shivered.

"We could do a little detective work," he suggested gently. "If she was buried in the English church here in Kuala Lumpur, there might be a record."

Now she was really shaking, the hand that held her fork trembling, her teeth chattering so that she had to clamp her mouth tight. Why hadn't she thought of that? Why did the idea frighten her so?

She stammered, "I thought everything like that was destroyed. I thought the . . . the Japanese deliberately removed traces of the English."

There was one nightmare, the nightmare of her father and Marike swallowed up in that terrifying stealthy wave of invasion. There was another dread, one she couldn't put a name to. Hadn't dared to. That there was more to her mother's death than could be explained away by the normal attrition of childbirth or disease, as though somehow it was the jungle that swallowed her up, this odd picture in her mind's eye of a white dress disappearing into thick, impenetrable undergrowth. Just her mother's back, that's what she could see. Fantasy, of course, dreamed up to answer unanswered questions, all mixed up in her mind: The invasion and the sudden end of what had been, until then, in the far reaches of the British Empire, a normal existence. The house in Kuala Lumpur, the abrupt disappearance of her mother, her adoration for her father. Her clinging to Marike. Her love for Ayala. A whirling kaleidoscope of events and people that constantly rearranged themselves in her mind. There was no accounting for that dread. No reason. Except somewhere in a childish mind. Except for something like the flash of terror she'd experienced on the veranda of the house, the hidden sounds of the ghosts she'd thought she heard upstairs. Her mother had been screaming. Why had she been screaming? Didn't all mothers scream at times? Hadn't she, Isabel, screamed at her children sometimes? Of course she had. Of course. All she needed was one person who could reassure her, could say, from firsthand knowledge, Your mother was quite normal, Isabel, just like any other mother, driven to distraction at times by her child. All mothers get that way sometimes.

Just one person.

Oliver Bailey couldn't tell her. He didn't know what her mother was like; he'd met her once at a party and been blinded by infatuation. Another foolish young Englishman. Like her father. The world was full of foolish young Englishmen in those days, setting off to the far corners of the earth, to foreign places they'd no business in, instructing Malayans and Indians and Burmese and Africans how to organize their lives. What strange people the English were, to think they knew the way the world should be run. And still doing it, even though England didn't know how to run itself. Men like Oliver Bailey, still here, still organizing someone else's country.

"I could take you there," he said. "To the church."

Isabel gazed at him. A kindly man who once was young and had fallen in love, as all young men did. But with a difference: it was her long-ago unknown mother he'd fallen in love with, however briefly. And he wasn't so old. He would be just over fifty now. It made her mind reel, this odd connection, this living proof, sitting opposite her at an ordinary table with a white tablecloth. Not a photograph, not a ghost, but a real live flesh-and-blood person.

"Church?"

"The Anglican church here in KL. She might have been buried there, don't you think?" He hesitated, asked as though it were a delicate matter. "Unless she was Catholic, perhaps?"

It should be something else she knew, what religion her mother was. "I suppose . . . I don't know. Church of England?"

"There'd be a record of your birth there, then, wouldn't there? Maybe your brother's too."

"Good heavens!" Isabel stared at him, lost in the sudden enrapturing idea that her own name might be recorded somewhere in this foreign land that was the land of her birth. "You know how exciting that would be for me? To find my birth written down. It would somehow make it real to me, all of it. I keep telling Victor how he has to remember he really did have parents, and yet I'm not sure I totally believe it myself. Good heavens!"

Bailey cleared his throat once more, a scratchy, strangled sound. "My dear young lady. I do think you have a lot of catching up to do."

14

HOSPITAL, VICTOR DECIDED, wasn't all bad. Not since his damn leg had stopped hurting so much and as long as they didn't put anyone with a foul foreign disease in the room with him. He trusted Bailey had taken care of that; he was relieved that Bailey had taken Izzy away. She'd been threatening to play her dutiful sisterly role and stay and entertain the wounded. Izzy was into duty.

He'd thought he'd be bored out of his tree, flat on his back like a beached whale, pinned down by weighted slings and a monstrous cast, nothing to do but read mindless mystery novels, if anyone ever thought to bring any for him to read. Instead, he found the experience strangely calming, even peaceful, his mind and ear growing attuned to the rhythms of the hospital, to the comings and goings of the little nurses on their silent soft feet, with their shining black hair and tiny brown hands.

Victor wasn't used to being touched by women. He'd cringed at the prospect of being handled and stared at by giggling females. Until now, he'd considered the term "cringing flesh" to be an exaggerated phrase of romantic novelists, and he was surprised to discover that his own particular flesh did its share of flinching away, involuntarily, the gingery hairs on his forearms standing on end at the threat of being meddled with. All his body, not just his leg, felt bruised and battered. At first he'd waved the nurses away when he saw them approaching, black eyes alive with glee, he was certain, at the idea of causing him pain and embarrassment. He dared them to lay their hands on him, but they ignored his protestations, pretending not to understand his muttered imprecations, his studied politeness: "Not today, thank you." Then he discovered that the hands didn't, after all, hurt him but soothed his aching body, and after the first few times he began to wait for their coming. Welcomed it, almost.

He became fascinated with the contrast of brown skin and white. He'd never had brown hands touch him before. His own skin, he began to notice, was extraordinarily pallid, as if it lacked some essential ingredient of life. It never had any color because he never exposed it to the sun; it turned an ugly blotched red under the sun's rays, burned too easily, would surely grow cancers if too many ultraviolet rays bombarded it. Victor didn't follow the example of his fellow Englishmen and take his holidays on the Mediterranean, didn't blast his flesh until it peeled and his nose burned, didn't return from vacation covered with relics of sunshine like labels on an old suitcase. When Victor took holidays, he went to Wales or Brittany, where the sun shone only fitfully and occasionally. He considered such places more sanitary.

The nurses' hands were surprisingly gentle, little fluttering movements on his large, ungainly frame. He'd protested the indignity of anyone rubbing his behind with alcohol and powdering him like a baby, but soon he discovered that the delicate areas at the base of his spine and along the knobs of his vertebrae were growing sore from the weight of his body; even the angles of his elbows had become reddened and tender from his pushing himself up on the bed. The nurses, in spite of his muttered curses, flung back the bedclothes and applied vigorous amounts of cooling alcohol in brisk circular motions to the painful parts, patted talcum powder on them, smiled at him and straightened the sheets and plumped the pillows and went away as quickly as they had come. They soon returned. They washed him frequently, laying cool wet cloths on his face and neck, massaging his shoulders and neck with lotion. It was oddly comforting. One of them even shaved him; she draped hot cloths around his face and soaped his cheeks, placed two fingers under his chin, stretching it to the ceiling, and to his terror drew a straight-edged razor against his neck. He didn't dare move or protest. Victor had never had anyone shave him before. He considered it a terrible indulgence, like having one's nails manicured. There were certain things one should do for oneself. But he had to admit that he felt incredibly more human once the prickly stubble was gone from around his face and neck.

He had to suffer the indignity of the urinal. There was no other choice. The nurses didn't seem to find such intimate procedures embarrassing, apparently accepting the process as part of their peculiar duties. It was such a relief to empty his bladder that he could only feel gratitude, but the idea of having to use a bedpan was appalling. Victor knew there was no escaping from the contraption that clutched the enormous cast in its grip, and he tried to calculate how long his bowels could hold out, reckoned that if he didn't eat any of the inedible food he might be able to get away with it for days.

He wasn't too sure how much English the nurses understood. They used certain phrases, rotelike, chirping like little birds. "Hello, Mr. Cartwright. How are you today? Feeling better?" But they didn't seem to respond to his answers or want to try out any other words on him. Perhaps all nurses everywhere were like that. Perhaps they never bothered to answer their patients' questions. He had no real desire to engage any of them in conversation anyway; what would they have to talk about, a stranded English accountant and an Asian handmaiden?

As he lay on his back, gazing up at the ceiling, Victor's mind was comfortably blank. Today he didn't feel any pain. He wasn't hungry. He was idly drowsy, probably full of dope. He'd have to ask that Indian chappie when he came, if he came, what sort of dope he might be full of.

The day drifted away. Sometime during the latter part of it, the Indian chappie came into the room with the air of a lord and master, trailing a retinue of white-coated minions. The small band gathered at the foot of Victor's bed and gazed at him with professional curiosity, as though he were a specimen on a lab bench.

"Hello again," the doctor said, with that posh English accent. "Remember me? I operated on your leg. How is it feeling this afternoon?"

Of course Victor remembered him. He wasn't quite gaga yet. He distinctly remembered that accent, though he was damned if he could recall the name.

"How does it feel?" Victor echoed. "Cast adrift, you might say." He decided that wasn't such a bad pun, all in all, and laughed at his own joke. Feebly.

The Indian doctor smiled indulgently. "Well, you must be doing all right if you can make jokes. How about your sister?"

"My sister?" Raising his head from the pillow, Victor stared at the group clustered around the foot of the bed. It seemed as if a hundred black eyes were peering back at him. "I wasn't aware my sister was ill."

The doctor's white coat crackled. "She was tired. Not surprisingly, I'd say."

"I can't imagine why she should be tired. She has the benefit of a comfortable bed in a comfortable hotel."

"Oh, come, Mr. Cartwright. Are you complaining about *your* hotel?" Without waiting for the obvious answer, the surgeon came closer and held a couple of X-ray films near to Victor's nose. "I thought you'd like to see your pictures," he said.

Victor attempted to focus on the blur of black and white before his eyes, but couldn't make head or tail of them.

"That's the tibia, there," Mr. Rei said, stabbing at the wavering film. Victor noticed how his fingers were a different shade of brown from the nurses', an inkier cast to them, thinner and bonier. "A nice clean crack. Nothing too serious. We didn't have to touch it; immobilization should take care of it. The fibula needed a bit of manipulation, but it'll heal in time. Time is the healer of all things, isn't that right?" The sycophantic gang at the foot of the bed nodded their heads in unison, starched coats rustling.

Victor began to feel sick. He felt even queasier when the surgeon lifted the wad of cotton wool out of the hole, peered into it, replaced it, and then tapped the pristine white plaster of Paris encasing his disembodied leg, remarking conversationally, "That was a pretty nasty tear in the calf muscles. We tidied it up, trimmed the ragged edges. Sewed them together. But loosely, in case there's some infection. That way any fluid can drain out. I'm afraid it means you'll have quite a scar there, but you probably won't complain about that, will you, if it means your foot isn't going to drop off."

He seemed very pleased with himself. "Any questions?" he asked, and didn't appear to expect any.

Victor resumed his gaze up to the ceiling. It was a very ordinary ceiling, plain and uninspiring, offering him no clue as to what he might ask. "What did you give me?"

"I beg your pardon?"

"Did you give me a shot of something?" But he didn't really care. He was only vaguely interested in the condition of his body, even if the discussion about it churned his stomach. He never could bear to listen to medical details. His body, rubbed and powdered, felt quite comfortable, thank you, like someone else's body.

"Ah, yes," the Indian chappie said. "A touch of morphine. Makes you feel good, does it?"

So that's what morphine felt like.

When Victor next opened his eyes, the starched band of inspectors had disappeared. He couldn't recall the end of the conversation. Against the white walls, the uncurtained window had become a rectangle of black velvet, and now the room was illuminated by a pool of light spilling in a dim circle from the lamp on the bedside table; the sounds outside the door had changed from a brisk distant clatter to a muffled hum. If he listened carefully, he could hear the soft slap of feet, the rustle of skirts, the murmur of subdued voices. Obviously the hospital had sunk into another night, but what time of night, he had no idea. The sounds were reassuring, comforting. Any minute now, another brown hand might be placed on his brow, might straighten the bedclothes again, offer him a drink of water from the spouted cup just beyond his reach. Victor decided he quite liked being taken care of.

When next he awoke, it was daylight once more, and his leg was throbbing painfully under the cast. Eventually a nurse came in and gave him a shot, which took the pain away, and for a while he slept, then he was washed and powdered and tidied up again. He thought he might lose total track of time at this rate. He should be making marks on the wall, crossing the days off like a prisoner in a cell. Except he couldn't reach the wall.

He wondered when Izzy was going to visit.

ISABEL WAS VISITING the English church with Oliver Bailey. Oliver Bailey had apparently decided it was his personal responsibility to entertain her and help her explore the lost past, a task he appeared to find almost as absorbing as she found it. It was as though he'd nothing better to do with his time. His attentive concern charmed Isabel; she thought it curiously affecting that a stranger should want to get involved. No one had ever taken such an interest in her former life—not Adrian, not her boys, not even Aunt Lucy. Certainly not Victor. Perhaps it was because Oliver Bailey had a connection with those vanished years; after all, those years were also his past, one he insisted he'd put behind him but which he now seemed more than willing to resurrect, as though he, too, had questions that had never been answered. Questions that maybe he'd never asked.

The previous evening, he'd arranged a small gathering of men and women from Parker and Dellworthy, treating them all to dinner in Chinatown. Isabel was sure it was a command performance for her benefit, middle management and their wives instructed to be on duty to pass a few hours with a stranded stray; she'd felt awkward at first, a liability who had no connection with the firm, but these were people accustomed to strangers dropping in from faraway points on the globe. Most of them came from distant places themselves, if anywhere could be said to be distant these days. Her presence evinced little curiosity, no searching questions, merely pleasant social chitchat. "Where did you say you live? Do you have children? What did you say happened to your brother? What do you think of Malaya? You should take a trip to Malacca." Perhaps she'd talked too much, drunk too much wine, had too good a time. At home, nowadays, her circle of acquaintances was limited to the village, to parents of children the same age as the boys, to Adrian's colleagues. None of them were very entertaining. They were all rather boring, in fact, as she and Adrian had become boring. Perhaps as they'd always been. But the people at dinner last night had made her feel lively and funny, had smiled at her as though she were witty and pleasing. Isabel couldn't remember when she'd ever been in the company of so many different nationalities at the same time, Australians and Malayans, Chinese and British, corporately smoothed into like habits and like conversation, set on entertaining her and each other. They were a new type of empire, a twentieth-century corporate empire.

After dinner, they had wandered through the teeming street markets. The tropical night was raucous and alive with the cries of vendors, with shrieking white cockatoos and green parrots in cages, with amicable shoving throngs, the thick velvety air redolent with the scents of spices and oils. Isabel kept pausing to peer at the heaping array of exotic fruits, at the stalls where food was being cooked on little flaring stoves, at the intricate silver jewelry and the woven fabrics and brilliantly colored paper kites and the myriad useless trinkets for sale. At one point, she murmured aloud, "It's so different from England," and knew what a foolish remark it was. Oliver Bailey laughed and took her arm. "Quite different," he agreed.

The English church, however, was astonishingly like England, dim, Gothic, and sedate, with stained-glass windows and a soaring arched nave, dark inside and cool, a refuge from the overbearing sun. But as their footsteps echoed on the stone floor, past the long, empty pews with red hymnals propped and waiting, little creeping chills shivered in Isabel's spine, as though she were smelling an old sad scent of homesickness, the rigid devotion to a distant God, the misplaced, unswerving faith in a British Empire. Along the walls were elaborate marble plaques commemorating empire builders who never made it home again and memorials to British soldiers who died fighting for that Empire. Above the choir stalls hung tattered banners of old regiments, faded with age. The building itself was a memorial to days that were gone, to an empire on which, the people who'd occupied these pews believed, the sun would never set.

What became of all those people who once prayed here? Of all the others who worshiped in similar churches in India or Burma or Africa, the thousands and thousands who'd lived and worked in all the distant places that once were colored pink on the maps of the world, those vast areas of former British domain? Where had they *gone* when it was decided those lands could manage quite well without them, thank you? How did a tiny country like Britain reabsorb them; what did they *do* when they finally returned to that small, damp corner of the world? What on earth did all those middle-class, run-of-the-mill British men and women busy themselves with instead of administrating and policing and soldiering and doctoring and deciding the fate of millions of other peoples?

Before the altar and cross, the silver candlesticks, the flower arrangements, the trappings of an English place of worship in a tropical land thousands of miles from England, Isabel was bemused by the consequences of the end of an empire, by a multitude of questions she'd never asked before, had never dreamed of asking. She couldn't help thinking about the people she knew personally who'd made careers in places like this: the doctor who'd run a hospital in Uganda; the solicitor's clerk who was a judge in India; the engineer who operated a mine in Sierra Leone; the bishop who was a missionary in Kenya. And her own father, of course. An endless list among the generations of Englishmen who grew up knowing they could leave behind small lives in a small island and go off into the big wide world, to adventures more exciting and responsibility far greater than any they'd have had if they'd stayed home. Adventure was how she should think of her parents' experience. Not as exile. Not as being trapped in a jungle. They must have gone willingly, even if in the end, like so many adventures, it turned out badly.

There was no doubt some sparkle had gone out of British life since those days. Boys like Edward and Jamie didn't have that kind of opportunity anymore. There they were, in that stupid school Adrian insisted on sending them to, a school founded especially to educate young men in the fine art of English fairness and justice in an empire that had vanished like dust. An empire that, adventure or not, had devoured her mother and her father.

Stumbling and fumbling her way around the silent church, her heart full of conflicting emotions, Isabel wasn't sure anymore how much she wanted to find out. As she agonized, caught between sorrow and hope, a not unusual state for her, Oliver Bailey went looking for someone to help in the search. He produced a tiny golden-skinned Malayan in the somber uniform of the Anglican Church, dusty black suit and yellowing dog collar, who listened gravely to Isabel's story. Then he told them how, in 1942, the vicar had hidden the records and how they weren't discovered until long after the war. The vicar, he said, perished in a Japanese camp. Disappearing into the vestry, the curate returned with a huge battered book. He fingered the leather bindings, mildewed and spotted. "A miracle, you might say. How wonderful someone wants to look at these old records."

Isabel turned the thick parchment pages, a litany of marriages, births, and deaths from 1910 until 1942, each year recorded on a separate page. The writing was a uniform distinctive copperplate, each letter elegantly defined in black ink with care and devotion. She wasn't sure why the word devotion sprang so easily to mind. She found the page for 1936. "To Eleanor and Rodney Cartwright. A daughter, Isabel Mary. May 12, 1936."

She turned more pages. "To Eleanor and Rodney Cartwright. A son, Victor Rodney. June 20, 1941."

But though she searched meticulously, running her finger up and down the years, again and again, she could find no record of her mother's death. Somehow it hardly surprised her.

15

VICTOR WAS BORED. *Very* bored. He couldn't think where the hell Izzy had got to. All that whining and moaning she did about family, and the very time—the *only* time—he could have used some family companionship, she was nowhere in sight. Wasn't that just typical? Hadn't he sacrificed a quiet little trip to the Far East for her? Wasn't he stuck in this damned hospital bed, with no one but a bunch of foreigners to talk to, all because of her? Everything was Izzy's fault, no denying it, *her* fault. If she didn't have such inane notions rumbling around in her head, if she weren't so compulsive and out of control most of the time, he would be sitting in a comfortable bar now, having a cool beer with a couple of chaps. Instead of which, he was strung up to a torture device, at the mercy of women who could hardly speak the Queen's English, while she was probably gallivanting around KL at his expense, flaunting herself in front of men. He'd seen the way they looked at her. That Indian surgeon. His eyes had clapped on her the first moment he'd walked into the cubicle. Did he look where he should've been looking, at his patient who was bleeding half to death? No, only at Izzy. And she flapped her eyes right back at him, fluttering her lashes like some unhinged schoolgirl. They all seemed to fall for it. Even Bailey, a respectable middle-aged man with a responsible position. She turned those huge shiny eyes on him and put her hand in his, and he'd straightened his tie and squared his shoulders and grinned at her foolishly as though she was some kind of gift to mankind. What got into them all? Why did she do it? Did she want to turn every man into a weak-kneed idiot? The answer was probably "yes." Women were all the same: devious, scheming, ensnaring. The mystery was why men who should have more sense, like Bailey, fell for it. And the Indian doctor seemed a sensible enough chap, educated in England, for God's sake, not some illiterate peasant; it couldn't be that he'd never seen anyone of Izzy's complexion before, but every time he came into the room, supposedly to examine his patient, the first thing he wanted to know was "How's your sister?"

It was exceedingly annoying.

Victor shifted on his sore behind. The very least she could do for him was bring him something to read.

By the second day in the hospital, the third if one counted the day of arrival, Victor had become bored enough to try engaging the nurses in conversation. It was an uphill battle, for he was at a shocking disadvantage, some of them so tiny they were barely higher than his head even as he lay in bed. Victor was used to speaking to people from a superior height. Another problem was that these women had seen more of him than almost anyone else in all his thirty-two years and as a result seemed to consider him as less than adult, as a child they had to humor. They smiled at him but shied away from his raised voice and involved sentences, though gradually he learned their names and even managed to have quite a decent chat with a couple of them. One nurse on the evening shift, unfazed by his foreign manners, was bold enough to laugh and joke with him, her English more than adequate, her idioms facile. Her name, she told him, as she busied herself with the unfathomable tasks of nurses, was Sundra, and she had learned her English in Singapore. "I went to school there. Grammar school, you know, Mr. Cartwright. My parents didn't care to live in such a restricted society as Singapore, so we moved back to Malaya. My father is baba, born here."

Sundra's eyes were black and uptilted, her skin was firm and golden. When she stood in the light of the bedside lamp, her face caught the incandescent glow and reflected it back, not absorbing it as white flesh would have done. Her little starched cap was perched on the very top of her neat shining head, like a flower, and her teeth gleamed as though there was light emanating from within her, not from an outside source. She was quick and precise and not to be messed with. "Now look here, Mr. Cartwright, while you're in the hospital, I am in charge. Don't tell me you don't want your dinner. You are to eat it up. Flesh and bones can't heal without adequate nourishment."

The way she spoke to him reminded him of Matron at school. Bossy. Except that Matron had been heavy and lumpy, with thick legs, gray permed curls, and an unbecoming navy uniform; nothing Matron wore could have made her anything but middle-aged and overweight. She had buck teeth, and her hair flew away from under the starched flowing headdress, years out of date even then. But she'd been quite kind, Victor suddenly remembered, especially the time he had scarlet fever and had to spend six weeks in isolation. He hadn't thought of her for years; no reason to. She must have had a name apart from "Matron," but no one ever knew what it was or would have used it if they'd known. It amused him that this snippet of an Asian girl reminded him of the matron of a boys' boarding school; the boys would have gone nuts if they'd had a nurse as quick and shining as this one. Which was precisely why the powers that be chose someone like Matron, of course.

But Sundra and the other nurses couldn't keep him amused all the time, so it was with some enthusiasm that he greeted the arrival of a visitor, a small man with heavy-lidded eyes, dressed in a dark-blue suit, correct and formal. The visitor came into the room unannounced, sidling through the door as though he preferred his entrance not to be noticed. At first Victor thought he must be a deliveryman of some kind, because he bore in front of himself a huge and elaborate arrangement of tropical flowers, but he was too well dressed and he carried his burden with an air of disdain. Also he looked vaguely familiar, though Victor couldn't imagine from where.

The little man bowed behind the extraordinary bouquet, inclining his sleek head. "Mr. Victor Cartwright. I am Dr. Cheng. From the Centre for Tropical Studies."

So that's where he'd seen him. Of course. On the visit to the Centre, a hundred or so years ago.

"We were so very sorry to learn of your unfortunate accident, Mr. Cartwright. Your escort, Singh, informed us, naturally. We would have come to visit you immediately, but when we conferred with the surgeon, he told us it would be better to wait until you had made some recovery from the operation."

Cheng set the flowers on the bedside table, a writhing mass of color, dazzling against the stark white walls. "A small token of the Centre's esteem."

Victor was at a loss for words. "How kind."

"We are at your service, Mr. Cartwright. If there is anything we can do for you, we will be most happy. We at the Centre feel most obligated. You were in the care of our driver. It was most unfortunate."

"Really, it was an accident. Nothing to do with him."

"You are very kind, Mr. Cartwright. Of course, he has been reprimanded."

Poor sod. Raising his voice in an effort to make the point clearer, Victor said, "It wasn't his fault. If it was anyone's fault, it was my sister's."

"Ah, yes, Mrs. Bennet. How is she?"

"As far as I know, she is quite well, thank you."

"Good, that is good. May I sit down, Mr. Cartwright? I will only stay a few minutes."

Victor gestured to the one chair in the room. "Please excuse me. I'm not used to having visitors in a hospital room. I've never been in the hospital before, as a matter of fact."

Perching on the edge of the plastic chair, Dr. Cheng folded his small hands in his lap and waited expectantly, as though he'd come to be entertained. Staring at him, Victor wondered what he was supposed to say. After several seconds of silence, Dr. Cheng said, "Mr. Cartwright, following the visit of your sister and yourself to the Centre, we have discovered some documents pertaining to your late father. We thought perhaps you would be interested in looking at them?"

Victor felt his mouth drop open, closed it with a snap, pushed his glasses back up his nose. "Documents?"

"Yes, Mr. Cartwright. Exactly. A box of documents."

He heard himself echoing the word, like a bloody parrot. "Documents?" The little man had taken him aback, dropped a bombshell, you might say. His mythical father had actually left something tangible behind? And they'd only just found them? It was too coincidental, too pat somehow. As an accountant, Victor didn't believe in coincidences.

"What sort of papers? How did you come to find them?"

Smiling a comfortable, conspiratorial smile, Dr. Cheng said, "My assistant, Dr. Vishnasi—perhaps you recall him from the day you came to visit? He was reminded by your name. After you'd gone, he remembered he'd once seen a box with the name Cartwright in a storeroom. It has most likely been there since the war. The papers appear to be items of a personal nature, though we have not examined them in detail."

Victor experienced the smallest stir of excitement. Perhaps more than a stir. "Well, that's interesting, of course. Very interesting."

He thought about it, a kind of coup, one giant step ahead of Izzy. "I'd be interested in looking them over, of course. Perhaps I could have a look at them while I'm here in the hospital? As you can see, I'm hardly able to get out and about. And I really don't have too much else to do with my time."

"We cannot let you keep them, you understand, Mr. Cartwright, as they are the property of the Centre, but if there is something you are interested in, we can always make some copies."

Victor decided not to argue as to whose property they might be, not yet. If they were personal, then they would belong to the heirs, not to the Centre. They'd belong to him. And to Izzy, he supposed.

Smiling and nodding, a small animated Buddha, Dr. Cheng unfolded his hands. "Very good, Mr. Cartwright. I took the liberty of bringing the box with me. The driver is waiting outside with it." He stood up, bowed again. "One moment. I will fetch him."

Victor pulled himself further up the bed—the weight at the end of his cast sinking in inverse ratio to his body—and he smoothed down the covers expectantly, almost eagerly, waiting for Cheng's return. Thank God for something to lift the boredom of the long day. Could the box possibly contain anything of importance? Or would it merely be full of obscure research papers, the sort of stuff he presumed his once-upon-a-time father spent his time writing? But Cheng had said "items of a personal nature."

Dr. Cheng reentered the room with a miserable Singh in tow. Singh, his eyes averted from Victor, was carrying a metal box, not large, the size that solicitors kept deeds in, painted black and gold, a handle in the middle.

Clearing his throat nervously, Singh said, "Tuan, you are well?"

Victor stifled the urge to reply, "No, I'm not bloody well," and instead said, "Oh, not too bad, thanks." He held his hands out for the box. Taking it from Singh, Dr. Cheng presented it ceremoniously, bowing again, and when Victor took the box between his two hands, he was disappointed that it felt so lightweight, and was surprised to be disappointed. On top of the lid, above the handle, a tarnished brass nameplate was engraved with the name Cartwright. Victor gazed at it.

"Extraordinary."

Dr. Cheng agreed. "Yes, it *is* extraordinary." He hovered beside the bed, breathing down Victor's neck. "That we found it. That Dr. Vishnasi should remember it." He smiled again with that conspiratorial air, somewhat slyly. "I think, Mr. Cartwright, your sister made a deep impression on him."

Singh was twisting his hands together, his thin, dark face an almost laughable picture of unhappiness. As if repeating something he'd been instructed to say, he said, "I am so very sorry, Tuan Cartwright, that you suffered your mishap when I should have been taking better care of you."

Victor said, impatiently, "It was an accident, Singh," and wanted both of them to leave now.

Singh said, "Your lady sister, she is okay?"

"When last I saw her, yes, she was okay."

"That is good, Tuan, very good. She is a very kind lady, your sister."

Not bloody kind enough to visit her only brother in the hospital.

Victor could sense that Cheng was expecting him to open the

box; he slid it under the bedclothes and leaned back against the pillows. "Well, Dr. Cheng, it was very kind of you to bring this to me. I'll have a look at what's inside and let you know if there's anything I should hang on to."

"I think your sister will be most interested, Mr. Cartwright. She obviously had great regard for your father. As do we all. Your father made a most important contribution to the development of other forms of rubber, as I'm sure you're aware. Until his work, we were almost totally dependent on *Hevea brasilicus*, one of the original rubber trees, which I'm sure you know was originally brought to Malaya from Kew Gardens by Sir Clements Markham in about 1875. That was when the plantations originally began, the foundation of the rubber trade in the British Empire."

"Yes, yes, very interesting. My sister will be very interested. You and she will have to have a further chat sometime. And thanks for the flowers. I've never seen such an amazing arrangement."

At last Cheng seemed to take the hint and was about to leave. "Please remember, Mr. Cartwright. If there is anything we can do . . ."

He bowed once more, for about the hundredth time, and departed, taking the unhappy Singh with him.

Victor lay with his hand on the box under the bedclothes, trying to decide what it might contain. He felt no urgency to open it. If it had waited for thirty years, another few minutes couldn't make any difference. He wanted to be prepared for what might be inside. Like conducting an audit, one's mind had to be flexible and open, but on the other hand, it didn't do to be surprised; unless one had an inkling about what might be coming, it was possible to miss the significance of otherwise obvious clues. It was all too easy to be misdirected, led astray. One had to tread carefully.

Finally he took the box out from under the covers and regarded it, tried the lid. It opened immediately, and he shut it quickly, surprised it wasn't locked. What was the point of saving papers if they weren't locked up? Maybe the people at the Centre had the key? Maybe they'd forced it? He looked for scratches at the edges and around the keyhole. No sign of forcing. It had lain in a storeroom for more than thirty years, unlocked? Well, maybe that wasn't so important. What was odd was that they'd found it, just when he and Izzy were in town. Pretty coincidental.

Victor didn't open the box until after the nurses had been in to make the bed and give him another back rub. When at last there was half an hour that he judged would be free of interruption, he opened the lid and looked inside.

A small package of papers was wrapped in something that resembled plastic but which he knew wasn't. There was a strangely nostalgic smell to the substance. Picking it up, sniffing at it, Victor was immediately reminded of school and of one of the masters who smoked a pipe. That was it, the stuff they used to make tobacco pouches from—what the devil was it called? The master, old Batty Bates, used to sit with one leg crossed high over the other, trouser leg pulled up to expose one gray sock and one pale hairy leg, and spend endless minutes fiddling with the pouch and pipe, stuffing tobacco into the bowl, pressing it down with his thumb, tapping it against his foot, a mesmerizing ritual that must have taken only four or five minutes but felt like four or five hours. What *was* that pouch made of? Victor could see it in Batty Bates's hands, smell the rich masculine odors that arose from it, the authoritative schoolmaster mystique of pipe smoking.

He was unable to unwrap the papers until he remembered the name of the substance. It was a sort of test, a kind of luxury to lie there and rack his brains about something useless. Whatever it was had long been replaced by plastic. Pipes were gone too, along with that kind of schoolmaster.

Staring past the sinister flowers on the bed table, Victor had an unusually generous notion—he would present them to Sundra—and then suddenly, out of the blue, the name came to him: percha . . . gutta-percha, that's what it was called. He felt inordinately pleased with himself. He'd have to ask if there was any significance to the stuff; perhaps his father had been leaving a clue? Perhaps his work had to do with gutta-percha?

At last he could unfold the package, and as he unwrapped it, four or five pieces of paper slid out onto the bedcovers. He picked them up, one by one. First was a birth certificate. Izzy's. On a long standard British form, filled in with a fine copperplate handwriting. A girl, Isabel Mary Elizabeth. Father's name, Rodney Harold Arthur Cartwright, of Khota Ruan Rd. Occupation, biologist. Mother's name, Eleanor Elizabeth, formerly Wellington, also of Khota Ruan Rd.

He'd not known what his mother's name was. Eleanor Elizabeth, formerly Wellington. It had quite a nice ring to it.

There was his own birth certificate. Victor Alexander James. Date of birth, June 20, 1941.

Victor tried to imagine himself as a newborn mewling infant. It was an impossible stretch.

A marriage certificate. Rodney Harold Arthur Cartwright, Scientist, to Eleanor Elizabeth Wellington, Spinster, of the parish of Marylebone. February 23, 1935.

It was almost forty years ago. But more than that, 1935 was a different era, a different world, before the Second World War, before Hitler's war and Hirohito's war, before the atom bomb, before jet airliners and television, before America became a world power and its President was assassinated, before Stalin destroyed Russia. Victor had never thought of himself as transcending history, but suddenly he realized he was as much a part of a huge shift in global powers and dominations and perceptions as if he'd lived through the French Revolution or the Bolshevik Revolution or the First World War.

It gave him an odd sense of . . . what could he call it? Destiny? An exaggerated concept: he'd been a mere bystander, not an integral part of the action. But he'd never before thought of himself as in any way connected to the paradigm shifts of mankind, and it altered his perception of himself, as though after all he'd been engaged in a grand scheme, in forming history. As though he were a character in *War and Peace.* It suddenly struck Victor that that was what history was, not only kings and queens and generals and armies, but a greater or lesser number of ordinary people moving or being moved around the chessboard of life, shaping and reshaping the patterns of the world.

It was overwhelming, really, to rethink his own place in history, the place of his father. And of his mother, Eleanor Elizabeth Wellington.

There was a very small piece of paper with nothing but a recognizable name and address, one he hadn't seen for many years. Lucy Tattersall, Groom's Cottage, Etherington, Somerset. Aunt Lucy.

Victor unfolded the remaining piece of paper.

Kuala Lumpur, January 20, 1942

This is, in effect, my last will and testament. Who knows if it will ever be read? Who knows what will happen to us? The world we have known is disintegrating around us. The children are gone, my work here is gone. With luck, my work will carry on, I hope and believe, but poor Eleanor is gone. There is only dear Marike left, and God knows what shall become of us. If He is willing, I shall live to complete my work in other places, but if I cannot, I wish my children to know that my thoughts were with them at this terrible time. May they reach safe haven and be fulfilled and happy in the future. I leave all my worldly goods to them, to Isabel who has been the light of my life and to little Victor who must never believe he was responsible for the disaster that overtook us.

To my dear Marike, who has shared these last months and who has taken care of my children so unselfishly, I have no wealth to leave. I pray that we will escape to continue our lives together. Perhaps we should try, like Eleanor, to follow Noone of the Ulu. Or perhaps we can reach Marike's father. If we survive, I shall take care of her, but she understands that I must first make provisions for Isabel and Victor. My solicitors in England are Dwight and Childers of Symington, Berks.

Signed,
Rodney H. A. Cartwright

Victor had never seen his father's handwriting before. It looked exactly like his own, small and neat and very clear, the same upright strokes, the same whorls and curls on the rs and the ds. This could have been a letter that he, Victor, might have written himself, few words wasted, no undue sentiment. The sight of the uncannily familiar handwriting, the feel of the paper, had a curious effect on him, as though he were holding his father's hand in his own. Victor felt his heart expand and contract within his chest, as if he'd made a connection and immediately lost it again, in one profound moment.

His glasses blurred and steamed. He had to take them off his face to wipe them clear. It was a strange, unnatural emotion, this feeling of nearness to someone who was a total stranger, with whom he'd never felt any connection. There *was* no connection. He, Victor Cartwright, was only a biological product, a seed, an offshoot. The rest of it was learned sentimental claptrap. He'd had a father, of course. Everyone had to have a father. And a mother.

Eleanor Elizabeth Wellington. It was a pleasing kind of name.

When he got back to England, he might look up those solicitors, if they were still around.

What the hell was Noone of the Ulu?

What disaster could he, Victor, possibly have been thought responsible for? A baby? Babies didn't *cause* disasters; they were merely disasters in themselves.

Where the hell was Izzy?

16

*I*SABEL WAS SPENDING the day with Oliver Bailey. Again. He'd suggested a visit to the mountains, to Fraser's Hill, an old colonial refuge from the heat and stickiness of the lower coastal regions, not so far from Kuala Lumpur. "It's where everyone went in the old days," he explained. "You'll like it." He would drive her there himself. "Really," he said, "this is like a little holiday for me. I'm kind of footloose and fancy free for a couple of days."

That their destination was yet another connection with the past tempted Isabel. It would take only a few hours, he said, but they should start early so they could arrive in time for lunch and have the rest of the day there. She'd accepted, almost too eagerly. It was getting to be a habit, letting someone take care of her, wallowing in a certain amount of luxury, cars and drivers and no decision making, a sort of escape, a frivolousness that she wasn't accustomed to. All her life she'd been serious and responsible, dedicated somehow. But to what? she asked herself now.

The car was a Mercedes, big, comfortable, smooth. The tape deck was playing Brahms, filling the interior with the soaring strings of the first symphony, in stereo, incongruously far from the cool lakes and mountains of Austria. She sank into the soft leather seat, stared out at the heaped green hills and the strange limestone outcrops that reared out of the surrounding land. "The Batu Caves," Oliver said as they swept past. "We don't want to stop to see them. Much too touristy."

It seemed unfair to her that this country, which had always been so remote in her mind, so far from civilization, was becoming a tourist destination. Nowhere was remote anymore; the whole world had turned into a "destination."

The road out of Kuala Lumpur was congested at first, huge lorries traveling at terrifying speeds, but once they turned off the main highway, the traffic was left behind and the snaking road was quiet and empty. It climbed upward, overshadowed by enormous tree ferns and giant bamboos and wreathing mists that shrouded the treetops.

"This is the old Gap Road," Oliver explained. "The British built it. When we get to the top, it's single track and there's a gate controlling the flow. We might have to wait our turn, but we can have coffee and cakes at the old rest house."

He was trying to entertain her, to be a tourist guide. Isabel realized she should be noting the scenery, drinking it in, remembering it for the future, and instead her mind wandered, idly.

"It looks as if there's a storm in front of us," he said. "But we'll probably drive out of it before we get to the top."

Isabel gazed up warily at the piled and roiling clouds ahead, at the sinister way they had lowered over the impenetrable trees, melding sky and forest into one thick gray mass, then she looked away from them to watch the profile of the man beside her, sideways, not wanting him to know she was watching him. He drove with arms straight out, like a racing car driver, the collar of his short-sleeved shirt open at the neck, his chin jutting forward, the skin below it firm and unwrinkled. His Adam's apple was smooth and rounded, not sharply defined like those of many men, and he was humming with the music, tunelessly. He seemed quite a different person now that he was in casual clothes, more accessible, no longer the correct middle-aged businessman in striped shirt and old school tie. She wondered what she was doing, driving up to the mountains with him.

The lush Brahms melodies filled the car and made the heat run into her face.

"I studied music once," she said. "I should've stuck with it. Perhaps I'll go back to it now my boys are away at school. Perhaps I could finish the course and then teach piano. I'll have to do something."

"You're very lucky if you have musical ability. I wish I did. Oh, I can strum a tune out on the piano, sometimes even with two hands. Why do you have to do anything?"

"Doesn't everyone have to do something? I can't spend the rest of my life being idle."

"I thought that was everyone's ambition."

"Is it yours?"

"Well, no. But then, like everyone else, I consider myself exceptional."

"You've probably been going to work every day of your life. I think I'd like to have a job for at least part of mine."

"Children are a job," he said.

"I never thought of them that way." She smiled. "And I didn't get paid very well. Do you have children?"

He didn't answer for a moment. "Twin boys. They're eleven. They live with their mother in Hong Kong."

"Why, they're almost exactly the same age as my boys. Edward and James. They're eleven and twelve. They've just gone off to boarding school. I miss them."

He nodded. "I miss my kids too. I only see them at Christmas and during the summer holidays. They might just as well be away at school. And they'll probably go off to school in England. Next year." He smiled this time. "Obviously I came to parenthood at a later date than you."

"Hong Kong," she echoed. She couldn't help being curious. "That's a long way away."

"It might have been easier if their mother had taken them straight to England." A touch of frostiness crept into the smooth, even voice. "But her present husband got transferred to Hong Kong, so that's where they are now. God knows where they'll end up eventually."

Now Isabel was really curious. She wanted to know if he'd married again. Who his former wife was. Had she run off with someone? From the company? Why did that suddenly leap to mind? He sounded slightly bitter—did anyone ever get divorced without being bitter? Was it worth it, to be bitter for the rest of one's life?

She'd been responsible for her children, of course. But someone else would be responsible for them from now on. If she disappeared into this jungle, they'd manage just fine, absorbed into their school routine, playing their manly games and learning their manly lessons, their mother only a fond and distant memory. She hadn't been dedicated to a career. She hadn't been all that dedicated to Adrian, not really, not when she thought about it carefully. She could've married someone else just as easily, another pleasant enough man, with other quirks and other annoying habits, and her life or his wouldn't be much different. Maybe she should have waited for a real passion, one that might have changed her, jolted her out of that careful construction of sober family responsibility. Maybe she'd cheated herself. And Adrian.

Once upon a time, when she was twenty, she *had* been in love. Madly, foolishly, wildly, a dizzying spiraling hormonal crisis, a roller coaster of joy and disappointment, one moment a black hole of despair, the next the soaring heights of blissfulness, and the experience had exhausted her, left her bruised and battered and betrayed. Betrayed because no one could survive the intensity of such desire. Her love had walked away from her, escaped from her, brushing his hands coolly, his heat and ardor vanished quite abruptly, unable, he said, to live up to that look in her eyes. "You're eating me alive," he said, and broke her heart. So she married Adrian instead. Adrian wouldn't betray her, because he wasn't capable of such passion, because he wanted what she thought she wanted: a quiet life, a nice house, nice children. Not a roller coaster.

Without warning, the Mercedes ran into the rain cloud. The sky disappeared and they were clamped into a heavy thick darkness, into great heavy lashings of rain that streamed off the windshield, buffeted the car, and obscured the road ahead, a thunderous downpour alarming in its intensity. Oliver Bailey slowed the car and turned the windshield wipers up into a mad whipping movement that added to the sound and fury. The road under the wheels suddenly became a river, a brown cascade of rushing water, so that their forward momentum, though much slower, made it seem as though the vehicle were hurtling along at an incredible rate. At first Isabel was exhilarated by the abrupt change of weather, but in a few moments she became alarmed by the volume of rain crashing on the metal roof, by a sense of being lost underwater, as though the waters would rise and drown them. She supposed Oliver Bailey was used to extremes of climate like this, but she longed to beg him to stop the car and wait out the storm and was afraid of behaving like an idiot, terrified of a little rain. Then he did pull the car off to the side of the roadway, bringing it to a halt but leaving the engine running so the air-conditioning still worked. He turned on the hazard lights and the red blinker flashed dazzlingly on the dashboard. He had to raise his voice to make himself heard above the clamor and noise of the storm.

"Five minutes, and the worst of it'll be over," he said, and silenced the wipers, leaned forward to increase the volume of the music. But the music, too, was lost in the thunderous banging, and soon he turned it off as well. "It seems that not even Brahms can compete with nature in all her fury." He smiled at her in the gray half-light.

It was impossible to talk. Isabel clenched her hands in her lap. In spite of the air-conditioning, she could feel the perspiration running down her neck, gathering between her breasts and under her arms. The car seemed so small and insignificant, an island, a tiny frail craft adrift on a raging sea, and she was frightened, just as she had been frightened when a child by the pounding thunder of the rain on the roof of the house, the world in disorder, the elements raging outside. She wanted to fling herself at Oliver Bailey, bury her face in the neck of his open shirt, just as she'd flung herself at her father all those many years ago. Save me, she wanted to cry. Help me.

She took deep sucking breaths to calm herself, trying to allay this foolish need to have someone's arms around her, Oliver Bailey's arms, anyone's arms, to soothe these wild and unreasonable fears. It was just an ordinary tropical rainstorm, for God's sake, the sort of storm they had all the time here, nothing terrible, nothing exceptional, nothing that could wash her away, not now, not now when she was an adult and sensible and in charge of herself. Then she could no longer stand the banging and the thundering, the sheer crashing chaos, and she thrust her hands over her ears and crouched forward, bent double, heard herself moaning, and then Oliver did put his arms out to her, and she fell across the seat and let herself be gathered in, his hands smoothing her hair, his mouth brushing her forehead, his gentle English voice murmuring in her ear. "Isabel, Isabel, it's all right. You're quite safe here. Don't be afraid, my dear. I'll take care of you."

Oh, God, that's all she'd ever wanted. To be safe. To have someone take care of her.

Folded against him, weightless, fragile, breakable, she could feel the sinewy, muscular arms tightening around her, could hear the beating of his heart, steady, strong, reliable. Pressing her face nearer to his chest for the comfort of that heartbeat, for reassurance, she clung to him, and he rocked her in his arms, his voice coming from deep inside the fortress of his rib cage. "Isabel, Isabel. Such a beautiful name. Beautiful. Like you. Like your eyes. Lovely, adorable Isabel. Isabel, Isabel."

It was as though he couldn't stop saying her name. She could say nothing, not his name, not anything, because what she really wanted to say was, Hold me, keep me, I am come home, I have found you again. I waited and waited for you all these years and searched for you and now I've found you. Don't ever let me go again.

A wonderful peacefulness stole over her, a stilling of those fears and those nerves that had racked her forever, and she closed her eyes and smelled the cool masculine smell of him and instantly fell asleep, like a child wrapped in a father's arms.

When she awoke, it was because the rain had ceased, suddenly, as if a tap had been turned off. It was the silence that awoke her, or maybe it was the sun striking hot through the windshield, or maybe it was the awkwardness of her position or the realization of where she was and whom she was with and how she had thrown herself on him. She straightened up, pulled out of the circle of his arms, turned her head away, and put her hands over her face. "I'm so sorry," she said. "I do apologize."

"For what?" Oliver tried to take her hands in his, and she shook them off.

"I think I have to get out of the car," and she scrabbled at the door. Leaning across, he opened it for her, and Isabel leapt from her seat, precipitously, almost falling onto the road. Outside, the roadway was still streaming with water, but the clouds had scudded away; steam rose from the road surface and curled from the dripping trees, and the sound of wetness was everywhere. The earth smelled mushroomy damp, ferny, primeval. Propping herself against the side of the car, Isabel felt the water on the road wash over her feet; her dress was limp and clinging to her thighs, and her hair was heavy against her neck; she stared down at her feet and then into the jungle of ferns and bamboo, the trees crowding around, their heads tall and thick and high above. She wouldn't dare take a step off the road. Everything seemed silent, breath-holding, as though the world were waiting to begin again, and then the sounds of the forest rose in renewed life, an echoing chatter of monkeys in the trees, crying out to each other, and birds calling, and the unmistakable melancholy honking of a bullfrog. After a while, Oliver Bailey got out of the car on the other side, closed the door quietly and carefully, came round to her side.

"Please don't apologize," he said. "Don't spoil anything by apologizing."

"It was the rain," she started to say, and he placed one finger on her lips, lightly, held it there.

"Don't explain, either," he said.

Isabel looked into his face and saw him blink, as though she was dazzling him. She was well aware of the effect her eyes could have on people: like undimmed headlights, that long-ago love had told her; she was usually careful not to use their unwanted power, but sometimes she forgot and was surprised when anyone flinched away in that fashion. She hadn't intended to dazzle him; she was merely concentrating on his face, trying to sort out her own mixture of emotions—this alarming peacefulness that had assaulted her, this terrifying sense of predestination. And she wanted to read his emotions, if she could. The expression on his face was one of faint puzzlement and uncertainty and yet gratified too, as though he'd received an unexpected gift, and she found something immensely endearing about that expression. And it was kind. His face was so kind. Quite suddenly he appeared to be much younger, bulkier and heavier, more substance to him, as though years and years had fallen away from him. Or was it that she had grown older and nearer to him in age? She had to look up to see into his face, because he was taller by several inches. His height reduced hers, made her feel less awkward, more feminine. Beside most men, she felt too tall. She took hold of his hand to remove his finger from her lips, held on to his hand for a moment, and knew she wanted to step back into his arms, needed them around her once more, and she thought: Why can't I? What's stopping me? So she leaned into him and he put his arms around her again and they clung to each other in the thickening sunlight, the humidity rising around them, a blanket of heat, sticky and sensuous, gluing the past and the present together.

Eventually, without speaking, they got back in the car and continued up into the mountains, as if they were embarked on a journey they had yet to complete. After a while, they began to talk. He told her about his sons and about his wife, who was also English, how he'd met her when she was working in Singapore, with one of the oil companies, and how, after a few years, they agreed, mutually, that they just couldn't live together anymore. "It's a very ordinary story," he remarked, ruefully, lightly. "It turned out we had little in common. She met someone she liked better, she said, and that was that."

Isabel wondered how he could say it so easily. "But it must be terribly hard to have your children in a different country."

"It's always been a fact of life for us colonial types, hasn't it? It was taken completely for granted in the old days. You and your brother, for instance. You'd have been sent back to England even if the war hadn't come along, wouldn't you? That's what boarding schools were invented for, to take care of all those children in distant places who wouldn't have a proper education otherwise. To get them out of those climates that used to be considered so unhealthy."

It was true. She and Victor would always have been orphans of a kind. She had a minor fleeting pang of guilt about Victor and then forgot him.

"I don't believe I could bear my children to be so far away from me. A hundred miles is too far."

Oliver Bailey took his eyes off the road and looked at her, thoughtfully. "A pity." Then, "Tell me about your life in England," he said, and she forced herself to think about it.

"You know, there isn't much to tell. We live in a beautiful house in a beautiful village, and I can't think of a damn thing I do that is of any significance."

"I don't believe that."

"I don't have a job. I don't make any contribution to mankind. I've let myself be turned into an ornament." That was the reality of her life. She'd traveled a long distance to acknowledge it.

"But you make a wonderful ornament."

"That's not what I want to be."

"What do you want to be, Isabel?"

She looked at him, at the slippery road ahead. "I don't know. That's the problem." She turned her face away from him. "I thought that maybe . . . if I could get this thing worked out about my parents, I might be able to decide where to go from there. As though it's a hurdle I have to climb over to be able to see the other side. Do you understand?"

"Perfectly," he said.

The clouds came and went among the hills, and now and then it rained again, but nothing like the downpour they'd just encountered. Suddenly the road flattened out on the very top of the mountains, and there was a line of cars stopped in front of them. At the side of the road stood a large Tudor-style building, even more out of place than the music of Brahms had been. "The rest house," Oliver said, and looked at his watch. "We've about half an hour before the gate opens to let us go on to Fraser's Hill. Like some coffee?"

When they got out of the car, the air was noticeably cooler. The jungle was still all around, but the air was thinner and the sun less oppressive, almost a tang in the air. Oliver took hold of her arm, just above the elbow, not in a commanding way but as though he merely wanted to touch her, be close to her, and Isabel felt unsteady, as if she was undertaking something she'd have trouble handling.

The rest house was cavernous, with high ceilings, lots of black beams, and an air of neglect. There were a few other people in the room, mostly white, tourists in shorts and khaki caps, perusing maps, sipping coffee. Isabel sat next to Oliver at a dark-brown table, and a Malay girl in a black dress and white apron brought them two cups of tepid coffee, sad-looking scones. Once the girl had slapped away in her rubber thongs, Isabel laughed, her burbling, cascading laugh. "So silly," she said, "to try and imitate England on top of tropical mountains," and he smiled at her, apologetically, and reached for her hand across the table, and she felt stupidly happy, ridiculously lucky, blessed by an unforeseen good fortune, as though she'd been set free, released from a prison she hadn't known she was in.

"I'm sure I could help you find out something more about your parents," he said.

"You *are* helping."

"No, I mean something more concrete. Maybe we should put an advertisement in the papers. I bet there are people still around who knew them. You'd be surprised how many people stayed on."

"I never thought of that," she said. "It seems too ridiculously easy."

"Why don't we try it?"

She thought about it. "Yes, why not? But the trouble is . . . I'm only here for another few days."

"Ah, well, yes. Perhaps we could discuss that?"

There was a sudden flurry of movement, and cars began to stream down the road past the rest house, and Oliver said, "The gates will be opening soon," and they abandoned the half-drunk coffee and the untasted scones and hurried back to the car. When they got in the car, Oliver leaned across the seat and kissed her, and Isabel thought: it *is* too easy. Nothing should be this simple. Then the cars began to slide through the gate, and they ground the few miles along the ridge to Fraser's Hill.

On the road, in the slow convoy of cars, Oliver told her something of the history of the place and about the aboriginal tribes who inhabited these mountains that ran up the spine of Malaya, about the way they lived in the high hills in the deep jungle, how these jungles still contained tiger and rhinoceros and had been quite impenetrable until fairly recently, how the natives still used blowpipes with poison darts that could kill a man in a few seconds and how they believed in spirits.

And when they reached the village of Fraser's Hill, it was beautiful, and Isabel absolutely knew she'd been there before.

17

*B*UT IT WASN'T UNTIL Oliver drove away from the new hotels and the tennis courts and the golf course, and up the hill to the old houses, that she was so sure.

The houses, low stone bungalows with ivy on their walls, were perched high on a hillside and surrounded by flower gardens: roses and hollyhocks, chrysanthemums and green, green grass. The total effect was charming and unreal, like a stage set attempting to imitate the English countryside. The houses produced in Isabel the same feelings of melancholy that the church in Kuala Lumpur had given her, a sense of the homesickness and nostalgia of the people who built these houses and so carefully crafted these gardens in the middle of the jungle.

"These bungalows were all there used to be at one time," Oliver said. She knew that by one time he meant the time she was interested in. "They're for rent—for the day, the week, as long as you want. You can get tea and scones served in your room before the fire. See, they have chimneys."

They did. She was astonished. "Are fireplaces really necessary?"

"You'd be surprised. It can get quite chilly up here at night. We're five thousand feet up, you know."

He stopped the car and Isabel got out. She was mesmerized, staring at the houses, the small windows, the lawns, then off into the near distance to the misty dark hills, layered one upon another, stretching to what seemed like infinity. She *knew* she'd stared at this view before.

"But of course you could have done," Oliver said when she tried to explain it to him. "I told you, everyone used to come here from KL in the old days. Mothers would bring their children and stay in these bungalows during the worst of the heat, and the husbands would come up at the weekend. There'd have been tennis matches and cricket matches and cocktail parties and games for the children. I'm sure it was all quite wonderful, and if you could remember, I'm certain you would have happy memories."

He took it so much for granted. There was nothing mysterious about it; for the British who lived in the heat of the lowlands, this was a natural escape. Oliver's matter-of-factness diffused the frightening sensation of a secret, enigmatic life threatening once again to crowd in on her; if he'd been with her on the visit to the house in Kuala Lumpur, she might not have been so overwhelmed. The outcome might have been different. For the first time, Isabel began to believe she could have normal, rational memories of her past. Her memories, when she found them, didn't need to be tragic and painful, she didn't need to be neurotic and unstable about them. She could and should appreciate those years for what they may simply have been—an escape from the cold rains of England, from dreary jobs in the city, a new life, a wonderful adventure, a stretching of horizons and talents and hopes, the making of a new land. Like being a pioneer, in a way. Isabel had always considered the stories of the pioneers in America to be tragedies of desperate people in search of a better life who found only hardship and suffering and death, but now, standing on a hillside in Malaya, she thought perhaps those stories weren't so sad after all. Not if you looked upon them as opportunities.

For Isabel it was a revolutionary way of thinking.

"If only they hadn't all disappeared." She intended to speak to herself but discovered she'd said the words out loud.

"Of course," Oliver said. "You have to find out what happened, otherwise you'll always wonder."

She turned away from her contemplation of the past. "Why is it you understand so well?"

"It's a universal theme, isn't it, the need to know our roots? Who our parents were, what sort of people they were or are. Most of us are lucky enough not to have to wonder about it." He grinned at her. "But how can we rebel against them if we never knew our parents? Who do you hate if you don't have a mother or father? Who will misunderstand you?"

Isabel laughed. "You sound exactly like a teenager."

"And that's really why people send teenagers off to boarding schools, isn't it? Not for all that nonsense about education."

"You know, when I was at school, it's all the girls talked about— how awful their parents were. When they weren't crying with homesickness, of course. I always felt left out."

"Poor Isabel." He squeezed her arm gently, a sympathetic touch. "When I get back to Singapore, I'll put a personal ad in the *Straits Times* for you. We can put one in the KL paper too. Anyone who knew . . . etc., etc. Let's go back to the village for some lunch and work on the wording. And afterwards we'll take a walk in the jungle. It isn't nearly so exhausting to stroll around up here as down in the lowlands."

She recoiled in dismay. "Oh, no. Please. Not in the jungle."

"There are wonderful trails near here. Quite safe, I assure you. If you like looking at birds, you can see the most marvelous varieties. An ornithological paradise. Wouldn't you like to see an Asian Fairy Bluebird?"

She tried to make light of her fear. "I'd love to see a fairy bluebird. But what about tigers and snakes?"

He laughed. "I assure you tigers give places like this a wide berth. And in any case, unfortunately, there aren't that many tigers left nowadays."

But it wasn't a laughing matter to her. The thought of walking into the jungle was quite terrifying: to be hemmed in with trees like that, the sunlight shut out, the ground alive with loathsome crawling creatures. The harder she tried to hide her terror, the more it overcame her, made her hands shake, her whole body tremble.

"Why, Isabel." He caught hold of her hands. "It does frighten you, doesn't it? Why should it frighten you so much?"

She had to clench her teeth to stop their chattering. "I don't know. Isn't everyone terrified of the jungle? Remember all those wartime stories? Soldiers who had to cut their way through it with machetes and were always getting lost because they couldn't see the sun, falling sick with awful diseases and being covered with leeches? Don't those kinds of stories frighten you?"

"No. But then I got very used to it. I lived in the jungle for three years. If you can call a prison camp living."

He held the door of the car for her and then drove down the hill to the village. She wanted to steer the conversation away from her unreasonable terrors, though what was unreasonable about a dread of jungles and snakes and leeches? It was as if she'd been born with such fears. "Tell me how you got caught, Oliver. How did it happen?"

"Oh, you don't want to listen to old soldier's stories. What sort of lunch would you like? There's a place just out of the village, on the other side. It probably won't be crowded."

"Anything," she said vaguely, letting him make the decision again.

Down in the village, they passed the golf course once more and went up the hill on the other side. Oliver stopped the car in front of a building raised on stilts, with a peaked thatched roof and long windows reaching down to the floor level. The sun was growing hotter, striking on Isabel's bare head, so she put on her Singapore market hat, and Oliver tucked her arm through his, held it with his other hand. He smiled down at her.

"One of the things I've always liked about living in the East," he said, "is that women wear hats like that. Those wide-brimmed affairs are so becoming."

His words sent an awful chill through her. She stopped abruptly, with the crazy feeling that she'd stepped into that photograph of her mother on her wedding day, the hat shadowing her face, the man holding her arm in this manner, the way he smiled down at her. Who were they, these two people walking in the sunshine? Was she her mother? Was he her father? She stared at Oliver, pulled her arm out from his, whipped the hat from her head.

"When you look at me," she said, "whom do you see?"

He frowned. "What do you mean?"

"Whom do you see? Tell me, do you see me, Isabel Bennet? Or do you see my mother? Is it her you're looking at? Was it me you kissed? Or her?"

He seemed confused. As well he should be, because she was confused too, wasn't at all certain what she meant. How honest was she being with him, or with herself? Whom did she see when she looked at him? Wasn't it her own vision that was clouded? Wasn't she the one who was seeking her past? Looking for her father?

"Whom do I see? I see a young woman with the most beautiful eyes I've ever seen. Her name is Isabel, and I'm honored and flattered that she allowed me to kiss her, and I think I may have fallen in love with her."

She was suddenly furious. "You said exactly the same thing about my mother. That she had the most beautiful eyes you'd ever seen. That you fell in love with her. Do you make a habit of this sort of thing?"

Oliver looked at her with amazement. "My dear young lady, I happened to meet your mother once about thirty years ago and I spent no more than three or four hours in her company. I'd hardly call that a habit."

Isabel glared at him with outrage, but his washed blue eyes were merely politely puzzled at her attack, and she realized how ridiculous she was, how absurd she sounded. Putting her hand over her mouth, she began to laugh, trying at first to stifle the laughter, then throwing her head back, laughing too loud. She thought she detected the faintest hint of hysteria in it.

"I'm sorry," she said. "Please forgive me."

"You're always apologizing to me, Isabel. You don't have to do that."

There were elaborate carved wooden pillars at the entrance to the restaurant, and a man in a sarong and a songkok hat showed them to a table. It was cool and almost breezy inside, the open windows catching the faint stirrings of the air. Leaning her arms on the table, Isabel looked into Oliver's face. "I *do* want to hear your old soldier's stories. I want to understand how you can keep so sane while I teeter on the edge of obsession."

Oliver ordered beer, and when it came he touched his glass to hers. The beer was cold and refreshing and slipped down her throat, and she was amazed to realize it was only two days ago that she'd drunk that beer at the restaurant in Kuala Lumpur with him. She felt as though she'd known him forever.

He said, "Perhaps because I still live here. I don't have to dream of it or fantasize about a long-lost distant place. Familiarity breeds contempt, remember. And I wasn't a child. My memories were intact. I had my mama safe home in England. She's there still, as a matter of fact. Eighty years old now. She likes to come out here. Says the heat is good for her bones."

The fact that he had a mother still alive made him seem even younger to her. "Why," she said, "you're still someone's little boy."

He was amused. "Only in a manner of speaking."

"I think if you explained what happened to you, it would help me understand what might have happened to my father."

He looked at her thoughtfully for a moment and then away. "Perhaps another time, Isabel. I hope there'll be another time? I have to go back to Singapore tomorrow. What will you do all by yourself? Your brother's going to be stuck in the hospital for another week at least."

Oh, God, she kept forgetting about Victor, poor devil. What *was* she going to do? The thought of Oliver Bailey's leaving made her slightly panic-stricken.

"Do you really want to stay in KL all alone?" he said. "Why don't you come back to Singapore with me? I don't mean . . . I mean, you can stay at the Raffles again. Until your brother is fit to fly back to the UK."

She was completely taken aback by the suggestion. Her first instinct was to dismiss it out of hand, but she hesitated and let herself contemplate the idea. A week ago, she wouldn't have allowed herself to contemplate it. After a moment, it seemed quite plausible. Almost sensible. What *was* the point of hanging around Kuala Lumpur all by herself? The city was so much bigger and busier than she'd ever imagined, it wasn't anywhere you wanted to walk around in, and the thought of being alone in it, with only Victor to pay hospital visits to, wasn't at all appealing. She would miss Oliver Bailey. Dreadfully.

"I couldn't do that," she said.

"Why not?"

"Why not? Because it's . . . it's . . ." She cast about for some reason. "It's not the sort of thing a respectable married woman should do."

"Oh, Isabel! How old-fashioned."

"That's not a good enough reason?"

"Of course it isn't. I'm not asking you to spend a week of sin with me. Just to have some company in the evenings. Go to the theater, maybe. Out to dinner. Show you Singapore. It could be . . . nice, Isabel." He made it a deliberate understatement.

It could be. "What would I tell Victor?"

"Tell him you're coming to Singapore with me."

"And what should I tell my husband?"

Oliver's eyes changed color, grew darker. "Do you have to tell him anything? He's a long way away, isn't he?"

She tried to think about Adrian. Not Adrian the man, but Adrian the husband. The father of her children, the keeper of the house. He seemed a remote figure, England a far-off country, fading rapidly from her memory.

"I don't have to tell him anything," she agreed.

"So you'll come?"

"Let me think about it." What in God's name was she saying? But she knew she would take up his offer.

"You know why I came with Victor, don't you? To find out about my parents. I'm not getting very far, am I?"

"Ah, yes, well," Oliver said briskly. "Let's have something to eat and get down to writing out the advertisement."

He ordered nasi campur and ulam. "You'll love it," he said, and she trusted him. She trusted him too much. He asked the man in the songkok hat for paper and a pencil, and they sat together and worked out the wording for the ad.

> *Anyone who knew Rodney and Eleanor Cartwright, or Rodney and Marike Cartwright, of Khota Ruan Rd., Kuala Lumpur, in the years immediately prior to the Japanese invasion in 1942, is asked to please contact Isabel Cartwright Bennet at Singapore 248-5592. She will be grateful for any information about the lives of her parents.*

The telephone number was Oliver's home number. "You can sit by the phone all day if you wish," he said. "Your name is better than mine. If there is anyone out there, they would sooner call a woman than a man, anytime."

Isabel watched the simple words shape themselves on the piece of paper. Shape her past, maybe her future. No, her past was already shaped. It was her future that was in doubt.

Probably, no one would answer the advertisement.

18

BY THE SECOND DAY of Isabel's nonappearance, Victor was almost beginning to worry. It had never occurred to him to worry about her before; she'd always done quite enough of that for both of them, thank you. But it was rather peculiar that she hadn't come to visit him for two whole days. Here he lay, helpless as a baby, his sister the one person in the whole of Asia to care whether he lived or died, and she was suddenly nowhere in sight. All his life, she'd been the one to watch over him, and now that he really needed her, she'd abandoned him, just as he'd been abandoned as a baby. He had information to impart, something that would really get her interest, and the longer she stayed away, the more he wanted to show it to her. He'd thought of keeping quiet about it, savoring it, but somehow it was no fun to keep a secret from her when she wasn't there to keep it from. Could something have happened to her? Of course not. Malaya was a safe country. People didn't disappear here. So where the hell was she?

He forced himself to ask Sundra to call the hotel. If there was a telephone in his room, he'd have called himself, of course, but apparently telephones weren't considered an essential piece of equipment for patients in this hospital. He'd begun to rely on Sundra for too many things, waiting for her to appear in the afternoons so he could talk to someone who really grasped the English language, someone who could translate his wants and needs to the other nurses, just to get them quite straight. Sundra also found books and newspapers for him. He had given her the awful flowers that Cheng had brought.

"Such beautiful orchids," she said when she first laid eyes on them, and Victor, who didn't know an orchid from a dandelion, waved his hand grandly. "You may have them, Sundra. Those kinds of flowers aren't my cup of tea."

She giggled. It was quite an endearing sound. "Flowers are nobody's cup of tea, Mr. Cartwright. But you shouldn't give them away. Whoever brought them for you will be upset to find them gone."

"You'll be doing me a favor. They make my head ache."

"Well, if you're sure, Mr. Cartwright."

She seemed doubtful, but when she picked up the enormous bouquet and her white teeth glistened above the strange blossoms, Victor realized he'd never given flowers to anyone before. The munificence of his gesture gratified him.

She weighed the arrangement in her small, capable hands. Her hands were very different from Isabel's. "Perhaps I'll take them later, when I go home."

He thought to ask her, "Where's home, Sundra?"

She shrugged her shoulders. Even a careless shrug of hers was graceful and pleasing. "Oh, one of those new condominiums, near Petaling Street."

Of course, he had no idea where Petaling Street might be.

"There hasn't been a message from my sister, has there?"

"Your sister? I don't think so, Mr. Cartwright. I didn't know you had a sister here in KL."

"I'm not sure I do anymore. Call the Hilton and ask for her, will you? Mrs. Isabel Bennet."

"And what do I say?"

"Ask her where the hell she is. If she's thinking of ever coming to see me again."

She frowned at him. "That isn't very polite."

"It isn't? She hasn't been to see me for two days."

"Perhaps she's busy."

"Busy? How can she be busy? She doesn't know a soul here."

Sundra said, "Do you have a proper message to give her?"

Victor thought she was splitting hairs. What was wrong in just asking Izzy where the hell she was? "Oh, all right. Tell her I've something interesting to show her."

"Okay, Mr. Cartwright. When I have time."

He'd kept the deed box under the covers, opening it now and then to check the contents, as though someone might steal them away from him. Not that there was anything particularly interesting or revealing about the small collection of papers, certainly not for anyone outside the family. He supposed his father must have stored them in case no one survived the war, as some sort of obituary. Family. It was a strange word for Victor to contemplate. He'd never felt part of a family. He'd thought for a while about the letter and decided it told him nothing. It was merely a curiosity, a memento that Izzy at least would cherish. He imagined handing it to her, seeing the look on her face, watching the inevitable tears fill her eyes.

Darkness had fallen outside, the abrupt disappearance of the sun that was so different from the lingering twilight of northern climates, before Sundra came back to report. "Your sister was not in her room, Mr. Cartwright, so I left a message asking her to come and visit you."

Well, he'd done his best.

He wasn't getting any more of the shots that had comforted and soothed him for the first couple of days, so he was beginning to feel irritable, sorry for himself. Even the Indian chappie hadn't been to see him today; instead, some young whippersnapper hardly old enough to be a medical student had checked on him, and it was patently clear to Victor that he hadn't a clue about anything. God knows whether the leg was healing properly. Bailey hadn't been back to see him. Nobody cared, that was obvious. It was damn difficult to read a newspaper lying on his back like this, and anyway the local papers were full of news he wasn't interested in. He'd asked Sundra to find him an English paper, and all she'd brought was a week-old Sunday *Times*, which he'd read in London, before he left. He let the newspaper drop to the floor, where it lay in a spreading heap until one of the nurses came in and picked it up, clucking her tongue in that irritating way of women. It wasn't easy to read books, either; he had to hold them up above his head, and the effort wasn't worth it, especially when they were thick and heavy like these potboilers Sundra had chosen. Why did writers think they had to write such *long* books? He should've told her he didn't care for American novels. Didn't care for novels at all, now that he came to think of it, though this Ludlum story wasn't bad—the damn thing was just too heavy. Well, he enjoyed Graham Greene. Next time Sundra came in, he'd ask her to find something by him, in a paperback. He wouldn't even care if he'd already read it.

God, the hours were endless. He was thoroughly sick of lying here, nothing to do but stare at the ceiling, pull himself up the bed, slide down the bed, pull himself up again, rattling the chain like a performing monkey. There was surely some better way to mend broken bones than to slap on a bloody great cast, string it up to the ceiling, and just leave it. The Indian chap *sounded* all right, but he'd probably taken the easy way out. If he, Victor, were in England, he'd almost certainly be walking around by now. If he were in England, he'd never have broken his leg in the first place. He knew whom he had to thank for that.

So when at last Isabel came to visit, late in the evening, Victor was in a very bad temper.

"Victor, darling. How are you?"

He glared at her. She seemed not the slightest bit embarrassed at her inexcusable absence. She looked, in fact, remarkably cheerful, eyes glowing, face soft and smiling.

"Don't darling me. Where have you been? Do you know I've been worried about you?"

She raised her eyebrows. "You have? How sweet of you, Victor." Pulling up the plastic chair, she sat close to the bed, smoothed the hair away from her forehead with both hands. "Frankly, I didn't believe you were capable of worry."

"You haven't been here for two whole days. I imagined you'd been raped or mugged or put in jail for drugs. In this country, they're always arresting Europeans for that sort of thing." Until that moment, he hadn't imagined anything of the sort, but the fact that it could have happened made him even crosser. "In this country, they hang people who deal in drugs," he said triumphantly. "Don't you read the papers?"

"Well, I haven't been arrested or raped or mugged. And I haven't been dealing any drugs. I didn't think you cared whether I came in or not. You weren't exactly friendly when I saw you last."

"Me? Unfriendly? You exaggerate as always, Izzy. But if I was, you can hardly blame me, can you? How would you feel, stuck in a hospital because of your damned fool sister who can't even be bothered to stop in and inquire after your health."

"Well, I've stopped in now."

"Thank you. So kind."

"So how are you? What do they say about your leg? How long before you'll be able to go home?"

Really, he was quite glad to see her. She was looking awfully well. The nervous tension that usually hung around her, tightening her lips, twitching her hands, seemed quite gone, smoothed away from her mouth and forehead. Her hands rested loosely in her lap and her eyes were peaceful, not anxious and strained. It struck Victor that his sister was not such a bad-looking woman, not when you added it all up, the light springing hair, those shining gray-green eyes. Especially when she sat quietly with this rare air of serenity. It was as if Malaya had worked some kind of magic charm on her, just as she'd always said it would. It was all in the mind, of course. Her mind, no doubt, was just as much of a mess as usual.

"Well," he said, "not only have you not been in to see me, but neither has that Indian chap. So I don't know the latest word. If there is one."

"I see." She looked down at her hands, looked up again. "Where did you get these orchids?"

"As a matter of fact, the director of the Centre brought them in. With his apologies. Seems to feel that the accident was their fault. Dr. Cheng. You remember him? Little Chinese fellow, rather self-important?"

"Oh, yes. That was kind of him."

Victor pulled himself up. "That's not all he brought, Izzy. If you'd come in before, I'd have shown you." Sliding his hands under the bedclothes, he produced the box, rested it on the side of the bed near to her, keeping his hand on it. "You know what this is?"

She glanced down at it, somewhat incuriously. He thought it surprising that she wasn't more curious. "What is it?"

He took his hand off the lid. "Read the label."

She bent nearer to the bed, looked up at him, frowning. "Cartwright? Is it yours?"

"Ours, Izzy. Yours and mine. This box, it seems, belonged to our father."

She gasped then, gratifyingly, the color running out of her cheeks, out of her eyes. She put her hand out for the box, and Victor didn't let go of it. "Who found it? How did they find it? Where's it been?"

"At the Centre. In a storeroom, Cheng said. If you ask me, it's pretty odd that they could come up with it just like that. They've probably known all along it was there and never bothered to find out who it belonged to."

She was still staring at the box, her eyes enormous. "What's in it?"

He let go of it. "Look for yourself."

Her fingers trembled as she lifted the lid and took out the small package wrapped in gutta-percha. "You know what that stuff's called?" Victor asked. She didn't answer but unfolded the yellowing material and the pieces of paper inside it, reverently, carefully, just as she handled those faded old photographs she'd kept for so long. "Gutta-percha," he said. "An interesting name. Malayan, I believe." She ignored him.

He waited to see her reaction to the letter, but it was a long while coming. She took her time reading the birth certificates, perusing each one as though it might contain words of wisdom and then laying it gently back in the box when she was done with it, as though it would get lost among the bedclothes otherwise. At last she came to the letter, she drew in her breath as she recognized it for what it was. A letter from her father.

She must have read it three times over. Eventually, putting it down, she sighed. "Oh, Victor. Isn't that sad? He must have written it just after we left."

She was much more in control than he'd imagined she would be. He'd expected tears at the very least, a wringing of hands, a beating of breast. Picking up the flimsy sheet of paper again, she peered at it.

"What does this Noone of the Ulu mean? What's that?"

"Beats me."

"You haven't asked anyone?"

"Who would you suggest I should ask? I'm hardly in a position to run around the town and find someone to ask, am I?"

"We could show it to Oliver," she said.

"Oliver? Oliver who?"

"Oliver Bailey. You know, your boss."

"Bailey? Since when have you known him as Oliver?"

The color ran back into her cheeks, pinking the soft flesh beneath her eyes. "Well, as a matter of fact, he's been showing me around. He took me to the English church, Victor, hoping we'd find a record of our mother's death. Then today he took me up to Fraser's Hill. It's a hill station, about seventy miles away, where the English used to go in the old days. It was beautiful there, Victor, quite cool, comparatively speaking. There were these old bungalows that looked just like England—touching, really—and I knew, just knew, I'd been there before. It was the strangest sensation, high up in the mountains but with jungle still all around, and it was almost as though I could hear the sound of cricket bats and balls and see the people who must have watched the cricket matches in their white dresses and hats, the servants carrying drinks. And Oliver said of course we'd have gone there for weekends and holidays, everyone used to, and then I thought: Perhaps they did have a good life after all, perhaps it wasn't just exile, it wasn't just my mother and father all alone together, getting on each other's nerves, stuck in the jungle, far from home. Hating it. Perhaps they *didn't* hate it, Victor."

Quite suddenly Victor could appreciate her anguish, as though for the first time. Feel it and almost understand it, an unexpected upsurge of empathy for his sister, who'd suffered with memories of those times he couldn't remember. But it was empathy mixed with a kind of envy, as if somehow he'd been cheated.

"I bet she hated it, didn't she, Izzy? Our mother. Eleanor Elizabeth. I bet that's where you get all these neurotic notions from. She hated it and she wanted to go home and she couldn't. That's what it was like in those days, wasn't it? You were stuck, thousands of miles from home, in the heat and the jungle. There was no going back. I bet you learned all that fear and dread from her, at your mother's knee, as they say. You were a little girl and you learned it from her."

Isabel stared at him—eyes wide and amazed, mouth slightly open—as though she couldn't believe what she was hearing. She put a hand on his arm, clutched it tightly, whispered, "I'm very afraid of the jungle, Victor. I think she must have been afraid of it too. Somehow I feel it and I don't know why."

She fell silent again, for a long while, her pupils huge, and then she said slowly, the words almost dragged out of her, "When we went to the church, we looked at the register. There wasn't any record of our mother's death."

Her eyes filled with the tears he'd been expecting. They brimmed over, spilled down her cheeks, and Victor, who couldn't stand the sight of her tears, said hurriedly, "And did you notice what else there isn't?" He tapped the lid of the box. "No death certificate for our mother and no marriage certificate for Marike and our father."

Isabel clasped her hands together, rubbing her fingers nervously. "I don't know what it means, Victor. So many records were lost. It's kind of a miracle that these were found, isn't it? Oliver thought we should put an ad in the newspapers. Here and in Singapore. To see if there's anyone around who remembers them. What do you think?"

What did he think? A door to the past had opened a chink for Victor, letting in the questions that had tormented Isabel for so long. But did *he* want answers? All this time he'd protested that he didn't want to know anything. What's done is done, he'd said, and he'd shut those people out of his life. Would he be any better off for knowing? Of course not. But maybe Izzy would. Maybe.

"You'd probably just get curiosity seekers, Izzy. Just think how nosy some people can be. It's not very likely there'd still be anyone who really remembers."

"There's Oliver Bailey, for one, isn't there? He actually met them. And he's not old, Victor. I suspect there are still plenty of others like him here. I suspect that if we advertised in the London papers, someone would come forward who'd known them."

"Then let's wait until we get back to London."

"I don't want to wait," she said. "Victor, I'm going to Singapore with Oliver. Tomorrow. Only until you're ready to come out of the hospital. I don't want to stay here in Kuala Lumpur, all by myself in that hotel. He's offered to help me with the search, with any replies we get to the ad. I'll have a few days there, before you get out of here. Maybe that will be enough time."

Now Victor was the one to gasp. "You're going to Singapore with Bailey? Bailey?" He saw the way her face flushed, a definite guilty look in her eyes, and his sense of decorum was outraged. "What is this 'Oliver' stuff? You talk of him as though he's some sort of boyfriend."

"He's a friend," she said, defensively. "Just a friend, Victor. I can have friends, can't I?"

But now he could account for the change in her demeanor, that silky self-satisfied appearance, the glowing skin. "Christ, Izzy, what are you thinking of? He's the head of my office, for God's sake. He's a respectable middle-aged man, old enough to be your father."

"No, he isn't," she flared. "He's fifty-two or -three. That's not so many years' difference."

Sweat broke out on Victor's forehead. He wiped it away with the back of his hand, enraged. "You've been working it out, haven't you? Totting up the years. I can't believe this. I take my eyes off you for five minutes, and I find you're out there running around like a bitch in heat."

Isabel's face went white. "Victor Cartwright! Don't you dare use terms like that to me."

"Well, it's true, isn't it? And why pick on Bailey, for God's sake? What are you looking for? A father? That's what you want, isn't it? A father. You've got a goddamned father complex."

Jumping to her feet, Isabel pushed the chair away from the bedside, a harsh, screeching sound on the vinyl-tiled floor, leaned her hands on the back of it, and stared at him with distaste. "And what if I do want a father? Is that so strange? A father might have done you some good, Victor."

"You've got a husband. Isn't that enough for you? Isn't one man enough for you?"

Her lips folded into a tight, unfamiliar line. She grabbed the box and flung herself away from him, headed for the door. "I'm leaving now, Victor. Perhaps I'll come back when you need to go home."

He shouted at her. "Don't bother. I can manage without you."

She was disappearing through the door, hair tumbling down her milk-white neck, skirt swishing. He yelled after her, his voice echoing down the hallway. "I bet our mother was like you. I bet that's what she did, catted around after other men. I bet that's what he had to put up with, our sainted father. Find that out, Isabel Cartwright, and then perhaps you'll be happy."

He wasn't sure she heard him. He didn't understand why he'd had to say it. He didn't think he really could manage without her.

19

SHE DIDN'T TELL Oliver what Victor had said. But the words dug into her like a knot, a tightness under her breast, and sullied the innocent little adventure of going off to Singapore. Isabel assured herself it *was* innocent. She didn't believe it was in her nature to have an adulterous affair. Oliver Bailey's attentions were flattering and, yes, intriguing, but she couldn't take him seriously. It was almost certainly a passing whim. He didn't need to get entangled with a suburban English housewife, and he was well aware she'd disappear from his life in a week or so. No, it was merely a pleasantly mild dalliance in the tropics, and Isabel didn't see why she shouldn't get to enjoy it. To hell with Victor.

And Oliver was being so helpful in the matter of her mother and father. She reminded herself that's what it was all about.

He'd changed back into his businessman persona for the flight to Singapore: linen suit, striped tie, expensive briefcase. She thought how sleek and assured he appeared, in charge, exuding authority, enveloping her in his aura of confidence. For the first time in her life, she flew first class, and though she protested the indulgence, she had to admit it was an agreeable luxury. "I always fly first," he explained. "It's written into my contract."

What exactly Oliver might do at Parker and Dellworthy was vague to Isabel, but then what did she know about the world of international trade? As soon as the plane took off, he delved into his briefcase and spread weighty documents over the tray table. "I have to read through this stuff before I get to the office. I'll be getting the sack if I don't look as though I know what's been going on lately."

Isabel glanced at the bound sheaves of charts and graphs, but it wasn't possible to decipher such important business matters with one casual look. She'd thought to show him the letter during the flight; the deed box was stowed in her carry-on bag under her feet, the photographs wrapped in their tissue with the certificates, but her papers seemed small and insignificant, of no consequence, beside those of Parker and Dellworthy. Instead, she looked out the window, down at the serried rows of rubber trees stretching in all directions, the misty islands in the near distance, the mountains covered in a thick dark tumble of forest, and she had the sensation of breaking free, of soaring above the jungle of her childhood, her life on the move at last, no longer handcuffed to the past. Her questions would perhaps be answered sometime in the near future, and she thought she was no longer afraid of the answers. She felt extraordinarily content, apart from the nagging throb of Victor's words. She wouldn't let him spoil it for her, she wouldn't.

Another car, sleek and black, met them at the airport. "I'll be losing the use of my legs soon," Isabel said.

Oliver settled into the back seat beside her. "What would you like to do this evening?"

The subdued tidy streets of Singapore slid past, sedate after the roaring chaos of Kuala Lumpur. "I don't know. I wish I could see Singapore as it used to be, before they sterilized it. Is anything left of the old city?"

He laughed. "Well, if that's what you'd really like, we should go to Bugis Street. Bugis Street is original sin city. However, I don't promise you'll like it, and you'll have to stay up late. It doesn't really get going until after midnight."

"Sounds just the job."

"I'll come to the hotel at . . . say eight o'clock? What will you do for the rest of the day? You can have the use of the car and the driver, if you want."

"Heavens, no! I couldn't think what to do with a car and driver. I'm not used to this sort of life, you know. Don't worry, I'll find something to amuse myself."

Taking hold of her hand, he squeezed it. "Isabel Cartwright, I think you're a lovely lady."

She withdrew her hand and frowned, very slightly. "It's Bennet. Isabel Bennet."

"Ah, yes. We mustn't forget that, must we?"

The car deposited her at the Raffles Hotel, and when she entered the wide, cool lobby, with the big white fans circling overhead, the slightly shabby palm trees in pots, it seemed extraordinarily familiar, as if she were returning to base camp after a long trip. The clerk at the desk smiled as though he recognized her. "Welcome back, Mrs. Bennet. Your room is ready. Mr. Bailey called to make sure." It was not yet ten o'clock in the morning, and she hadn't given a thought about being too early for normal check-in. Another small act of dependence. They gave her a different room this time, not a suite but still airy and comfortable, with another enormous bathroom, and as soon as she unpacked, she took a bath. She lay immersed in warm scented water up to her neck, hair piled on top of her head, adding a little more hot water now and then, idly, putting off the rest of the day because she hadn't decided what to do with it. Only a week ago she'd lain in the tub in this hotel, in just this fashion, and though she'd achieved very little in the week, it felt as if she'd traveled an enormous distance since then. She'd gone to the house in Kuala Lumpur and faced the ghosts. She would no longer hold herself responsible for Victor.

On her way out of the hotel—to do what? perhaps shop a little, or sightsee a little—a rack of postcards in the lobby caught Isabel's eye and reminded her she hadn't so much as written a postcard to the boys. Or to Adrian. Stricken with guilt, she immediately backtracked to the room and put in a call to Adrian. Before she changed her mind. Or forgot. She sensed she was in danger of forgetting all about Adrian, as if he were merely an acquaintance from a life only peripherally associated with her.

Telephone calls didn't come easily to Isabel. Disembodied conversations unsettled her, unable as she was to judge words and reactions, the subtle nuances of expression, unless face-to-face with the speaker. Even someone she should know as well as a husband. If she weighed the pros and cons of calling Adrian, she'd never get around to it, and therefore she didn't stop to consider the time difference between Singapore and England, not until the melancholy ringing tones persisted for too long in that faraway house. Was she eight hours ahead or eight behind? Singapore was east and therefore ahead, of course. Of course. Which meant it was three in the morning in England, an absurd and dislocating hour to be calling. She was about to drop the receiver, before being discovered in more forgetfulness, when Adrian answered, sleepy and cross. "Who is this?"

"Oh, God, Adrian, I'm so sorry. I totally forgot it's the middle of the night there. I didn't mean to get you out of bed."

He'd have had to get out of bed, because the phone was at the foot of the stairs. She pictured his bare feet on the Hamadan runner in the hallway, pajamas rumpled, hair standing on end.

"Isabel?" His tone changed to anxiety. "Where are you? Is something wrong?"

"No, not really. But I won't be coming back when I said I would. Victor's broken his leg. It was a silly accident, really, but he's in a hospital in Kuala Lumpur, and it'll be at least another week before he can travel."

He was trying to interrupt, and she kept talking, fast. She didn't want to tell him the accident was five days ago. She didn't want to tell him she was in Singapore, not Kuala Lumpur. She realized, with a sliding lurch of her gut, that she didn't particularly want to talk to him at all.

"I'm fine," she assured him, though he hadn't had a chance to ask if she was. "And Victor's fine, really. Grumpy, of course. But that's to be expected, isn't it? Poor Victor. He doesn't handle it very well. I think he must be difficult with the nurses. He's being taken care of by a really nice Indian doctor who trained at Charing Cross, so we don't have to worry about his treatment. The hospital's really modern and up-to-date. Better than NHS hospitals. How are the boys?"

Her voice echoed over the line. She could hear it bumping back at her from space, bounced off a satellite or other mysterious interplanetary device, so that her last words hung for a moment in the ether, as though she were talking in a cave. "Boys, boys, boys," her own voice said back to her.

At last she gave Adrian a pause in which to speak. He sounded bewildered. "The boys are fine, as far as I know. Why shouldn't they be? When will you be back, then?"

"I'm not too sure. I'll call you again, as soon as the doctor gives Victor the say-so. Another week, I should think. Adrian, I'm so sorry to have got you out of bed. Please forgive me. Go back to sleep now. Good night, darling."

She put the phone down abruptly, her hands shaking and sweaty.

Oh, God, that was unforgivable. To call him up from all these thousands of miles away and not let him speak, not tell him the complete truth. Not even tell him where she was or what hospital Victor was in or anything. So what should she have said? "I've left my brother alone in the hospital and gone off to Singapore with his boss. I'm going out with him tonight, for a bit of sin." She knew then she was already unfaithful in a way, not telling the whole truth, just the same as lying. You didn't have to sleep with someone to be unfaithful. First it happened in your heart and mind, before the flesh got involved.

Getting up off the bed, she smoothed the covers compulsively, erasing the marks of her body, and sat down again. Perhaps Victor was right. Perhaps both she and her mother were dissolute loose women. That the same man had touched both their lives, over the span of years, was bizarre. Through Oliver Bailey, Isabel felt as though her shadowy mother were drawing closer to her, laughing over her shoulder, as a sister might, comparing notes. "My darling," she might say. "He's all right, isn't he? But you should've seen him when he was young. He was quite lovely then; you know how young men are. Really, Isabel, I could have fallen for him myself, hook, line, and sinker."

It was as if Isabel could hear the voice, light and throaty and slightly affected, as if someone really had spoken aloud to her, and she recognized, without knowing how she recognized it, that her mother had talked in exactly that manner, an actressy kind of voice, not totally top drawer but near enough, a little nervous tremor to it, verging on the edge of laughter, or tears, difficult to know which. An amused voice, a seductive voice, a desperate voice.

The flimsy white curtains at the windows fluttered in the languorous movement of the overhead fan; the fan clicked and turned, turned and clicked, hypnotically; the sun lay hot and yellow in a streak across the shiny wooden floor; the scent of the bathwater still hung in the steamy air. Near the window, a rattan chair creaked and sighed, ever so gently, as if a slender body had settled itself into it, had leaned against the cushions and crossed narrow, arching feet. "Try to be happy, my darling child. I forgot how to be happy myself."

Of course she hadn't heard the voice. Of course she hadn't. There were no such things as ghosts. Ghosts existed only in one's own mind, manifestations of the brain, the temporal lobe or something. She hadn't heard her mother's voice here in this room, she hadn't heard the voices at the house in Kuala Lumpur; it was all conjured out of her own imagination, her own longing. They were dead and gone, as Victor insisted, brutally but truthfully. Dead and gone.

Isabel could have sworn she felt the faintest, briefest touch of a hand on her arm.

SHE BOUGHT A new dress to go to dinner with Oliver Bailey. She saw the dress in a shop window and knew it would be exactly right, a soft smoky green almost the same shade as her eyes. She didn't think of it matching her eyes, not as aware of them as other people were, only that she desired that dress, and when at last she ventured into the tiny store to try it on, the skirt flowed and swirled around her hips and made her appear delicate and fragile, which she certainly was not. The assistant wore a brilliant pink sari and a diamond in her nose and smiled approvingly. "This dress is most beautiful on you, miss. It could have been made to go with your white skin." The assistant was more elegant and colorful than Isabel could ever imagine herself, even in her new dress, and she hesitated, then rationalized that she was buying a relative amount of beauty. With her own money, not Adrian's. It would definitely have been treacherous to use his money for such a purpose.

When Oliver came to the hotel, he said, "How nice you look."

They went outside to have a drink on the lawn, and the silk dress billowed and rustled satisfyingly in the humid airless night. He looked up at the sky and said, "It's going to rain soon. You've been lucky so far."

People were gathering for dinner, moving languidly and slowly between the tables. Several of them spoke to Oliver as they passed by, nodding and smiling at Isabel when he introduced her; she thought how different it was from a mere week ago, when she and Victor had sat here, strangers in a strange land, nobody but each other to talk to. "Poor Victor," she said, thinking aloud. "I do hope he's all right."

"Your brother? I'm sure he's just fine. He'll be well indoctrinated into Asia by the time he gets out of the hospital. Maybe he'd like a job here? Perhaps we'll offer him one."

Isabel was caught off guard. "Do you mean that?"

Oliver shrugged, careless in his largesse. "Why not? Parker and Dellworthy can always use a good, steady accountant."

"I can't imagine what he'd say." She frowned and fiddled with her glass, and was filled with surprising reactions, and recognized that jealousy was paramount among them. Jealous because Victor might get a job here? Yes, damn it. Victor didn't give a shit about this country. Why should he be offered a job? Why shouldn't she, who felt almost as though she belonged? Almost but not quite. But then she didn't have any qualifications, did she? Even this dress was paid for not with money she'd earned but with money she'd inherited. She'd have to go back to cold, dark England whether she wanted to or not, because she had nothing to offer anyone, and if she had to go back, she was going to make damned certain she trained for something for the future. The word "if" sounded a tiny warning knell in her mind. There was no "if" about it.

"But it's not anything we have to think about just yet, is it?" Oliver said. "By the way, your advertisement was in the paper today. The phone might even start ringing tonight."

Isabel stared at him in dismay. She wasn't ready for that yet, not prepared. "I didn't think it would be in the papers yet. I thought perhaps . . . tomorrow."

"You can spend tomorrow at my house, waiting for the calls."

Who would call? Would anyone call? What sort of person might read a notice in the newspaper and immediately pick up the telephone? Not someone like herself. She would sit and agonize about it for days, weeks. Were there really people out there who'd share old memories so easily with a perfect stranger? Would the names mean anything to anyone? So long ago, such a different world.

"I have a swimming pool," he said, as though she needed an inducement. "And a houseboy who'll answer the phone and fetch you if it's for you."

Her ghosts, her precious ghosts, might be disturbed. Why was she alarmed at the idea? What had changed her, once so eager to remove the layer of dust that covered the past, and now wary and uncertain? Her father's letter was in her bag and she'd meant to show it to Oliver, and she still hesitated, putting off the moment.

The crowd grew thicker on the lawn, swirling and laughing, settling like butterflies into the white chairs, at the white tables. Isabel said, "I'm awfully hungry."

She wasn't, of course. She needed to move, not think about the letter in her bag, the ad in the paper, the past she was avoiding.

Later, much later, after dinner, the letter was still in her bag, lurking like a threat. Oliver drove across town and parked in a dark, narrow street in a network of other dark, narrow streets, and the sound of Bugis Street was loud before they turned the corner, a humming and buzzing in the air. When they came around the corner, the scene was like something out of a Hogarth painting, a touch of madness that surely didn't belong in the puritan strictures of Singapore: tables crowded the middle of the street, with hundreds of people drinking and eating and moving about—sailors in uniform, well-dressed men and women, tourists in T-shirts and shorts; tiny open stalls lined each side of the shadowy street, the flickering light of flaring torches and cooking stoves casting a fitful glow over the myriad assorted faces, and among the throng, food vendors and hawkers ran, crying their wares. The smells of beer and hot oil and cheap perfume were thick in the wreathing smoky atmosphere, and there was a roar in the night air, a fetid scent of something Isabel didn't quite recognize. Oliver pushed through the crowds and found a seat at one of the tables, ordered a beer from a sweating Indian, and after they'd been sitting awhile, Isabel saw, along with the vendors and hawkers, a steady parade of extraordinary girls in heavy makeup and foolishly false eyelashes, dressed exotically in elaborate saris and sarongs and tiny miniskirts, rounded hips swinging, long legs flashing, painted fingers beckoning, teeth gleaming, hair piled high on delicate necks or cascading over bare shining shoulders. Sashaying one by one past Isabel, ignoring her, they leaned on the table and whispered in Oliver's ear. He waved them away with an amused grin, and they moved on with shrugs and no apparent ill will to other tables, other men, blatant in their sexual overtures.

"What do you think?" Oliver said.

"What am I supposed to think?"

"Do you recognize them for what they are?"

"Isn't it obvious? They're prostitutes, of course."

"They're men," he said.

She turned to stare at the parading figures again. "Men?"

"Transsexuals, transvestites. They come here to Bugis Street to earn money for their operations. They hustle here and then go to Thailand and Australia for the surgery. You hadn't recognized that they're not women?"

Of course she hadn't. As far as she'd known, she'd never seen a transsexual in her life. She'd hardly ever seen a prostitute in action before. "But look at them," she said, disbelieving. "Their breasts, their skin, their shapes. They *are* women."

"Hormones," Oliver said. "Implants."

That's all it took to be a woman, hormones and implants? Isabel felt dizzy, watching the men/women, and she was overwhelmed with some sort of shock and yet pity for them, trapped inside bodies they felt compelled to change. It was bad enough to be born a female without needing an operation to change into one.

"Watch them," Oliver said. "They use the public conveniences as changing rooms. They go in and change and come out again in some other fantastic garb. They're drag queens; this is a stage for them. It's theater. And a living."

"And you mean that the men here pay them for sex? Even when

they know they are other men?" She looked around among the onlookers, trying to see if any of them walked away with any of the "girls." But the men who weren't drunk and incapable seemed, like Oliver, impervious. "What do they think they're buying—men or women?"

"Oh, I think men know the difference, don't you?" He was amused at her astonishment. "That's what it's all about on Bugis Street. I warned you that you might not like it. But it's something to see, isn't it?"

It was something, all right, and she didn't think she liked it, appalled at the bizarre complications of other people's lives. She could hardly bear to be another voyeur who came to be amused at an outlandish parade that a moment ago seemed merely colorful and risqué. Prostitution was surely pathetic enough; this was some sort of degrading travesty. Yet she had to admit there was something heady about the outrageousness of it all, like a Mardi Gras festival, a flouting of preconceptions.

"It won't last," Oliver said. "The government is going to clean it up. It's not the image Lee Kuan Yew wants to project to the rest of the world. They'll all go somewhere else, the girls, the drunken sailors, the druggies, and then Bugis Street will be somewhere you can bring your maiden aunt, and a little more color will have gone out of life."

"Maybe a good thing," Isabel said tartly.

"Maybe. But somehow Bugis Street *is* Singapore, sin and all. It won't be the same when it goes. People have always come to gape at the goings-on. I bet your parents came here."

Once again it came back to them, their footprints all over this country, everywhere she went, a child following footsteps in the sand, hurrying to put small feet in larger imprints before the sea washed them away. But she wasn't a child anymore. She was an adult, a married woman with children, and she couldn't think what she was doing here at one o'clock in the morning, flirting with the notion of adultery and watching men playing at being women.

20

*O*LIVER STOPPED AT his house on the way back to the hotel. "Just for a minute," he said. "There's something I want to show you. And maybe, just maybe, there'll be a message for you."

There wouldn't be, of course, but Isabel accepted the excuse. Reluctant to let go of the evening, or of him, she drifted passively in his wake. Somehow she should be less compliant, free herself of this growing dependency, but she was curious to see how he lived, even if going home with him at past one o'clock in the morning hardly seemed the way to go about freeing herself from anything.

She said, "How can you stay up so late and still work in the morning?"

"It's Saturday tomorrow. Today. Had you forgotten?"

"It is? I guess there's been nothing to remind me."

Oliver's house was large and white and imposing. Lights shone from every window, so it was ablaze in the darkness of the tropical night, the house illuminated, the circular driveway, the flight of low curving steps to the front door. "My God," Isabel exclaimed. "It's a palace. You really live here all alone?"

"Just me and a few dozen servants. As befits my station in life." Taking her arm, he walked her up the steps. "It's a company house, actually, not mine. I get to keep it as long as I have the job. I'm supposed to entertain and show the flag. There's a strict hierarchy about these things, you know. Like being the ambassador. The ambassador has to have the biggest house, otherwise the world would come to an end."

A wide hallway led into an enormous sitting room with overstuffed sofas, wing chairs, Oriental rugs, brass lamps, portraits on the walls, even a fireplace, an ornate carved marble affair with a Chinese screen in front of it. Isabel's initial reaction was disappointment. This wasn't a home; it was a showplace. She'd learn nothing about Oliver from it. Her second reaction was that at least the servants would be accustomed to his entertaining, so they'd think nothing extraordinary about her being there. Isabel wasn't used to servants anymore. She was nervous of their opinion of her.

No servants appeared. Oliver steered her beyond the big formal room, out to a screened veranda, a dim casual space much like the sitting room at the house in Kuala Lumpur: chintz-covered rattan chairs, glass-topped tables, a deep softness to the night, the clicking of fans, the rustling of palm fronds.

"Like a brandy?"

She shook her head. "No, thanks. Can I see what you put in the paper?"

He handed her a newspaper, folded and refolded so that the section of personals was uppermost, one column ringed in black ink. It was just as they'd composed it together at Fraser's Hill. *Anyone who knew Rodney and Eleanor Cartwright*... Gazing at the announcement, so bald, so definite, so laden with threat, Isabel wished, in a way, that it weren't there in black and white. She put the paper down, exhausted already by the implications of it, walked to the edge of the veranda, and pressed her face close against the screens. "I suppose there's a garden out there?"

Somewhere near at hand, Oliver must have flicked a switch, because suddenly the dark void beyond was flooded with light, a breathtaking, spectacular transformation. Tall dramatic trees, low shrubberies and brick walkways and curving flower beds, were thrown into brilliant relief, and directly below the veranda, another flight of steps spilled down to an ornate blue-and-white swimming pool. It all sprang into glittering, opulent existence, like an overdone Hollywood extravaganza. Isabel laughed aloud.

"My God! What sinful luxury."

"Sinful?" Oliver sounded surprised. "Merely the legitimate fruits of a successful capitalist system."

"Same thing, isn't it?"

"Oh, Isabel." He pressed the theatrical scene back into darkness. "Don't tell me you're a believer in any other kind of system?"

She said primly, "As long as you're not exploiting the workers."

"But of course we are. That's the nature of capitalism, isn't it? However, the workers aren't nearly as exploited now as they were in the good old days of the Empire. These countries were really bled dry when the Union Jack flew here. The Brits sucked their lifeblood and sent all the profits back to England."

"Oliver Bailey! That's some kind of heresy!"

"You think they did it just to spread fair play and justice and religion? No, my dear. It was all for profit then, just as it is now. The difference is that nowadays, the countries themselves get a slice of the cake as well. Perhaps the Brits didn't always do harm, but believe me, they weren't in places like this just to do good. The East India Company, for example, was hardly a missionary organization."

"Well, I don't know." Isabel sighed doubtfully. "It's hardly what I learned at school."

"We were fed an awful lot of hypocritical cant about empire in the old days. Would you like to see around the house?"

"I think I find your house rather intimidating."

"Remember, it isn't my house. When I leave this job, I'll settle for something considerably less grandiose. Though I do like the swimming pool."

He made it sound as though leaving his job was somehow imminent.

"What will you do then? Will you stay here in Singapore? Or go back to England?"

He looked horrified. "Oh, my God, no. My blood's much too thin for the English climate. I'll probably go to Australia. I like Australians, they're so bloody-minded. Ever been there?"

"I've been to Malaya and England. An occasional trip to France. I want to go to Italy and India. I've always wanted to see India."

"More empire nostalgia?"

"Oh, dear. You think that's why?"

Suddenly she noticed a shadowy figure in the doorway from the sitting room, an unobtrusive man in a white jacket, black hair sleeked back, round, closed-up face. He stood quietly, waiting to be noticed, and she had no idea how long he'd been standing there. Uncomfortable under his steady, patient gaze, she had the distinct feeling he didn't approve of her presence. Looking up, Oliver saw him too. "Oh, Leong, you're still up? Were there any calls for Mrs. Bennet?"

When he said, "Yes, Mr. Bailey, sir. I have written them down," Isabel exclaimed aloud with surprise. And trepidation. The man handed a small piece of paper to Oliver, not to her. "This one, sir, the maid spoke to me. She said it was most important that Mrs. Bennet call as soon as possible." He paused. "Will you be needing me anymore tonight sir?"

"No, Leong. Thank you. It's high time you were off duty."

The man nodded and slipped away like a wraith, as silently as he'd appeared.

"Messages?" Isabel couldn't believe it. "Already?"

Oliver put on the half glasses he'd used when she showed him the photographs in the restaurant; the careful gesture of placing them on the bridge of his long, narrow nose seemed astonishingly familiar. He peered at the paper, passed it over to her. "Do these names mean anything to you?"

The writing was large and spidery, sprawling across the paper in inky black strokes, not unlike Chinese calligraphy. *Colonel Ambrose Gill, Singapore 983-2236. Call anytime. Jennifer Sweeney, will call again. Mrs. John Partington. Very urgent. Please ring for appointment. Malacca 5923.*

"I can't believe it! People really called!" She sat down suddenly, her legs unsteady. "I wonder who they are. And this one? Why should it be urgent?"

Oliver's voice contained a warning note. "It might be unwise to put too much store in them. You might get a few crank calls."

"I know. I understand. But still . . ." She stared at the strange names. "I really didn't think anyone would respond."

"People don't forget. Those times are etched in their memory. How about that brandy now?"

Crossing to the bar in the corner, he poured them both a drink. "Wait there a second. I told you I had something to show you." He disappeared through the sitting room and in a few minutes was back. "This is why people don't forget."

He handed her a photograph, framed as though it was important, and she brought it nearer to the light. Half a dozen men sat on the dirt ground somewhere, staring into the camera with lusterless eyes, their bodies horribly shrunken and collapsed, bony necks protruding above hollowed chests, every rib visible, stick-thin legs angular and so fragile they couldn't possibly hold the skeletal frames upright. But the men were trying to smile, ghoulish unlovely grins, teeth too big in the skull-like heads, mouths smeared with sores, the muscles of the emaciated faces stretching and cracking painfully, no light reaching the dulled eyes.

Oliver stabbed at the photograph. "That's me," he said. "The day we were released from the camp."

He wasn't totally unrecognizable, which somehow made it worse, as though she were looking at the corpse of someone she knew who'd been dead a long while. "My God," she said, inadequately. She stared from the photo into his present-day face, smooth and well fed, the lines of laughter flaring away at the corners of his blue eyes, his neck filling his shirt collar, his jacket hanging comfortably from his shoulders. She put a hand on his arm. She could feel the firm muscles under her fingers, remembered the strong beat of his heart when she'd rested her head against his chest. "How are you so sane now? How did you recover so well?"

"Oh, I don't believe anyone ever quite recovers from those sorts of experiences, do they? I still get nightmares sometimes. Though who knows what sort of person I'd have turned out to be if I'd not been in the camp? It's a question that obsessed me once. If there'd been no war, I'd not have gone into the army. If there'd been no Japanese invasion, I might have returned to Europe. I could have ended like your father, disappeared. I could easily have died in the camp. Maybe surviving it made me more determined to survive anything. Would I have this job today if it wasn't for the camp? Who knows? I've got over it now. Once I faced up to working with the Japanese, I think I was cured."

"Where was the camp?"

"On the Malay-Siam border."

"You worked on that railway? The Burma railway?"

He sighed. "Yes. And I didn't die. But thousands and thousands did."

"I know. How could you bear to return to this country? Weren't the memories too dreadful?"

"That was part of the cure. To come back, not to let the memories take over your life. To replace them with something else."

"That's what's happened to me. I've let the memories take over."

He corrected her. "Your problem is that you've not yet found the memories." He pointed a finger at the scrap of paper. "Ring those people tomorrow, Isabel, and perhaps you'll soon know what to remember."

"Look," she said, fumbling for her handbag, pulling the letter out. "Look what the people at the Centre found. I want you to read it and tell me what some of it means."

Oliver turned the yellowing paper between his fingers, delicately. "What is it?"

"A letter written by my father. It was in a storeroom or somewhere, with a few other papers—our birth certificates, his marriage certificate. The director of the Centre gave them all to Victor."

He glanced over the top of his glasses at her. "Are you sure you want me to read it?"

"Oh, yes, please. You'll see there's something I need explained."

It took him only a few minutes. "How very touching," he said, and read it over again. "Extraordinary that it was found like that. But it doesn't really help explain what happened to them, does it?"

"What does that phrase mean: no one of the Ulu?"

"It isn't no one. It's Noone. It must refer to Pat Noone, an English anthropologist who disappeared in the jungle during the war. Everyone used to call him Noone of the Ulu; he was a legend in Malaya during the thirties. Ulu means . . . well, it's a Malay word that means the deep jungle. The upper reaches of a river, which is the same thing, really. At the top end of the rivers is uncharted mountain jungle, a place where white men never went. Noone was interested in the aboriginal tribes who lived up there. Nobody knew or even cared much about them before him. He went to study them, even married a girl from one of the tribes, I believe. They were extremely primitive people, still used poison blow darts in those days and believed in spirits, but during the crisis in the fifties, they became of interest to the British antiterrorist forces. It seemed the Communists were using them to maintain their bases. Without those tribes, the Communists could never have survived in the jungle."

Isabel struggled to understand. "But why do you think my father used his name in his letter?"

Oliver frowned. "Who knows? Perhaps he thought he could escape the Japanese by hiding in the jungle. As a biologist, he must have been fairly familiar with it."

Isabel held her hand out for the letter. She saw how her hand shook. "He says, 'Perhaps we should try, like Eleanor, to follow Noone of the Ulu.' What do you think that means?"

Oliver looked at her. He said, gently, "It does seem rather obvious, doesn't it? That she had followed Noone into the jungle."

The veranda fell into a small crackling silence. Beyond the screens, she could hear faint noises from the garden, rustlings and creakings, a stirring of the heavy air, the beginnings of rain, drops spattering on the roof. "Yes," Isabel said at last. "I think that's right. I think that she disappeared into the jungle. I've always known that somehow. Somewhere deep inside me."

Once she said it out loud, she knew it was true. As though speaking made it so. As though, once again, she was responsible. Except she knew she wasn't. Now that she was an adult, she knew it hadn't been her fault. But until she said it aloud, the terrible secret had festered within her, hidden even from herself. Now it was spoken out loud. At last.

Isabel wept then. Not as she had wept at the house in Kuala Lumpur, with unresolved sorrow and longing, but with relief that she was able to acknowledge something never spoken about before. The tears ran down her face and dripped into the brandy, and Oliver took her glass and put his arms around her and she cried on his shoulder.

She said, "I don't really remember it. All I know is that she was suddenly gone and no one ever told me what happened to her. Except I believe it must have happened somewhere like Fraser's Hill. Somehow I imagine we went up together to a place like a hill station and came back without my mother. Do you think that's possible?"

Oliver's arms tightened around her. "It's possible. People have disappeared in the jungle. Fraser's Hill itself was named for someone who vanished mysteriously up there, a long time ago; only a few years back, an American went missing in the Cameron Highlands. He was fairly notable, and his disappearance created an enormous flap. There was a huge search, but not a single trace of him was ever found. It can happen. The Malayan jungle is a terrifying vastness. There's not as much of it around as there used to be, of course, but it can still swallow people very quickly."

His voice was somehow soothing and reassuring, even though what he was telling her only reinforced her worst fears. Isabel tried to concentrate on the image of a woman in a white dress walking away from her and thought her mother and Marike were mixed up in her mind.

She said, "The question is why, isn't it? Why would anyone walk off into the jungle?" But she was too exhausted to think about it, drained by tears and the lateness of the hour, the conflicting emotions, that awful picture of Oliver starved to a skeleton, the raucous scene in Bugis Street. She closed her aching eyes, and the silence of the tropical night, which was not ever quite silent, descended around her.

Oliver murmured in her ear. "Stay here with me, Isabel. Let me look after you."

It would be so easy to say yes. "Yes," she could imagine herself saying, "Yes, please." He would take her hand and lead her upstairs to a room with a great wide white bed and she could lie down on it with him and he would wrap his arms around her and comfort her and erase her doubts and fears with his warm strong body, which had once been too weak to stand upright. And she knew the comfort would be mutual, because in the unburdening pleasures of lovemaking, it was possible to forget everything, all the self-inflicted sorrows of the world, all the wars and deprivations and cruelty, the separations and dislocations, all the questions that maybe had no answers.

"Try to be happy," her mother's ghostly voice had seemed to tell her in the hotel.

She would try.

21

THE SUN CAME thundering through the window and into his eyes, and Victor knew immediately that something was wrong. Apart from his leg, of course. He was becoming accustomed to the absurdity of having a leg strung up to the ceiling, taking it almost for granted, as though he'd been lying in this bed for most of his life. No, what was wrong now was Izzy.

He couldn't really believe she'd walked out on him like that. She'd be back. She never could stick to anything—she wouldn't stick to outrage, either. Just because he'd called a spade a spade. She was hardly the one who should be outraged. Running off with Bailey—quite unconscionable, an act of betrayal. Lucky for her she had a brother who wasn't the type to tell tales, but he'd like to know how she thought she could get away with it. Did she never consider that in years to come, he might one day let slip to Adrian about his wife's adventures in Singapore? With a man old enough to be her father? Well, of course he wouldn't let anything slip; she knew her brother was close-lipped. Tell him a secret and you'd be safe for eternity. It wasn't as though he particularly cared about Adrian's sensitivities; Adrian had never sat down with Victor and chatted, the way people in other families no doubt did every day.

Victor tried to recall if anyone had ever confided a secret to him.

Soon after breakfast, the Indian doctor breezed in, accompanied, as usual, by the sycophantic retinue. He peered at Victor through his glinting glasses.

"Well, good morning, Mr. Cartwright. How are we today?"

"We are well enough," Victor said.

"Looking forward to getting that leg down from the ceiling?"

"First I've heard of it."

"Did you think it was going to stay up there forever?"

He was so damned patronizing, exchanging little pleasantries with the poor dumb patient. Victor gritted his teeth.

"As a matter of fact, I *was* beginning to think that."

"No, my dear fellow." Mr. Rei's smile was brilliant in the thin, dark face, the gold tooth glistening. "It's off to the X-ray department with you. If all is well, we'll put you in a lighter cast—not one you can walk on, mind you, but at least you'll be able to get out of bed. We'll give you some crutches, and hey presto! You'll soon be on your way."

"On my way where?"

"Why, back to jolly old England, of course. Isn't that what you want?"

"You mean . . . get on a plane? When, exactly?"

"As soon as you like. Provided that tibia of yours is healing properly."

He made it sound entirely Victor's responsibility. If there was anything awry with the healing of the tibia, it was obviously not going to be the surgeon's fault.

"You might have given me some warning," Victor protested. "I mean, one minute I'm lying here helplessly, and the next minute you're expecting me to jump on an airplane."

Mr. Rei's eyebrows met in a thick, fierce line above his aristocratic nose. The little crowd around him rustled nervously, as though any hint of criticism was akin to blasphemy. "Exactly how much warning would you like to have had, Mr. Cartwright? Medicine isn't a matter of hours and minutes, you know. We can't set a stopwatch on the healing process. We are not automatons, Mr. Cartwright."

"Yes, but . . ." Victor was nonplussed. "You're telling me I could be leaving the hospital tomorrow?"

Mr. Rei shrugged, as though it was a minor issue. "Perhaps the day after tomorrow. If the bone is healing according to plan. I'll see you in the X-ray department in an hour or so, and then we can discuss how to proceed from then on. You can arrange for your charming sister to take you out of here. I'm sure you'll both be glad to get on with your lives."

He swept away, the white-coated brigade following behind, exactly like a herd of sheep, Victor thought. Damn it, he wasn't sure he wanted to get on with his life. Surely he wasn't expected to rise from a bed of infirmity and leap about on crutches without time to adjust? He felt a small sense of panic, as though he was about to be thrown out into a cold hard world that he wasn't prepared for. Leave this hospital and all the little brown nurses? Leave Sundra, whom he'd come to rely on? With Izzy roaming around somewhere in the wild blue yonder, doing God knows what? This would teach her to run off and leave him. Now she'd have to come crawling back from her gallivanting and apologize. He'd make jolly sure everyone knew about it. The Indian chappie wouldn't consider her so charming when he heard what she was up to. When Victor found her.

He'd have to ring Bailey in Singapore. The idea made Victor perspire, having to call someone like Bailey, the big white chief of Parker and Dellworthy, to ask for his own sister. It would be demeaning, embarrassing, confrontational, practically an accusation of adultery. Bailey had seemed a decent chap, honorable, a gentleman, and Victor couldn't understand what the hell he was playing at, taking a married woman off with him like that. Surely he had a wife of his own. There'd be a scandal. He, Victor, would be the laughingstock of Parker and Dellworthy, allowing his sister to accompany him on a business trip and then to carry on in this manner. Accountants weren't supposed to get embroiled in messy scandals; they were supposed to be reliable, steady, sober. He'd be blacklisted. He'd have to get out of the City, where everyone knew everyone else's business, skulk away to some hole-in-the-wall company so desperate for an accountant they wouldn't care about gossip.

Izzy had ruined his life.

By the time the stretcher came to take him to the X-ray department, Victor was extremely anxious. There was always a hope, he thought, watching Mr. Rei wield an alarming-looking buzz saw along the sides of the cast, that his bones wouldn't have mended correctly;

then all this worry would have been for naught. He could return to his bed and let the nurses look after him again. He wouldn't have to confront anyone.

The sight of his leg as it emerged from under the plaster of Paris comforted him: exceedingly unhealthy-looking, pasty white where it wasn't black and blue, thinner than his other leg, a long bright-red scar along the side, with large black stitches in an untidy row. It was obviously unfit to be allowed back into the world.

Mr. Rei caressed the sickly pale skin with his glowing black hands. "Excellent," he announced, with satisfaction. "A very nice result. Looks very good."

Flabbergasted, Victor convinced himself this was some doctor act, like reassuring a dying patient that he looked exceptionally healthy today.

"We'll remove these skin sutures and then take the X ray."

Submitting to the quick snip-snip of the nurse's scissors, Victor watched the stiff black stitches fall away and began to pray the X ray would save him. But it didn't. He was shunted under a machine that appeared ready to devour him, and several clicks later, his tibia was declared in "good shape." Mr. Rei's slick hands wrapped another cast quickly and expertly around the unpleasant sight, so that it was hidden from view once more, which was some relief.

His surgeon put the X rays into a lighted box and pointed out the medical miracle he'd apparently performed on Victor's bones. "See," he said, "the crack in the tibia is stable. There's a nice collection of callus. Here and here. Around the fibula too. In a few weeks, you'll be as good as new."

The new cast seemed dangerously flimsy compared to the previous one. Victor regarded it with doubt. "Am I going to be able to walk on this?"

"Oh, you can't put any weight on it. You'll have to get around on crutches. For six weeks or so." Rei was cheerful, as though six weeks of hobbling around on crutches was of little consequence. "We'll let you practice for a day, and then we can release you. You'll be all right to fly back to the UK, if that's what you want to do. I can give you the name of an orthopedic surgeon in London. I'll send your X rays and some notes with you."

Victor was being dismissed, cast out of the womb. He was measured for a pair of crutches and wheeled back with them to his room, allowed to scramble from the wheelchair to the blue plastic chair beside the bed. It groaned under his weight. Victor sat staring at his freshly made bed, the traction devices removed, the sheets stretched pure and white, the pillows plumped, the yellow cotton cover smoothly pristine, as though he were already past history. He longed to crawl back under the covers and close his eyes, and after a while, when no one came in to inquire after his well-being, he managed to do just that.

He was still there when Sundra came on duty. When she saw him in the bed, she clapped her little hands disapprovingly. "Oh, now look here, Mr. Cartwright. You're supposed to be up and about. Where are your new crutches? How are you ever going to manage if you don't try them?"

His new crutches were leaning against the wall in the corner. "How could I get to them?" he protested. "They weren't thinking when they put them out of my reach."

Sundra pressed her lips together. "Come on," she said in her best matron manner. "Get out of that bed at once and get moving. You can't possibly leave tomorrow if you don't get with it."

She held out the ugly metal crutches, and very reluctantly Victor swiveled his legs over the edge of the bed, caught hold of them.

"You'll have to put your one good leg to the ground," Sundra ordered. "You have to be upright first of all. Lean on me."

She planted her own small feet firmly, and when Victor straightened up, with great trepidation, he found himself ludicrously taller and bigger than she was. He hadn't realized how little she was. He would crush her with his weight, fall to the ground helplessly, be stranded like a fish, humiliated again. This whole Malayan business had turned into nothing but indignity and degradation. He was sick to death of it.

22

MRS. JOHN PARTINGTON'S house was different from any other house that Isabel had seen so far. The whole town was different: terra-cotta, not modernized, almost European in appearance at one moment, and at the next, a pagoda-shaped minaret appeared, a mosque with a huge tiered roof.

When Isabel had called the number in Malacca, the voice at the other end of the telephone had whispered urgently. "You must come quick, Mrs. Bennet. Mrs. Partington is very, very sick. She has something very important to tell you, but you must come soon. Soon, mem." Oliver had said, "But of course you should go," and put her on the flight himself. She was growing dizzy from traveling.

The house was stuccoed, with heavy dark beams, shuttered windows, and an arched foyer; a long green lawn was surrounded by lush and tropical plantings. The house and garden exuded tranquillity and security, as if they had been lived in for a long time, as if wars and political changes had swept by and left them unscathed, marooned in a colonial past.

Isabel didn't know what to expect. She was apprehensive as she stood before the carved black door, and was startled when it was opened immediately, by a Malay woman in a sarong and tunic, as if she'd been waiting behind it. Tears glimmered in the woman's eyes, and her old face was lined with fine, soft wrinkles. "Oh, mem," she cried, "I am so glad you have come. Mrs. Partington has been waiting for you. I will take you to her room immediately."

Leading the way through a hallway and up a wide, dark staircase, the woman spoke in a hushed voice that was barely audible. Isabel had to bend her head to hear her. "Mrs. Partington is very sick, mem. Please be gentle with her."

Isabel wanted to say, Wait, who is she, this Mrs. Partington? Why does she want to see me? But the amah was scuttling ahead, not pausing, opening a door along the landing, beckoning. Isabel entered cautiously. The room was large and dim, and on a high bed with an ornately carved headboard, a ghostly figure lay among a heap of pillows. Not until Isabel was quite close could she really tell the figure was that of a woman, the body so thin and frail it barely mounded the silk covers, no hint of female shape to it. Against the pillows, a head rested lightly, barely denting the feathers, the hair fallen away so that a fragile pink skull showed beneath, such flesh as there was on the face more like crinkled tissue paper than skin. The woman seemed incredibly old, ancient beyond life, but surprisingly, her eyes were dark and flashing, fixing on Isabel's face as she came close to the bedside.

Holding up one skeletal hand as though shading her eyes from sunlight, the woman spoke in a harsh, dry whisper. "It *is* Isabel, isn't it?" and then she extended the thin hand. Isabel took it in hers, very gently.

"Yes. Isabel Bennet. Cartwright."

"Thank God. Thank God. You've come just in time."

Isabel, towering above the bed and the woman in it, felt gigantic, tall and gangly and fleshy, bursting with indecent health and strength. The amah drew up a small chair for her, right beside the bed, and Isabel perched on the edge of it, carefully, because it, too, seemed delicate and breakable. Now her face was at the same level as the woman's, and she peered into the dark eyes, sunk far into their bony orbits. "It was kind of you to see me. I can tell you're not well."

"I'm dying. That's why I needed to see you. The message in the newspaper was like a message from God."

It was hardly possible she had enough strength to lift a newspaper, let alone read it. "You saw the notice in the paper?"

"Raminah read it to me." Pausing, the woman rubbed the back of her hand across her lips. "You don't know who I am, do you, child?"

Isabel shook her head. How was she supposed to know who she was?

"You're not so difficult to recognize. Those eyes. That hair. You've become a beautiful young woman, Isabel. Just like your mother."

"You knew my mother?"

"Yes. And your father." The black eyes lit for a quick moment with what seemed like amusement. "Well, it's been a very long time. You were a child, and God knows I've changed since those days. Just a little." Plucking at the bedcovers, a nervous agitated gesture, she said, "I believe I can make my peace with God if you can forgive me."

A sensation of dread crept through Isabel, heavy and cold, and she began to shiver, though the room was almost stiflingly warm. "What do you mean? Forgive?"

The woman stared as though she was trying to look into Isabel's heart.

"Darling, I was Marike Van Deuman."

Isabel heard her say it, quite clearly, but couldn't believe the name actually had been spoken aloud. It was as if an imagined sound had come through the ether, just as she'd imagined she'd heard her mother's voice. She felt as though someone had punched hard on her sternum, a great thumping blow that took her breath away and nearly stopped her heart from beating. Her heart did stop for a moment, a half second, lurching irregularly in her chest, then it began again, with a sickening bang, bang, bang, so the blood roared in her ears. Marike? Marike was dead long ago, with all the other people who'd died. The room grew foggy around her, the bed, the old woman, and Isabel was trapped in a nightmare, a bizarre dream from which she'd surely wake at any moment. She let go of the woman's hand and clung to the edge of the chair.

"It's true," the woman said. Flatly, undramatically. "After all this time." The dark eyes flickered, the head turned away on the pillows.

Isabel found the name impossible to form with her mouth. "You can't be," she whispered, her voice low and cracked. This woman was so old, so ancient. She couldn't possibly be the beautiful young woman Isabel believed she remembered; there was nothing left in this feeble relic to re-create the image captured in the photograph— the smile, the grace, the springing black hair. Isabel couldn't bear to look at her, couldn't bear not to. She stared, horribly fascinated, then looked away around the room, at the rich silky draperies and glowing dark wood, at the silver-framed photographs, the cut-glass vases, the paintings on the walls, as if the normality of these objects could convince her that this wasn't something out of her imagination. Her eyes wandered back to the diminished figure among the pillows. Her beloved Marike absolutely could not have ended up like this, aged and wizened like this. And yet when she had said "darlink," it was exactly how she'd said it all those years ago, and it awoke instant recognition.

Bending closer, Isabel could smell the acrid breath. There were so many questions she should ask, yet she could only say, "What happened to you? How did you get to be . . . like this?"

The woman closed her eyes and was silent for a long time, and suddenly Isabel was terrified she'd slipped away from life entirely. Obviously she was going to die soon. Why not now? At the moment before truth. Catching hold of the inert hands on the coverlet, Isabel felt them cold and dry beneath her own, as though she were clutching a dead bird, and she forced herself to speak the name. "Marike?"

The hands stirred in Isabel's, fluttered. When the dark eyes opened again, Isabel thought she could perhaps recognize something familiar in them, a faint echo of laughter and love.

"Will you forgive me?" the woman whispered.

Isabel whispered back. "For what?"

The desiccated lips curved upward for a second, the shadow of an incredulous smile. "For what, you say? For not going with you that day. And the baby. Little Victor. That poor baby. Two little children. So selfish of me. What could I have been thinking of?"

Isabel's arms and legs seemed to solidify, her body stiff with disbelief, her mind refusing to accept what she was hearing. Eventually she managed to stammer, "We got back to England. Victor and I were fine. You were right—someone else took care of us. I never blamed you for not coming with us."

"You didn't?"

"No. Never." She could state it quite firmly. It was the truth. She'd never blamed Marike. Had she?

"Say you forgive me."

"There is nothing to forgive."

"Say it."

But Isabel couldn't say it. She and Victor weren't really so fine. Victor had needed someone to love him and care for him; you didn't abandon little babies and expect them to grow into normal human beings. Twice he'd been abandoned: first by his mother, then by Marike. But how could she say that to this dying woman? Whatever sin of omission she'd committed, she'd suffered for it. Look at her!

"That little baby," the woman murmured. "That darling red-haired baby. I'd give anything in the world to see him again." She closed her eyes wearily. "But it will have to be soon."

Isabel found she was rubbing the birdlike hands between her own large-knuckled hands, trying to be gentle, trying to bring some warmth to them, to herself.

"Promise not to leave me now. You have to tell me what happened, I have to know. That's all I ask of you now. I'll tell you about my life and about Victor if you'll tell me about yours. About my mother and my father. That's all I need. Please, please."

She *had* to will her to stay alive, had to breathe life back into the wasted body, had to convince her to keep living long enough to lift the curtain. "Tell me what happened to them, and then I will forgive you."

Isabel felt rather than heard the sound of a door opening behind her, soft footsteps across the floor, a figure hovering beside her left shoulder. When she looked up, the small Malay woman in tunic and long sarong was standing beside her, her hands folded together, and Isabel's heart gave another lurch. For a moment, she believed it must be Ayala again, come for her out of the past, like Marike.

"Mrs. Bennet, excuse me, mem," and of course it was not Ayala. "There is a telephone call for you. Mr. Bailey, from Singapore."

Attempting to withdraw her hands, Isabel found them held with pathetic, surprising strength, the woman on the bed stirring into forgotten life.

"I'll come back," Isabel promised, "in a minute. Then we can talk?"

"Yes," the woman said, with a sigh that fluttered in the air. "We can talk. You can stay as long as you like. Raminah, bring us some tea." Suddenly the voice had more vigor, more timbre to it.

Raminah lifted her mistress's head, plumped the pillows, pulled the agonizingly fragile body further up the bed and rested it back down very gently. "Yes, mem. But the doctor said you must not get too tired."

"Oh, damn the doctor." Marike laughed, a wheezy travesty of a laugh, but laughter nonetheless. "Show Mrs. Bennet where the phone is, there's a good girl."

The phone was at the foot of the stairs, just as it was in her own house, and when Isabel picked it up, she wanted to weep with gratitude at the sound of Oliver's voice.

"Oh, God, Oliver, you can't believe what has happened! Who this Mrs. Partington has turned out to be," and she started to tell him, rushing and stumbling over the words, hardly believing them herself. "Isn't it the most extraordinary thing? But she's dying, Oliver, so sick she can hardly speak."

"But that's wonderful, my darling. That you found her. Amazing!"

"She's told me nothing yet. I have to stay."

He was silent for a moment. "I'm calling because I've heard from your brother. He's looking for you. He's going to be discharged from the hospital tomorrow."

"Tomorrow? Oh, no!" She couldn't leave here now, she couldn't. Confused and indecisive, Isabel said, "Perhaps I can go up to Kuala Lumpur and get him tomorrow. Mrs. Partington—I can't really think of her as Marike, you know—she said she would give anything to see him again. But I'm afraid she might not last that long."

"Listen," he said, in his take-charge voice. "Leave it to me. I'll get someone to pick your brother up at the hospital in the morning and drive him down to Malacca. Why not? And then the car can bring you both back to Singapore."

"Oh, Oliver, that's brilliant."

"I'll let you know as soon as it's organized. Isabel, are you all right?"

"I'm all right."

"Take care, my darling," he said. "I'm thinking of you."

As soon as Isabel put down the phone, the unreality of being in this house, talking to someone she'd believed to be dead for so long, swept over her again, made her feel weak and dizzy. She thought she might be in a state of shock. She was numbed, unable to grasp the reality of someone resurrected from the grave, like Lazarus—raised from the dead but still more dead than alive.

The house was very quiet, muffled, no sounds anywhere. She needed a drink, something to steady her hands, to calm her churning stomach. Raminah came slipping silently along the hallway, carrying a tray with a china teapot and two cups and saucers. "Do you have any whisky or brandy?" Isabel asked, desperately. Normally she never thought of having a drink during the day, but this was not a normal day.

Taking her into a dining room with a huge table and thick, soft carpets and a carved sideboard, the amah gestured to cut-glass decanters on a silver salver. The furniture was dark and gleaming, and each decanter had a silver label hanging round its neck. The whole house smelled of sandalwood and middle-class comfort.

"Dr. and Mrs. Partington used to have many dinner parties," Raminah said, and rubbed the surface of the sideboard with one wistful finger. "There were more servants then. Now there is only me and a houseboy and the gardener."

Life out here hadn't changed much, not as it had in England. Isabel poured herself a slug of brandy and knocked it back, the alcohol jolting through her veins and restoring her to some sort of sanity. "He was a doctor?" she asked. "Mrs. Partington's husband?"

Raminah nodded her head. "A very fine gentleman," she said, and led the way up the stairs again.

Isabel dreaded reentering the room of death, but the woman who claimed to be Marike was sitting up in the bed now, a lacy shawl around her wasted shoulders. As though she could read Isabel's mind, she said, "I have good moments as well as bad. I'm stronger than I look. And now that you've come, well, I know I'll last a bit longer. It's not time yet."

Isabel sat down in the chair beside the bed. She didn't know how to ask the question tactfully. "What's wrong with you?"

The woman wheezed with laughter again, the sound of it painful. "What isn't wrong is more like it. I've had it all, darling: malaria, beriberi, dengue fever, amoebic dysentery. I'm a walking textbook on tropical diseases. Well, not walking anymore. The poor old body gives up after a while."

"I'm sorry." It was very inadequate.

"Oh, don't be sorry. I suppose I'm bloody lucky to be alive at all, frankly. It's all from the damn camps, you know."

Raminah poured a cup of thin tea and handed it to her, and Isabel watched the teacup and saucer tremble dangerously in the frail hands. But the hands managed to raise the cup to her lips steadily enough, and the tea seemed to put a faint touch of color into the deadly-pale face. "Come on," she said to Isabel. "Join me."

Isabel's own hand shook as she lifted the teacup. God knew how much time there was. Never had she before been so near anyone who was dying; she had no idea how long the process took. She must begin somewhere.

"Tell me what happened after Victor and I went away. I remember that day. I suppose I'll never forget it."

The woman sucked in a shallow breath, shuddered, and her eyes grew distant. "I have tried to forget about it, you know."

"But you have to tell me," Isabel cried. "Why did you want to see me if not to tell me?" She guessed, of course, that she'd been invited to dispense some kind of forgiveness, but even in the Catholic Church you had to confess before your sins could be forgiven. She wondered if Marike had a religion. The Dutch, she thought vaguely, were Protestants of some kind, and Protestants weren't into confessions.

Mrs. Partington sighed, handed the cup back to the amah, who hovered, concern in her face. "Really, it's not much of a story. We didn't last long, Roddy and I. You children got away just in time. I remember how silent the house was after you'd gone. We spent the rest of the day gathering some things together, and we had to drive to the Centre so Roddy could make sure nothing important was left there, that his research wouldn't fall into Japanese hands, and then we started down the road to Port Swettenham. I thought we'd find a boat to get to Sumatra. My father was in Sumatra. He was a tea planter there, did you know that? But we'd lingered too long at the Centre, and somehow we were behind the Japanese instead of in front of them, and quite suddenly, without any warning, we drove round a corner into the middle of a group of Japanese soldiers, and it was all over. Just like that. Phfft! They took Roddy one way and me the other, and I never saw him again."

That was it. Baldly. What Isabel had always supposed might have happened. A routine tragedy of war. Gone, just like that. Phfft! If he hadn't gone to the Centre, could they have escaped? Did he sacrifice his life for rubber? It seemed an inadequate cause to have to die for.

"You never found out what happened to him?"

"There was much we never found out. You can't imagine what it was like, darling, marching from camp to camp, women and children, never enough to eat, people dying all the time, not even allowed to speak to each other most of the time. If we talked among ourselves, the soldiers got angry, you see, because they didn't understand English. And afterwards, no one could ever tell me and I didn't have the strength to find out for myself. I was very sick. I stayed on here because there was nowhere else to go. I would've gone to my father, but he vanished too, in Sumatra. After the war, it was chaos here, even after the Japanese left, people trying to find each other, so many sick and disabled, different relief organizations trying to identify their own nationalities, trying to repatriate them. So many prisoners. So many dead."

She shrugged her shoulders under the silky nightgown, slightly, as though it was of no great importance.

"And Dr. Partington? Who was he?"

Marike smiled briefly. "John? He was Australian, a doctor who helped in the camps. He knew all about tropical diseases and malnutrition. You see, he'd been a prisoner too."

She closed her eyes, wearily, as if the effort of talking had exhausted her. Which Isabel was sure it had. She waited awhile, but Marike seemed to have drifted into sleep; moving very quietly so as not to disturb her, Isabel went to the window and gazed out through the wooden slats. She could see the roofs of other houses beyond the dark-green hedge, the oily waters of the ocean in the near distance. It was from Malacca, she suddenly remembered, that the ship had sailed, the ship that took her and Victor away to England. She had no recollection of it, only the smell of diesel fuel and seasickness. It was in this place, at that moment, that her old life finished and her life in England really began; as though she'd boarded the ship one person and immediately become another, the two halves never quite linked; as though the dangerous oceans had washed her former self blank.

She wouldn't try to picture what it might have been like when the Japanese were here, but she tried to imagine what it might have been like in this town after the war, after the Japanese left. A comfortable life, she supposed, if the way this house was furnished was anything to go by. Had John Partington practiced medicine here? What sort of person had he been? Someone like her father? Glancing at the bed, she saw that Marike's eyes were still closed, her breathing was shallow and slow. Isabel wandered around the room, peering at the photographs that stood on the chest of drawers, on the dressing table. This must be John Partington, this intense-looking man with a thin face and dark hair that had turned white in other photos. There were several with Marike, a recognizable Marike, as if that person lived only in photographs: black curly hair, bright shining eyes, young and pretty. Isabel wondered if she'd ever looked for the two lost children, Isabel and Victor, if she'd ever really thought about them before she got old and sick, or if it was something that came at the end of her life, when, it's said, sins come back to haunt one.

Isabel stared down at the sleeping figure, wondering how long Marike would sleep. But she was prepared to wait, all day and all night if necessary. There was more to learn. The door opened, and Raminah stole silently into the room again. "It is another phone call for you, mem." Isabel had heard no sound of a telephone ringing.

It wasn't Oliver, as she expected, but Victor. His voice was loud and furious.

"*Now* what the hell is going on, Isabel?" He called her Isabel only when he was really angry. "I get this message from your friend Bailey to say I'm going to have to drive down to Malacca tomorrow. I'm struggling around on crutches like a benighted cripple, I've just got out of a hospital bed after a week, and you expect *me* to come and fetch *you* in Malacca. Malacca, for God's sake! Why the devil should I go to Malacca?"

Isabel took a deep breath. "Victor, the most extraordinary thing has happened. You know that advertisement we put in the paper?"

"We? We? I didn't put any advertisement in any paper. What paper?"

"I told you about it in the hospital, but you never listen to me, do you? Anyway, someone answered. That's why I'm in Malacca. You won't believe who it is, Victor. I mean, it's quite unbelievable even to me." She paused, hardly able to speak the name. "Victor, it's Marike."

"Who?" His voice didn't convey any recognition.

"Marike, who was married to our father."

"Jesus Christ! Are you sure?"

"She's very old. She seems much older than she really is, I suppose." It suddenly occurred to Isabel that Marike must be about the same age as Oliver Bailey, and the thought astonished her. "She's ill, Victor. She wants to see you."

There was a small silence. "What makes you think I want to see her?"

"She's dying, Victor."

"So? If I remember the story correctly, she was the one who didn't care whether we lived or died. Why should I bother to see her now?"

"To forgive her."

"*You* forgive her, Isabel. You're the one into that sort of stuff."

"Victor! It can't hurt to show a bit of charity to a dying woman. And apart from that, she can fill in some of the blanks. I need to know, Victor. I'm staying here until I find out."

"And what about me, may I ask? I may not be dying, but running around this damned country with bloody crutches and a bloody cast is no joke, I can tell you. I mean, what am I going to do if I come to

Malacca? Are you expecting me to sit beside a sickbed while you wait for some deep, dark secret to be revealed?"

"Yes. That's just what I expect. Oliver's giving you a car and driver. He'll drive us on to Singapore. What more can you expect? Remember, Victor, he's your boss. I'd do as he says, if I were you."

That wasn't really fair, but it served him right, the selfish bastard. She could practically hear Victor's thought processes at the other end of the phone. He breathed heavily into the receiver.

"Oh, well, I suppose Malacca is halfway to Singapore. Then we can get on a plane and go home."

"I'll see you tomorrow," she said. "Oliver knows this address."

Oh, God. Home to England, to Adrian. To the boys, of course. Of course. She could visit them at school, stand around the playing field and watch them play games. Speak to the housemaster. Take them a Care package. And then go home again, to Adrian. Oh, God.

23

ISABEL LOST TRACK of the time she spent at the bedside. Hours and hours, doing all the talking herself because Marike was too tired to talk, recounting her life since the day they were taken from the house in Kuala Lumpur: about Aunt Lucy and the boarding school, about Adrian and the boys, about her home in England; and as she related thirty years of her personal history, she heard how ordinary and mundane it was. She'd escaped from the war to accomplish what? Only the war had given her life any drama. But wasn't that how life should be—undramatic? Wasn't that what people thought was so wonderful about peace? The woman in the bed appeared to listen with rapt interest, as though she couldn't get enough of ordinary life, her eyes closing and opening, her breathing barely disturbing the air. Her amah came and went with medicine and tiny helpings of food, and the sun descended abruptly outside the room.

"And Victor?" Marike asked at last. "What about him?"

Isabel wasn't sure why she waited so long to say that Victor was near at hand, but when she did, the wasted figure in the bed became almost animated, excited.

"Ah, I loved that darlink little red-haired baby."

Isabel sighed. "He's not a darling red-haired baby anymore. He's a tall, bad-tempered man. You may not like him."

"I will love him," Marike said firmly. "But he will have to come soon."

"Tomorrow," Isabel promised. It might be good for Victor to have someone love him unconditionally, but it would surely have to be very soon. Such strength as Marike had seemed to be fading, inexorably, and it was a relief when the amah suggested, in her hushed voice, that Isabel allow her to sleep.

Marike's eyes flew open. "Don't leave me. I have no one else."

"Mem, you have me," Raminah said.

"But Isabel is family," Marike said.

Raminah turned to Isabel. "I have made the guest room comfortable for you, mem. I will make Mrs. Partington ready for the night. I am used to sitting with her."

Isabel hadn't imagined she would go to bed here. She'd pulled one of the easy chairs up to the bedside and thought she might sit in it all night, but she could tell that Raminah wanted her out of the room now. She wondered at the devotion the amah showed, but thought how sad it would be to have only a servant sitting beside you when you died. Except that people died in hospitals all the time without anyone as devoted as this gentle amah near to them. So she let Raminah show her the room where she was to sleep, where there was a nightdress laid out on the bed, a new toothbrush wrapped in plastic in the bathroom.

"You're very kind," Isabel said. "And very kind to Mrs. Partington. She's a lucky lady."

Raminah bowed her head. "She is a very unhappy lady. But now she is dying, and we must let her go so she will have peace in the next world."

"You will call me if she wants to speak to me, won't you?"

"She will wait now, until your brother, Tuan Cartwright, comes. She has told me often about her two little lost children. It is like a dream that you have appeared. Your spirit has always been with her."

When Raminah left her, Isabel lay down on the bed, stretching out, her muscles cramped after so many hours of sitting. She thought she'd lie awake, waiting to be called back to the sick woman's bedside, worrying that Marike might die in the night, but she fell asleep almost instantly. She stayed awake just long enough to hope that Victor would be kind when he came. If he came.

He did come, around midday, climbing awkwardly out of the car with his crutches, his leg in another cumbersome cast. His face was haggard and worn, unfamiliar lines etched down each side of his mouth, and when he straightened up, balancing unsteadily on the crutches, Isabel could see he'd lost weight. He still towered above the driver who was trying to assist him, but he no longer had that overbearing, pompous manner. Even his hair seemed thinner and paler, flaring in the midday sun.

She reached out to put her arms around him. "I'm so glad you came, Victor. I know you'll be glad you made the effort."

He waved her away. "Steady, for God's sake. Don't knock me off these damn things. I'll never get up again if you do. And I've still got to get up those steps, haven't I? Why does everywhere have to have steps? I'm beginning to understand what being a cripple means."

Isabel and the driver and Raminah, like tugs nudging a tanker, maneuvered Victor with a great deal of difficulty up the steps to the front door. He'd always been physically uncoordinated; now the crutches and the cast seemed to have destroyed such sense of balance as he'd possessed. Sorry for him, inept and stumbling, Isabel wondered how on earth he could climb the stairs to the bedroom.

Victor's arrival caused upheaval in the quiet, mournful, female household. Eventually they got him settled on a sofa in the living room, where Isabel hadn't been before, his leg raised on one cushion, his head on another, and Raminah fussed and rearranged the furniture around him and brought him a cool drink and a plate of little biscuits, setting them on a table by his elbow. She clasped her hands together under her chin, and her black eyes glittered with fresh tears. "Mrs. Partington will be so happy, tuan, to see you. So very happy. I will go and tell her now, this very minute, that you are here."

"How's he going to manage the stairs?" Isabel asked.

"What stairs?" Victor dropped his head back against the cushions and looked exhausted. "There's no way I can get up any stairs."

Raminah's mouth drooped with dismay. "Oh, what shall we do? But I will go and tell her you are here, this instance," and she glided from the room on her soundless feet.

"Nice place, this," Victor said, craning his neck to stare around the room. "She seems to have done pretty well for herself, our Marike."

"Please, Victor," Isabel said. "You must do your best to go up and see her."

"Listen, Izzy, I'm only here because I had no choice in the matter. You think I want to talk to a dead woman? I've come this far, but I can't and won't go up any stairs. You want me to fall and break the other leg? My neck, perhaps?"

"Sometimes I think that wouldn't be such a bad idea."

"Well, I'm not going to. Not to please you or anyone else. Especially not someone who dumped me when I was a baby."

"You've got to forgive her for that, Victor."

"Why?"

Isabel thought she knew why. She recognized now that Victor held grudges from that time before he could remember anything. If he could forgive Marike, he might learn to forgive other women. Perhaps he'd even learn to like his sister.

Raminah came back into the room. "Please, mem, Mrs. Partington wishes to speak to you."

Earlier that morning, Marike had been sleepy and disoriented, forgetting that she had talked to Isabel the day before, but now she was wide awake, sitting up in bed, her dark eyes bright, the yellow skin smoother and firmer, as though she had woken from a deep, peaceful sleep, as if there were still plenty of life left in the frail body.

"He has come," she said, as though she were speaking of her savior. "Raminah explained that he cannot come up the stairs to me. Therefore I must go downstairs to him. You, Isabel, you are young and strong. You can carry me down the stairs."

She would weigh nothing. "Of course I can," Isabel said. "If you're sure."

So Raminah dressed her mistress in a silk dressing gown, and Isabel lifted the wasted figure out of the bed. Marike wrapped her arms around Isabel's neck, and as Isabel cradled her in her arms, she could smell a long-ago perfume in her clothes and remembered the day she'd thrown herself against this very same body, begging not to be sent away. The body had been strong then, young, as her own was now. How beautiful she'd been. How cruel life was, that it ebbed away and left such shadows behind. How fortunate Isabel was to have caught this shadow just in time. Holding her close, cherishing her, Isabel carried her carefully down the staircase, like a breakable treasure.

Marike wept when she saw Victor, and Isabel wept too, of course, while Victor stared in horrified silence, his face reflecting revulsion at the sight of the sick woman. But Marike didn't seem to notice, or to care if she did notice. Isabel set her in a chair beside Victor on the sofa, and she reached out to clutch at his big, fleshy hand with her clawlike fingers. "Little Victor. Little Victor. You have grown up to look just like your daddy, did you know that? I can't believe it. Just like him, the way you hold your head, the way you look at me through your glasses." She held his hand tight, stroking it, and Victor's face reddened, but he didn't pull his hand out of hers.

"I was punished, wasn't I? I let you go by yourselves, and so I lost everything. I lost you and Isabel, who I loved, and Roddy, who I loved, and I nearly died of all the fevers and sicknesses and the beastliness. In the camps, in all the different places the Japanese moved us to, I thought about you, little Victor, and about Isabel, and I prayed that God would someday forgive me for not going with you. And now here you are, just in time, to show me you made it safely."

After a long pause, Victor said, "No thanks to you, was it?"

"Victor!" Isabel protested.

He pulled his hand away from Marike, roughly. "Well, it's true. Let's not beat about the bush. You did your best, Izzy, but you were only a baby too. What did she think would happen to us, two babies? What the hell was she thinking of?" He stared into Marike's face, and she flinched away from him. "What about the Japanese? What did you think was going to happen to you when they caught up to you?"

Her eyes darkened and glistened. "My darling boy, I was much more afraid of the Germans than the Japanese. I thought the English had lost the war. I thought it was madness to try to go back to Europe." She put her hand against her trembling mouth. "My father, you have to understand, was Jewish. I knew what was happening to the Jews in Europe."

The irony of it took Isabel's breath away. Marike had been *afraid* to go with them? It was fear for herself that made her stay, not love for her husband? But if she'd gone with his children, she'd have survived, just as they survived. She could have taken care of them, and they would have loved her.

"Don't blame her, Victor," she cried. "Nobody knows what they'll do in a war. Nobody. That's what's so terrible about war. It makes people do things they'd never do otherwise. She loved us, I know she did."

"I loved you," Marike said. "I still do."

"Love?" Victor said scornfully. "What sort of love do you call that? Tell me, did you ever look for us afterwards?"

Marike shrank back into the chair, her eyes bleak. "What was the good of that? It was years later. I tried to forget all the terrible things that had happened. To you, to me, to your father."

"And you forgot, all right, didn't you. You married this Partington. Didn't you have to wait to find out if our father was dead?"

"Ah, but I was never married to him, you see. Not to your father."

Isabel gasped. "Not married? But . . . I always thought . . ."

"Of course you did, my darling. You were a child. But how could I marry him when we didn't know if your mother was really dead?"

This was it. At last. Isabel held her breath, looked at Victor. He wasn't looking at her. He was still staring at Marike, contempt in his eyes. A long silence stretched around the room. Isabel could hear Marike's quick, shallow breathing.

"My mother," Isabel said. "What, exactly, happened to her?"

Marike looked at her mournfully. "Your mother went to be with the spirits, Isabel. She went off alone into the jungle. Her head grew full of strange aboriginal ideas, and one day she walked away from the hill station where she and your father had gone for the air, and she was never seen again."

Isabel knew it was the truth, of course. She'd always known it, even before she admitted it to Oliver. But as Marike spoke it out loud, the sudden memory of what had happened came sweeping over her. She knew much more about it than Marike did. Staring at Marike, at Victor, Isabel leapt from her chair and stumbled blindly around the room. Her poor, poor mother. Lost in the terrifying jungle. She wanted to weep for her, grieve for her properly, and knew there wasn't time, not now, not before Marike told them everything. Taking a deep breath, she knelt down beside Marike. "What did it have to do with Noone of the Ulu?"

"How ever do you know about Noone of the Ulu?"

"My father wrote it in a letter."

The woman, whom Isabel still could not call Marike, stared into a distance, and the worn lines of her face melted into compassion. "He told me how she became obsessed with the myths of the jungle. She used to read everything about this Noone, about the work he was doing with the aborigines. She went crazy, you know, Isabel. Quite crazy. She was beautiful and desirable, and your father loved her too much, and she just went crazy. A young Englishwoman too alone, too far from home. Especially after the baby. She went into one of those depressions women can get after a baby."

"What can you mean?" Victor demanded. "He loved her too much?"

Marike leaned forward, nearer to Victor, and he recoiled from her. "How can I make you understand? Some men want to possess every part of a woman—her mind, her body, her heart. Some men are like that, perhaps because they don't trust their wives. I'm not sure. But why do you think they lived so far from the city? So that no one else should look at her. All the English lived close together, except for the plantation people. Sometimes they came to the city, not often. I saw her there once or twice. I saw how delicate she was. In the end, she went mad with loneliness, with the rain and the heat and only the jungle all around her. She began to believe in all those spirits those primitive Malays believed in, up in their deep jungle. She was drawn to them, a kind of compulsion. Afterwards, Roddy realized what he had done, and he couldn't forgive himself."

"Oh, so it was our father's fault, was it?" The color raged up and down in Victor's face. "He drove her to it, is that what you're saying? What did you have to do with it? Where were you when she was going crazy, as you call it?"

"Oh, Victor." Marike sighed again, gently, regretfully. "Now you sound like your father. Angry. Suspicious. I didn't come until after your mother disappeared. To help look after you. And Isabel. He had to have someone else beside the amah."

The room was quiet as they each retreated into their own thoughts. Even Victor subsided, his head resting against the cushions, gazing up at the ceiling, lips pursed, one hand clenching and unclenching. Marike closed her eyes. "But your father was really a good, kind man. I don't want you to think he wasn't. He just didn't understand how lonely she got. He went off to work every day, and he didn't know what effect having a baby and being alone all the time, in such a strange place, could have on someone like her. He just didn't understand about women."

She opened her eyes again. "For me it was different. I was born in this kind of world; I was never afraid of it. I had no roots in Europe. My father was Dutch, but I'd never lived there. That's another reason why I couldn't think of going back with you children. And somehow I felt my poor Roddy needed me more than you did."

Isabel held the sticklike fingers between her own. "Marike, I understand."

"And Victor? You think he understands now?"

"Do you, Victor?"

Victor groaned aloud. "Understand women? Who the hell can do that?"

Marike turned to Isabel, a hopeful, twisted smile. "And can you forgive me?"

Isabel said, "Marike, I forgive you."

And as soon as she said it, a kind of peace filled Isabel, a lifting away of the sorrows and regrets, as though her soul had taken flight, as though she could forget all the missed years and the weight of responsibility that had burdened her for so long. It was like being reborn, fresh and new and unwrinkled. When she forgave Marike, she forgave her mother. And Victor. And her father. And herself.

24

*I*T WAS QUITE the most luxurious room Victor had ever had the prerogative of sleeping in, even more spacious and airy than the suite at the Raffles Hotel, with even more evidence of wealth and privilege: Chinese rugs on the dark wood floor, tall windows opening onto a balcony, his own private bathroom. Bailey certainly lived in grand and ostentatious comfort.

Victor eased his aching body onto the wide, soft bed, thankful to get his leg off the ground at last. He contemplated the day and the conduct of his sister. She'd sat in the front of the car beside the driver on the way down from Malacca, leaving the entire back seat for Victor, so they couldn't discuss the extraordinary business of the Marike woman. Not that he wasn't glad for the peace and quiet, able to go over it all in his head without Izzy telling him what he should be thinking. He shuddered now to think of that woman, dying in front of his eyes, just skin and bone, her sickly yellow color, the obscene way her hair barely covered her scalp. Izzy hadn't seemed to notice. She'd held her hand and breathed into her face, even kissed her. The thought of kissing a reeking skeleton like that made Victor want to puke.

She'd surely die within the next couple of days. He'd been panic-stricken, he had to admit, afraid he might be forced to stay there and wait for the end. He'd more than half expected Izzy to insist on some grand deathbed scene, but thank God he'd been spared that. And once they arrived at Bailey's house, he understood why she hadn't lingered for the finale. He could instantly see that Izzy and Bailey had taken a ridiculous shine to each other; couldn't bear to be away from each other, was his guess. Pretty obvious even to someone like himself, who didn't care to take note of that side of life. The way Bailey fawned over Izzy—pathetic, really, a man of his standing, holding the chair for her at dinner, touching her hand at every available opportunity, smiling into her eyes. She loved it, of course. Ate it up. You'd never believe she had a husband of her own and children at home. He'd like to know what she thought could come of it all. Though when Victor compared Oliver Bailey to Adrian Bennet, he had to say he couldn't entirely blame her. Bailey was a smooth charmer, all right, and Adrian Bennet a cold kind of fish. Bennet probably wouldn't notice she'd gone. He was far more interested in his house and his bits and bobs. He'd probably go out and collect another wife, one who'd match the furniture.

Victor had to admit he was surprised his sister had done so well for herself, snagging someone like Bailey, with this grand house, a couple of servants waiting on them at dinner, candles and flowers and good china on the table. No wonder she'd lost her head. Luxury like this didn't exist in the UK anymore, not in their circles anyway. Though, after all, if he hadn't brought her with him to Malaya, she'd never have met Bailey, would she? Victor was struck by his hand in his sister's fate. If Izzy and Bailey remained enamored of each other—though there was no telling whether Izzy had any kind of sticking power—it surely couldn't hurt her brother to have such good connections. Izzy had got what she wanted, a father figure, and one Victor couldn't help admiring, a man who'd survived what Bailey had survived and got to the top in spite of it. Perhaps got to the top because of it. Toughens a man, that kind of hardship. And if Izzy didn't seem to want Bailey as a father, well, maybe Victor could adopt him for the role. Not that he needed anyone like that, of course. The idea made him want to laugh.

He supposed it was just as well they'd got all that old stuff about their parents cleared up. If you could trust someone like that Marike woman to be telling the truth, someone who'd saved her own skin instead of doing the right thing, looking out for two little children. Forgive her? How could he forgive, when he thought of the grief she'd caused? How could Izzy show such . . . generosity? Surely it was merely weakness on her part. He'd managed not to feel too much pity for Mrs. Partington, pathetic though she appeared. She'd suffered, all right, no doubt about that, but as far as he, Victor, was concerned, she deserved what she'd got. Everyone got what he or she deserved in the end. It was one of Victor's abiding beliefs.

His eyelids grew heavy, but now his damned leg was beginning to hurt like hell again. He wished he could ring the bell for Sundra. She'd bring him a pill and lay her little brown hand on his forehead just before he slipped into sleep. He wondered whether Sundra was missing him. If there was a bell to ring in this room, one of the servants might come. Or he could climb laboriously out of bed and find the pills they'd given him when he left the hospital. Victor regretted having to leave the hospital.

Recognizing he'd never sleep unless he took something, he struggled out of bed, limped on the wretched crutches across the shining floor, around the rugs, to the bathroom, washed a couple of the pills down with water from a carafe, started his slow way back to the bed. Wide awake now, Victor could hear a soft murmur of voices somewhere below, so he shuffled over to the window and pushed the filmy curtains aside to maneuver himself onto the little stone balcony. Outside, the night was balmy and warm, soft and gentle on his sweaty skin, and in the velvety darkness, a huge amber moon was rising over a fan-shaped palm tree, a picture-postcard scene, a dream of tropical paradise. The sight of it almost took his breath away. Really, it wasn't so bad in this part of the world, especially when he compared it to the chilly streets of London, to the scruffy pubs, to his cheerless flat in Fulham, where there weren't any small Asian women to soothe his aching flesh and laugh at his jokes.

It was Izzy's voice he could hear down below, having an intimate little chat with Bailey, he supposed. He couldn't make out what she was saying. Teetering on his crutches up on the balcony, Victor felt as if he was being deliberately excluded, that the two of them were down there together discussing their future, sharing secrets, leaving him out. He wished he could hear what they were talking about. Quite suddenly, Victor couldn't bear not to know what Izzy was talking about, what her plans might be. She was *his* sister, after all. She'd always shared everything with him, whether he wanted her to or not, and it was unexpectedly alarming to realize that she might not be around much longer to burden him with her neuroses and anxieties. He wasn't sure he could face the prospect, not when he truly contemplated it. Suppose she remained here with Bailey while he, Victor, had to go back alone to a cold and friendless Britain? She wouldn't cast him adrift, would she? Izzy had always been with him. Always. She wouldn't let him go now, would she? Could she?

Inching nearer to the parapet, Victor strained to hear what she was saying.

"The thing is," Isabel was saying, sitting close to Oliver on the dark veranda, "that of course I hadn't really forgotten what happened to my mother. Or even blanked it out. What I'd done was shovel it aside, bury it in some way. The memory was waiting for me, lurking somewhere in my subconscious. As soon as Marike confirmed it, I could remember what happened. Quite clearly."

Oliver took hold of her hands and cradled them in his as though they were precious objects. He stared anxiously into her face. "Isabel, are you sure? Recovered memories? Such an unknown quantity. Dangerous too. You should be very careful, my dear."

But now that she was with Oliver, she wasn't afraid. She thought she would never be afraid anymore. "I want to tell you about it, now, in case it slips away again. Though it wouldn't, would it? But I might prefer to forget it, now that I understand what it is I need to forget. All the way from Malacca, I went over and over it in my mind, and I couldn't wait to get here so I could tell you. I feel I can tell you everything, Oliver, that there's nothing I need keep hidden. You don't know what a relief that is, not to have to *pretend* about anything anymore. We spend so much of our lives being someone or doing something other than what we really want to do or be, don't we?"

He seemed to think about it. He always seemed to listen to her. It was wonderful to have someone who really listened.

"Pretending is often merely politeness, isn't it? Sometimes I have to pretend to be interested in what some bore is saying. Women, they say, do a lot of pretending in bed."

She blushed in the darkness, suddenly uncertain. "Are you insinuating that I fit into either of those categories?"

He grinned down at her. "You weren't pretending, were you, Isabel?"

"I wasn't pretending, Oliver."

"And you don't bore me. Not at all. Tell me what you remember."

Her head was against the steady reassuring beat of his heart. She took a deep breath. "The first thing I remember is being surprised that my mother was driving the car. Perhaps she never drove, because that's what leaps immediately to my mind, that I was surprised to see her behind the wheel. I can't imagine where my father was or why Ayala wasn't with us, but I do know my mother was driving us away from the house. And it was away from the house in the hills, not the one in Kuala Lumpur, though I can't recall what anything looked like. I was sitting beside her, with Victor on my lap, and she was talking, talking, talking, leaning over the steering wheel, staring through the windscreen, never looking at me or at Victor, just straight ahead, talking all the time. 'We'll be all right, Isabel, you and me and the baby,' she kept saying. 'We'll be looked after. They all live together up there, always together, never alone. We won't be alone anymore.' And I had no idea what she was talking about, but I wasn't frightened. Why should I be frightened? It was just a ride in the car. We went further and further up into the hills, and then the road died away and there was only the jungle all around us and ahead of us, and it was already dark and creepy and breathless and heavy. My mother stopped the car—I can see her now, yanking on the hand brake; she needed two hands to do it—and then she got out of the car and took Victor off my lap and caught hold of my hand and started walking into the trees. And then I did get frightened, because the trees were so close around and the vines hung down from them and the sun was blocked out and there were all those secret noises. Victor began to cry and my mother began to cry as well and I remember pulling at her hand and saying, 'Please, please, don't let's go in there, Mummy,' and she said, 'But they have dreams like I do, Isabel, they will understand. The people up here live together in one big house and they take care of each other and they never do anything unless their dreams tell them to do it, and that's why we need to go and live with them.' And then she said, 'I can't stand the way this baby keeps crying,' and she just plonked Victor down at the foot of a huge tree, among the roots, as though he was some kind of parcel, and she left him there, just like the story of the Babes in the Woods. She kept on walking further and further into the jungle with me, and I was pulling at her hand, pulling and pulling. 'Victor, Mummy—we can't leave Victor.' But it was as if she didn't hear me, as if she was in some kind of dream, and after a while she just let go of my hand and I ran back to where I thought Victor was. But I couldn't find him, already I couldn't find him, because there was so much undergrowth and so many trees and the light was so dim, and then I heard him crying and I thought I could follow the sound. But I couldn't decide which way to go, after my mother or to Victor, and when I looked around for my mother, I could just see her white dress, flickering in the shadows, disappearing. And then she was gone, and I tried to find Victor. And I did, because of his crying. I carried him out of the trees and got back in the car, and we just sat there, waiting until someone came looking for us."

Oliver groaned and clutched her close to him, tight against his chest. "Isabel, are you sure you remember this? Those things your mother said?"

She pulled away to stare into his face. "Sure? How can I be sure? How can I be certain that's what the truth is? But I think I remember it. Isn't that enough?"

There were deep creases in his forehead and around his mouth, and his eyes were very pale. "I don't believe you can suddenly remember something like this. I don't believe you can have forgotten it for thirty years and then have it surface again with no warning, complete with dialogue."

Who was he to tell her she might not be remembering correctly? He hadn't been in the cool dank trees with the slithering dripping sounds all around, her heart banging loudly with terror for her mother and the greater terror of where she was leading them; he hadn't seen

Victor's bright head among the snakelike roots; even he couldn't understand the choice she had to make, her mother or Victor. It hadn't seemed so difficult then. Now it was impossible to decide whom she should have chosen, her mother or her brother, the grown-up woman or the little baby, and she supposed anyone would choose the baby.

Pulling herself out of Oliver's reach, Isabel paced along the veranda, stared out into the night. A gigantic moon was rising above the palm trees, bathing the whole house in a shimmering ivory glow. She could see the balcony of the room where Victor was sleeping off the effects of the long drive, if his poor leg wasn't keeping him awake. All her fault. "Oliver," she said. "I never want Victor to know."

"To know what, exactly?"

"That I let our mother walk away into the jungle."

Oliver jumped up from the sofa, practically shouting at her. "Never say that again, never. Even if your memory is halfway correct, you were only a child. Just a little girl. It wasn't your mother who was *your* responsibility. You and your brother were *her* responsibility. And you absolutely should share this memory with him."

"My poor mother," she sighed. She leaned her head against the screens, dazzled by the moon. "I don't want Victor blaming her. He's very unforgiving sometimes. I think he must be like his father in that respect, though who will ever know? And I don't want him blaming himself. I suspect that's what my father meant in the letter, wasn't it? That it was somehow Victor's fault, that it was the baby who drove her over the edge, and that a baby shouldn't carry the blame. Women can get very strange after having babies. Puerperal depression, that sort of thing." She looked back at Oliver, anxiously. "Now that I've told you, that's enough."

"No, it isn't." Oliver's voice was firm and loud. "You have to tell him. You've been carrying that burden around for too long, too heavy a weight, my darling. In any case, it should be his memory as well. He's an adult now. You don't have to go on protecting him."

But it was a lifetime habit. She didn't think she could break it now.

He hugged her to him. "It wasn't Victor's fault, Isabel. Or yours. Or even your father's. It was probably no one's fault. Things happen and later we want to assign blame. That's human nature. But sometimes we have to let go of the past, forgive ourselves and other people."

She understood that he was speaking about his own past too.

She felt so light and peaceful here with Oliver, the sound of cicadas loud and familiar in the garden, the rustling of the palm trees, the clicking of a gecko somewhere near, as though she'd never lived anywhere but in the velvet blackness of a tropical night. His hand was firm to her touch, comforting and reassuring. She felt as though she could trust her life to him. His closeness wrapped her in security, a strangely unfamiliar feeling, which she hadn't missed until he had given it back to her. She could stay here forever. She could live with him and love him, her journey come full circle, her duty done. To have remembered and be able to forgive. And be forgiven.

Above her head, Victor struggled to get himself back into bed. He hadn't been able to hear all that much, except for Bailey's voice raised at Izzy, as though he was angry with her. Didn't bode well for their future, in Victor's opinion. And what memory was she supposed to share now? Hadn't there been quite enough memories already? Sometime, he supposed, he might have to find out, though. Sometime. How important could it possibly be, after all these years?

25

IT WAS COLD in England. Freezing. Frost lay in a white vapor over fields and hedgerows, blurring the gray sky, a chill December dankness that froze the breath from the lungs into a tangible mist. Isabel huddled into her thick winter coat, the wind whipping at her hair, bringing tears to her eyes.

"You'll feel the cold, I expect," Adrian said, turning the key in the front door. "Good job you didn't stay away any longer."

"Yes, good job."

"I bet you're glad to be home." He carried her suitcase in from the car, setting it in the hallway. "There's nowhere like home, I always say."

"Nowhere," she said.

"Like a cup of tea? I'll put the kettle on."

"Yes, that'll be good. I must get into something warmer."

She went upstairs to the bedroom, her legs stiff after the flight, not working properly, stumbling on the staircase. She had to catch hold of the banister to steady herself. The room was incredibly tidy, the covers smooth on the bed, no clothes left around. She wanted to take a hot bath and instead changed into a thick pair of pants, a turtleneck shirt, and a wool sweater. She still felt cold.

The kitchen was warm, the Aga pumping out heat, and it was tidy in there too, unnaturally so, all the surfaces neat and shining, the dishes stacked in the glass-fronted cabinets, the newspapers folded away, the chairs pushed under the pine table.

"It looks as though you've been having a clear-up," Isabel said. "It looks as though you managed fine without me."

"You know me," Adrian said. "I like to keep things under control. I must show you what I found for that corner of the sitting room, where that old plant was." He poured tea into a china mug, pushed it across the table to her.

"The ficus? I liked that ficus. You haven't thrown it out, have you?"

"It was just gathering dust. So are you going to tell me about Victor?"

She'd fallen asleep in the car as soon as the heater warmed it up. She'd hardly slept on the plane.

"He's staying on, like I told you. Until his leg is healed. His boss is putting him up in his house. That's kind of him, isn't it?"

"Kind? I'd say it's masochistic. Who'd want Victor as a houseguest for more than a couple of days?"

"He's offered Victor a job in Singapore. He's thinking about it."

"Unbelievable," Adrian said. "Still, I suppose he's probably quite a good accountant. Unimaginative. That's what you need in an accountant."

She sat down at the table, wrapped her fingers around the hot mug. "You've never liked Victor, have you, Adrian?"

He shrugged. "If he wasn't your brother, I wouldn't give him the time of day."

Suddenly Isabel found herself laughing. "You know, if he wasn't my brother, sometimes I don't think I would, either."

"My God, Isabel! What do I hear you saying? What on earth did the two of you do out there?"

She drank the tea, waited for it to unfreeze her body, to warm up her heart, bring the tidy house back to a home again. The tea slipped hot down her throat, and the house remained just a house, beautiful, shining, impersonal, a picture in a magazine. She waited for Adrian not to seem like a stranger to her. She felt like the ficus, gathering dust.

She'd have to tell him the truth sometime. She could tell him now. She could say, "Adrian, I fell in love with someone out there. He wanted me to stay. He offered Victor a job because of me, let him stay in his house because of me. Victor's a kind of hostage, a pawn in the game."

But Isabel had had enough truth for the time being. She'd decided that perhaps Victor had been right all along. What you didn't know didn't hurt you. She'd thought the truth would bring release, but now she wasn't so sure. Invented answers were sometimes easier than real answers. It might take more time than she'd realized to win release from all the ghosts of the past, and now she had the future to contend with. She'd got on the plane to come back to Britain because she couldn't deal with the future just yet. Because she wasn't totally sure if Oliver was real or a figment of her imagination, another ghost. Could you fall in love with a ghost? Though when she thought of it, there was nothing spectral about Oliver.

"I have to go back," she'd told him. "I have to see the boys. And Adrian. I can't just stay here without telling them face-to-face. That would be cowardly."

The boys must know their mother didn't just disappear. They must know what she was thinking and feeling and wanting. She'd have to tell them so maybe they'd understand in the future. She'd have to tell them sometime. Perhaps soon. Perhaps not so soon. Sometime.

"If you don't come back," Oliver had said, "I'll come looking for you. Don't think I'll give up easily."

"Australia," he'd said, "is a wonderful country. Lots of sunshine. The country of the future. Your boys would love it there. Mine too."

```
FICTION

Morgan, Mary, 1931-

The house at the edge of
the jungle /
1999.          $21.95     6/3
```

MAR 2 3 1999